MOLLY CL

MRS. LORIMER'S

MARY 'Molly' Clavering was born in Glasgow in 1900. Her father was a Glasgow businessman, and her mother's grandfather had been a doctor in Moffat, where the author would live for nearly 50 years after World War Two.

She had little interest in conventional schooling as a child, but enjoyed studying nature, and read and wrote compulsively, considering herself a 'poetess' by the age of seven.

She returned to Scotland after her school days, and published three novels in the late 1920s, as well as being active in her local girl guides and writing two scenarios for ambitious historical pageants.

In 1936, the first of four novels under the pseudonym 'B. Mollett' appeared. Molly Clavering's war service in the WRNS interrupted her writing career, and in 1947 she moved to Moffat, in the Scottish border country, where she lived alone, but was active in local community activities. She resumed writing fiction, producing seven post-war novels and numerous serialized novels and novellas in the *People's Friend* magazine.

Molly Clavering died in Moffat on February 12, 1995.

TITLES BY MOLLY CLAVERING

Fiction

Georgina and the Stairs (1927)
The Leech of Life (1928)
Wantonwalls (1929)
Susan Settles Down (1936, as 'B. Mollett')
Love Comes Home (1938, as 'B. Mollett')
Yoked with a Lamb (1938, as 'B. Mollett')
Touch Not the Nettle (1939, as 'B. Mollett')
Mrs. Lorimer's Quiet Summer (1953)
Because of Sam (1954)
Dear Hugo (1955)
Near Neighbours (1956)
Result of the Finals (1957)
Dr. Glasgow's Family (1960)
Spring Adventure (1962)

Non-Fiction

From the Border Hills (1953)

Between 1952 and 1976, Molly Clavering also serialized at least two
dozen novels or novellas in the *People's Friend* under the names
Marion Moffatt and Emma Munro. Some of these were reprinted as
'pocket novels' as late as 1994.

MOLLY CLAVERING

MRS. LORIMER'S QUIET SUMMER

With an introduction by

Elizabeth Crawford

DEAN STREET PRESS

A Furrowed Middlebrow Book

FM69

Published by Dean Street Press 2021

First published in 1953 by Hodder & Stoughton

Cover by DSP

Shows detail from an illustration by Eric Ravilious

ISBN 978 1 914150 51 7

www.deanstreetpress.co.uk

INTRODUCTION

Mrs. *Lorimer's Quiet Summer* was hailed on publication by the reviewer in the *Coventry Evening Telegraph* (16 March 1953) as 'a pleasant first novel', remarking that 'this new author has a woman's gift for detail for recording ordinary little happenings and making them add to the general interest'. Doubtless the author, Molly Clavering, allowed herself a wry smile, for this was in fact her eighth novel, although the previous four had been published under the pseudonym of 'B. Mollett.' Now, with her new publisher, Hodder & Stoughton, she was relaunched on what was, in effect, the third stage of her literary career.

Born in Glasgow on 23 October 1900, Molly Clavering was the eldest child of John Mollett Clavering (1858-1936) and his wife, Esther (1874-1943). She was named for her paternal grandmother, but was always known by the diminutive, 'Molly'. Her brother, Alan, was born in 1903 and her sister, Esther, in 1907. Although John Clavering, as his father before him, worked in central Glasgow, brokering both iron and grain, by 1911 the family had moved eleven miles north of the city, to Alreoch House outside the village of Blanefield. In an autobiographical article Molly Clavering later commented, 'I was brought up in the country, and until I went to school ran wild more or less'. She was taught by her father to be a close observer of nature and 'to know the birds and flowers, the weather and the hills round our house'. From this knowledge, learned so early, were to spring the descriptions of the countryside that give readers of her novels such pleasure.

By the age of seven Molly was sufficiently confident in her literary attainment to consider herself a 'poetess', a view with which her father enthusiastically concurred. In these early years she was probably educated at home, remembering that she read 'everything I could lay hands on (we were never restricted in our reading)' and having little 'time for orthodox lessons, though I liked history and Latin'. She was later sent away to boarding school, to Mortimer House in Clifton, Bristol, the choice perhaps dictated by the reputation of its founder and principal, Mrs Meyrick Heath, whom Molly later described as 'a woman of wide culture and great character [who] influenced all the girls who went there'. However, despite a congenial environment, life at Mortimer House was so different from the freedom she enjoyed at home that Molly 'found the society of girls and the regular hours very difficult at first'. Although she later admitted that she preferred devoting time and effort to her own writing rather than school-work, she did sufficiently well academically to be offered a place at Oxford. Her parents, however, ruled against this, perhaps for reasons of finance. It is noticeable that in her novels Molly makes little mention of the education of her hero-ines, although they do demonstrate a close and loving knowledge of Shakespeare, Dickens, Thackeray, and Trollope.

After leaving school Molly returned home to Arleoch House and, with no need to take paid employment, was able to concen-trate on her writing, publishing her first novel in 1927, the year following the tragically early death of her sister, Esther. Always sociable, Molly took a lively interest in local activities, particu-larly in the Girl Guides for whom she was able to put her literary talents to fund-raising effect by writing scenarios for two ambi-tious Scottish history pageants. The first, in which she took the pivotal part of 'Fate', was staged in 1929 in Stirlingshire, with a cast of 500. However, for the second, in 1930, she moved south and in aid of the Roxburgh Girl Guides wrote the 'Border Historical Pageant'. Performed in the presence of royalty at Minto House, Roxburghshire, this pageant featured a large choir and a cast of 700, with Molly in the leading part as 'The Spirit of Borderland Legend'. For Molly was already devoted to the Border country, often visiting the area to stay with relations and, on occasion, attending a hunt ball.

In the late 1920s Molly published two further novels under her own name and then, in the 1930s, another four as 'B. Mollett'. Centring her fiction on life in the Scottish countryside, particu-larly in the Borders, with occasional forays into Edinburgh, the novels reflect the society of the day, with characters drawn from all strata, their gradations finely delineated, the plots fuelled by sherry parties and small-town gossip, rendered on occasion very effectively in demotic Scots. *Touch Not the Nettle*, the last of her 'B. Mollett' novels, was published in 1939 and then, on the outbreak of the Second World War, Molly joined the Women's Royal Naval Service, based for the duration at Greenock, then an important and frenetic naval station. Serving in the Signals Cypher Branch, she eventually achieved the rank of second officer. Although there was no obvious family connection to the Navy, it is noticeable that in her fiction, both before and after the war, many of Molly's most attractive male characters, such as 'Guy' in *Mrs. Lorimer's Quiet Summer*, are associated with the Senior Service.

After she was demobbed Molly moved to the Borders, to Moffat, the Dumfriesshire town where her great-grandfather had been a doctor, and in 1953 published a paean to the surrounding country-side. This, *From the Border Hills*, was her only work of non-fiction. She lived in Moffat for the rest of her life, sharing 'Clover Cottage' with a series of black standard poodles, one of them a present from D.E. Stevenson, another of the town's novelists, whom she had known since the 1930s. Thus, it is not by chance that *Mrs. Lorimer's Quiet Summer*, the first of Molly Clavering's novels to be written in Moffat, features two women novelists living in a small Border town. 'Mrs Lucy Lorimer' ('that quiet woman') is clearly based on D.E. Stevenson and 'Miss Grace ("Gray") Douglas' on Molly herself. Furthermore 'Gray Douglas' may well have been named in homage to another Border novelist, 'O. Douglas' (Anna Buchan), and, taking self-reference a stage further, D.E. Stevenson gave the name 'Freda Lorimer' to a character in her own 1953 novel, *Five Windows*. *Mrs. Lorimer's Quiet Summer* proved to be one of the most successful of Molly Clavering's novels, popular on both sides of the Atlantic.

While affirming that the adult children and their entangle-ments, which rendered Mrs Lorimer's summer rather less than 'quiet', bear no resemblance to D.E. Stevenson's real-life family, her granddaughter, Penny Kent, well remembers how 'Molly used to breeze and bluster into North Park (my Grandmother's house), a rush of fresh air, gaberdine flapping, grey hair flying with her large, bouncy black poodles, Ham and Pam (and later Bramble), shaking, dripping and muddy from some wild walk through Tank Wood or over Gallow Hill)'.

During these post-war years Molly Clavering continued her work with the Girl Guides, serving for nine years as County Commissioner, was president of the local Scottish Country Dance Association, and active in the Women's Rural Institute (meetings of which feature in many of her novels). She was a member of Moffat town council, 1951-60, and for three years from 1957 was the town's first and only woman magistrate. She continued writing, publishing six further novels, as well as a steady stream of the stories she referred to as her 'bread and butter', issued, under a variety of pseudonyms, by that very popular women's magazine, the *People's Friend*.

When Molly Clavering's long and fruitful life finally ended on 12 February 1995 her obituary was written by Wendy Simpson, another of D.E. Stevenson's granddaughters. Citing exactly the attributes that characterise Molly Clavering's novels, she remembered her as 'A convivial and warm human being who enjoyed the company of friends, especially young people, with her entertaining wit and a sense of fun allied to a robustness to stand up for what she believed in.'.

Elizabeth Crawford

CHAPTER ONE

1

It was generally considered that Mrs. Lorimer, that quiet woman, was not at all a sentimental person. Therefore when Nan Gibson, her valued and trusty and frequently tiresome cook-housekeeper, announced one morning as she twitched back the bedroom curtains, "I hear Harperslea's been sold," the pang which her mistress felt must have been simply because another suitable house—a house she would have liked for herself, had been bought by someone else. Stifling her annoyance at being roused by such unwelcome news—for Nan was not to know how unwelcome it was—Mrs. Lorimer asked who had bought Harperslea.

"I wonder the Colonel didn't mention it, seeing he was at the Legion meeting last night," replied Nan, one of whose more irritating habits was never to return a direct answer to a question.

Through long years of use it had ceased to irritate Mrs. Lorimer. She said mildly, "He didn't mention it, Nan. Perhaps he hadn't heard."

Nan sniffed. "He'd hear all right. The Legion meetings get all the news that's going. They just sit there and blether like a lot of old sweetie-wives. It's a stranger that's bought Harperslea, a widower with a daughter. Better drink yer tea before it gets cold."

She stumped from the room, shutting the door rather noisily. Mrs. Lorimer poured out a cup of tea, and as she drank it, reflected that Jack probably had known about Harperslea when he came in on the previous evening. He had been unusually discursive, even for him, about the British Legion meeting, had indeed gone on and on until his wife's ears had ceased to convey the sound they received to her brain, and her mind became a blank. This experience befell many who listened, or tried to listen, to the Colonel's long and involved statements, but it did seem to Mrs. Lorimer that yesterday evening he had deliberately talked her into a daze. In anyone but Jack she would have been certain, but her dear Jack was not capable of considered subtlety. It was more likely that he had done it in an instinctive desire to conceal knowledge which he knew would distress her.

Mrs. Lorimer was distressed. "I am as sick as mud about it!" she thought, using one of the children's phrases which she heard so often in their conversation, though they were apt to sound incongruous on her lips. "I *did* so want Harperslea! Not just because it's the right size and is lovely, and has a good garden, but because I love it. It's meant to be my house."

Only in her private thoughts, and then only rarely did she indulge in the sentimentality which she never displayed and was credited with not possessing at all. She was sentimental about Harperslea, she admitted it; but leaving that aside, their present house, Woodside, was no longer big enough to hold them. Now if the whole family wanted to gather for any special occasion it was impossible to have them all under one roof: Alice and her husband Vivian Fraser, Phillis and her husband George Gordon, Thomas and his wife, with Alice's three children and Phillis's two; and then dear Guy, who, though he was not married yet, sounded as if he were thinking of it. Some of them had to be farmed out to the hotel or a boarding-house at the other end of the town, a mile away. "Whereas if we had Harperslea we could all get in, and it wouldn't even be a squeeze. I do wish Jack weren't so unreasonable about moving," thought Mrs. Lorimer, sitting up in bed with her hands clasped round her knees which she had pulled up very inelegantly almost to her chin below the sheets.

Woodside stood high, and through the open window she could look straight across to a line of rolling green hills, bright in the morning sunlight which gilded the newly-shorn sheep feeding on their flanks. It was June, and the gayer green of young bracken sprawled in big irregular patches over the grass. It was the sort of landscape which can be seen over and over again in the Scottish borders, but which yet succeeds in avoiding mere repetition by an individuality owned by each hill, each burn, each tree. Mrs. Lorimer loved the outlook from her bedroom window. She knew it at every season of the year, in every change of weather, and never tired of it. She consoled herself now by remembering that Harperslea was shut in by tall trees on this side, and she would miss her view badly if she were deprived of it.

There was a perfunctory knock, the door flew open, and an elderly black Labrador bitch burst into the room, charged up to the bed, panted loudly in Mrs. Lorimer's face, and sank on the floor with an air of utter exhaustion. She was followed less exuberantly by Colonel Lorimer, who advanced and saluted his wife's cheek with a somewhat bristly kiss.

The bristliness was due to an arrangement of the Colonel's called "saving Nan trouble," by which he postponed shaving until he was almost dressed, when he took an ancient pewter tankard down to the kitchen, filled it from a kettle (which had to be kept on the boil for this purpose) and retreated with it to the bathroom full of a glow of unselfishness. As Nan appeared to be resigned to the procedure, Mrs. Lorimer had never tried to baulk her husband of this simple pleasure. His day was made up of routine of this kind and if he liked it that way, why should he not enjoy it to the full?

"Good morning, darling," said Mrs. Lorimer, accepting the kiss. "Give June that tea in my cup, will you? I forgot to drink it and it's cold."

This also was routine, and if Mrs. Lorimer sometimes wondered what would happen if she finished her tea one morning herself, she was too kind-hearted to put it into practice.

"Nan tells me that Harperslea has been sold," remarked Mrs. Lorimer.

"That great barrack of a place stuck down in the bottom of a bog!" was her husband's instant reply. "Can you imagine anyone being such a fool as to buy a place like that? They'll regret it, mark my words. I said to Turnbull last night at the meeting, 'Mark my words, Turnbull,' I said, 'the fellow that's bought Harperslea will regret it.' The place must be infested with midges, down in the hollow like that. Infested. Mosquitoes too, I shouldn't wonder. And damp! Lord, how damp it must be!"

"So you heard about it last night," murmured Mrs. Lorimer.

"Somebody mentioned it—Browning, I think. What a size that fellow's getting, Lucy! He ought to do something about it—take up gardening, or something. Yes, he said he'd heard Harperslea had been bought by some stranger, from Glasgow, I think. I meant to tell you, knowing you had a notion of the place, but it slipped my mind. It would never have done for us, m' dear. Never. Damp as it is, you'd be riddled with rheumatism in a few months. I'm willing to bet it's full of dry-rot, too. I don't envy the fellow that's bought it. He'll regret it."

"I expect he had it thoroughly surveyed before he bought it," said Mrs. Lorimer.

"I hope so. I hope so," said the Colonel gloomily. "Not that a survey will tell him about the midges. What are you going to be doing today, Lucy?"

"Gray is coming along to see me this morning and staying to lunch. She got back from London yesterday," Mrs. Lorimer said.

"Good! You and she will have a lot to talk about. I'll make myself scarce."

"Well, Jack, you'll be in for lunch, I suppose? Gray will want to see you too, you know."

Colonel Lorimer, who so seldom ate a meal away from his own house that the event was one of almost international importance to him, agreed that he would be in for lunch. "I have to go down the town this morning," he added. "Anything I can do for you, Lucy?"

This was a daily occurrence, and therefore a daily inquiry. Mrs. Lorimer was sometimes hard put to it to think up errands for him. It was useless to ask him to bring home the fish or mince for that day's luncheon, since his discussions with acquaintances met in the street made him oblivious to the passage of time so that the meal would be late and Nan exasperated. But a semblance of necessity, of affairs, had to be given to what was really a social expedition, and Mrs. Lorimer had become adept at asking him to do things which appeared important without taking up very much time.

"Yes, Jack. Would you leave a small parcel at Miss Fleming's for me as you pass?" she said. "It's that book she lent me weeks ago, of very dull reminiscences, and I have read as much of it as I can bear. Why will people insist on lending me books? They are never the ones I want to read. It is on the chest in the hall, tied up and with her name on it."

Colonel Lorimer accepted the mission, promised to carry it out to the best of his ability, and prepared to leave the room, calling loudly on June to accompany him.

Mrs. Lorimer decided that she might as well get up. While she dressed she wondered what the day would be like. It had begun disagreeably with the news that Harperslea was now really beyond her reach, but Gray was coming, which was pleasant. Gray and she could always find something to laugh about together.

2

The town of Threipford is quite small and compact, lying in a sheltered position with hills all round it except where the valley widens southward and flattens out into a land of rich pasture and fine woods. The hills on east and west are cut by smaller valleys which streams made thousands of years ago when the great glaciers finally melted and sent streams of water on their way to join Threip Water flowing past the little town.

Woodside, the Lorimers' house, was on the north side of Threipford, and Thimblefield Cottage, where Miss Grace Douglas, whom her intimates called "Gray" lived, was on the east. To go round by the road from one to the other meant a walk of over a mile, but the distance could be halved if one climbed the wall at the back of Thimblefield's garden and went across the meadows, jumping two burns and scaling two more walls, and finally coming out on the road opposite the garden gate of Woodside. It was not a route to be recommended in wet weather, when the fields, in spite of extensive draining, reverted to their original bog, and the streams became torrents, but the morning of Miss Douglas's visit to Mrs. Lorimer followed a week without rain. Gray's shoes were thick, and she was rather late in starting—she was often rather late in starting—so she took the short cut without hesitation.

Though she was a large woman she moved lightly, and quarter of an hour saw her at the Lorimers' heavy iron sidegate, and wondering for the hundredth time, as its hinges shrieked piteously under her vigorous push, why Jack didn't oil them.

Lucy met her where the path ended and the level gravelled stretch in front of the house began.

"Come in, dear," she said. "I heard the gate and guessed it was you."

"How lovely to see you, Lucy. Do you keep the gate un-oiled so that you are warned of the enemy's approach?"

The two soft, rather faded cheeks touched in an affectionate kiss. Lucy linked her arm through Gray's and laughed.

"It is Jack's affair—the gate's being so squeaky," she said.

"Then it is certainly to give warning of the enemy's approach," said Gray. "I never met anyone who viewed the arrival of visitors with the horror that Jack does. He always makes me think of a beleaguered garrison."

"Well, he doesn't consider you the enemy."

"No, and it's a blessing, because I couldn't keep away from seeing you, and it would be very awkward, wouldn't it?"

"Gray, I *am* glad to see you." Lucy's voice held a warmth which only a few of her real intimates heard. "I was feeling gloomy, and you have made me laugh already."

They went into the pleasant rather shabby drawing-room and sat down companionably side by side on the sofa.

"Why are you gloomy, Lucy dear?" asked Miss Douglas. "Or don't you want to tell?"

"Oh, yes. It's just—you know how I've always hankered after Harperslea? Well, it's been sold," Mrs. Lorimer said sadly.

The two were friends and had been for many years before Miss Douglas, a little battered by war experiences, had settled down in Threipford, to Mrs. Lorimer's quiet content. Not only were they genuinely fond of one another, but they had many mutual interests; but neither had ever tried to probe into her friend's innermost reserves, and this reticence seemed only to have strengthened the friendship. Both wrote; each admired the other's work. Lucy possessed what Gray knew she herself would never have, a quality which for want of a better name she called "saleability." Lucy had made a name by a succession of quiet workmanlike novels, redeemed from any suggestion of the commonplace by their agreeably astringent humour and lack of sentimentality. Now she earned a comfortable income, and if she did not actually supply the family bread and butter, the family jam and cake depended largely on her. If, then, she had been so anxious to own Harperslea—and Gray quite saw that Woodside was too small—why had not she bought it herself?

As if the thought had been given shape in words, Lucy answered it. "Jack simply won't *hear* of our leaving Woodside," she remarked. "We could afford a bigger house quite well, we *need* a bigger house if the children all want to be at home together, but there's such an uproar whenever I speak of it that I always give in. I like a quiet life."

"Once you get over the shame of being an old maid, there is something to be said for single blessedness," said Gray.

"There's a great deal to be said for it," answered Mrs. Lorimer with feeling. "Besides—an old maid, Gray! You know you could have married if you'd wanted to."

"Not exactly. I've had an offer or two, but never from the men I wanted them from," said Gray candidly. "Besides, one can hardly go about wearing a placard with 'I've had a proposal but I didn't choose to accept it' printed on it."

"Ridiculous old thing!" Mrs. Lorimer laughed.

"I know I'm an old thing, love, but don't dwell on it," entreated Miss Douglas.

"Well, I'm far older than you—"

"And there's no need to boast about that, either."

Then they both laughed a good deal and felt quite young, knowing that however grown-up and even elderly they might appear, say, to the young Lorimers, it was all humbug, for they really knew very little more than the coming generations. They were making so much noise, this quiet reserved Mrs. Lorimer and her friend, that the sound of the front-door bell was not heard by them, and when Nan opened the door of the drawing-room, remarking, "Here's Mrs. Young!" they were smitten into petrified silence.

Mrs. Young marched in, her determined tread making the Dresden shepherdesses in the cabinet opposite the windows tremble. "Well, Lucy, it seems that I've managed to find you in at last!" she said in trenchant tones. ("And find you out, too, sitting here giggling and gossiping with that Douglas female when you say you're writing and mustn't be disturbed!" her cold eye added accusingly.) "Good morning, Miss Douglas. I heard you were in London."

"I'm back," said Gray meekly.

"So I see. Now, Lucy—" Mrs. Young turned a sternly tailored tweed back on Gray. "It's your husband I want to talk to, really. About the Show. He'll have to get the Legion to do a bit more than they did last year, you know."

"Sit down, Margaret, and have a cup of tea," said Mrs. Lorimer, once more quiet and calm and low-voiced. "I'll give Jack your message if you like, but you know I don't interfere with his affairs. I think he must still be in the town."

Gray, who was steadfastly avoiding Lucy's eye by looking out of the window—for she knew that she might quite easily disgrace herself otherwise—caught sight at this moment of a spare soldierly figure slinking rapidly down the path to be lost to view among the rhododendrons. "The garrison beating a strategic retreat," she thought. "Nan must have warned him. I suppose he'll go to ground in the garden until Mrs. Young's gone. What cowards men are!"

"Tea, Gray?" It was plain from Mrs. Lorimer's voice that the offer was not being made for the first time, and Gray turned round guiltily, met her glance, and realized that Lucy had a very good idea of her husband's whereabouts. But not a flicker disturbed her gentle gravity as she handed the glass to Miss Douglas.

In silence, complete on the part of Miss Douglas, broken only in civil monosyllables by Mrs. Lorimer, they sat while Mrs. Young issued the instructions which she wished passed on to Colonel Lorimer.

At last, at long last, the flow dwindled to a trickle and then ceased. Mrs. Young drained her cup, twitched her good felt hat further over her eyes, and rose. "Must be getting on. I've a lot to do," she announced. "You won't forget to tell your husband, now, Lucy? It's important." She sketched a gesture of farewell to Gray Douglas, took Mrs. Lorimer's hand in a firm clasp, and left.

Tramping feet were heard in the hall, with much wheezing and grunting from June, and the Colonel made a brisk military entrance.

"Ha, Gray! Good morning to you. You and Lucy been having a crack, eh? I would have come in sooner, but I didn't like to disturb you," he said, shaking hands.

"I suppose Nan told you that Mrs. Young was here and that's why you stayed in the garden," observed his wife. "You great baby! And it was you she came to see."

"Too bad! Too bad!" said the Colonel, his tone of regret deceiving none of his hearers, for if June's expression of disapproval meant anything, she was no more taken in than the other ladies present. "Was it about the Show?"

"It was. And as I've forgotten half of what she told me you had better ring her up after lunch," said Mrs. Lorimer.

"But Lucy, I can't. She says so much I forget the beginning before she gets to the end," said her husband pitifully. "And anyhow, it's none of her business. She knows quite well that the Show committee will let us know what they want the Legion to do."

"Then you had better tell her that too," said his wife callously. "I have been a buffer state for forty minutes when I wanted to talk to Gray, and most unpleasant I found it. Be a man, Jack!"

"I'll ring Turnbull up and put him on to her," said the Colonel, brightening. "He's the man for the job. I have a great deal to do in the garden this afternoon. I was talking to Turnbull about these turnips of mine, you know, Lucy, that didn't get a prize last year, at the Show, though they were fine turnips. But they had a slight purplish tinge round the top, you know, and Turnbull suggested that *that* might have been against them in a class for *white* turnips. Turnbull, as a professional gardener, knows all about these things, and he advises me to try Addisan's White Pearl this year. I always believe in taking an expert's advice, Gray. As I said to Johnstone when he asked my opinion on a matter, 'My dear fellow,' I said, 'that's the Town Council's job. Ask the Town Council.' And so I've got my expert's advice on my turnips, you see."

"I didn't know they discussed turnips at Town Council meetings," said Gray, greatly bewildered but interested.

Colonel Lorimer looked equally bewildered, and his wife began to laugh.

"I must have misled you, my dear Gray," he exclaimed in courteous distress. "Quite unintentionally. Surely I didn't tell Gray that we were talking about turnips at the Town Council, Lucy?"

"I don't know what you thought you were telling us, Jack," said his wife.

"It was to *Turnbull* that I was talking about turnips," began the Colonel, when fortunately the gong was sounded for lunch, and he hurried away to give June her dinner first.

"I'm sorry, Lucy," said Gray. "I suppose I am extra dull-witted today, or something."

"It's with being away. You're out of practice," Mrs. Lorimer consoled her. "The children always say it takes them three or four days to get accustomed to Jack's grasshopper conversations. Come and have lunch."

3

After the meal had been rounded off by excellent coffee—Nan had a real gift for making coffee—Mrs. Lorimer suggested that she and Gray should go for a walk.

"Aren't you supposed to rest after lunch?" Gray demurred.

"I shouldn't rest if I spent the afternoon thinking that we've hardly had a chance to talk to each other, and remembering all the things I want to tell you and ask you. We needn't go far, just up the hill where we can sit in peace without interruptions."

So they took a rug and an old burberry to sit on, and after walking a short distance up the road which led to a shepherd's house at the head of the valley, left it for the rough grass and new springing heather of the moor. In a sheltered dip, where a huge rough boulder, its face softened by growths of lichen, grey and yellow-brown, offered support for their backs, the two spread their burberry with the rug above it, and sat down to enjoy the afternoon air, balmy and warm, yet fresh. Though their announced intention had been to talk undisturbed, the two sat in companionable silence for a long time, each enjoying their surroundings in her own way.

"What a pity it is," said Lucy suddenly, her eyes on the tiny shape of a gull which was flying slowly overhead, immensely high, "that people have to sleep in houses."

"Well, they don't *have* to," Gray pointed out. "But the alternative, in our climate at least, is often very uncomfortable. Of course there are tents or caravans—why do you think it's a pity?"

"Because if they were like birds they could sleep out quite comfortably without tents or anything. And as far as I can see, if the family wants to come here in force this summer—and they always choose the time when the hotel and all the boarding-houses are full to the doors—that is what they will have to do," said Lucy. "I don't see Jack allowing tents to be pitched on the lawn, or caravans standing about the garden."

"I didn't realize that you were speaking of it from a practical angle," murmured Gray. "I thought it was on a general back-to-Nature principle."

"I'm really speaking of the impossibility of cramming them all into Woodside."

"The children could all go into Jack's little sitting-room," began Miss Douglas in a brisk sensible manner. "Alice and her husband could have the spare bedroom, Thomas and Mary Guy's room—"

"Phillis and George and Guy could all sleep under the dining-room table and the two Nannies on the drawing-room sofa, I suppose. How jolly it will be!" finished Mrs. Lorimer bitterly.

Entering into the spirit of the game, Gray suggested: "Alice and Phillis and Mary in the spare room, Thomas and Vivian and George and Guy in Guy's room, on the dormitory system."

"But Gray, dear, do be *sensible*. This is serious," begged Mrs. Lorimer. "It's dreadful to think of having to tell them they can't all come at once. It is their best chance of seeing each other, and for me of seeing them all together, and it just happens that for once they could all get off at the same time."

Gray pulled herself together and demanded to be told exactly what the capacity of Woodside was in terms of guests. After a lengthy discussion, during which all possible and some impossible permutations and combinations were discussed, they found that Alice and Phillis with their husbands and families could be accommodated.

"But we still haven't found room for Thomas and Mary, or Guy," said the anxious mother.

"Yes, we have. I've had a perfectly good idea for that," Gray said. "They can come to me. It's not exactly under the parental roof, but it isn't *too* far from it."

"To Thimblefield?"

"Yes. Why not? Bed and breakfast, and they can spend the rest of the time at Woodside."

"Oh, Gray dear, bless you!" said Lucy. "Are you sure you could bear it?"

"I'll try," said Gray in the quavering tones of hard-pressed courage. "You silly creature, of course I can! I'm fond of Thomas and Mary, and *very* fond of Guy."

"Guy really is rather a dear," Lucy agreed in a tone that did not succeed in sounding quite impartial.

"He's the most like you of your four," said Gray thoughtfully.

"Yes, I believe he is," said Lucy. "He's the one who likes books and pictures and poetry. The others never seem to read at all and pictures to them usually mean the cinema."

"Lucy! They aren't so bad as that!"

"Very nearly. But Gray, to go back to your suggestion of having some of the family at Thimblefield, it really would be marvellous. You see, they have made up their minds to be at Threipford at the end of June—quite soon now, and I haven't broken it to Jack yet! I'd particularly hate to have to put Guy off. He sounds from his letters as if he had an idea of getting married," said Lucy. "And I do want to *see* him. Letters tell you so little, and he doesn't write very often. If he were here I could find out about this girl who is always creeping into them. I do hope she is nice enough for him—"

"You won't think any girl is nice enough for Guy," observed her friend.

"Yes, I will, if she is! But this Iris doesn't sound his kind at all. I do so want Guy to be happy, Gray, and there can't be much chance of happiness in marriage with an absolutely unsuitable girl."

"Suppose you consider her unsuitable and Guy considers her suitable, what are you to do?" asked Gray drily.

"Yes, that's the trouble," said Lucy, and her intelligent sensitive face looked pinched with maternal worry.

"It's no use crossing bridges that haven't even been built, before you come to them," said Gray. "Guy hasn't actually proposed to this Iris yet, has he?"

"I don't know. He may have by now, but I haven't had more than a few lines from him for three weeks," Lucy said with a sigh. "I do hope it will be all right."

Gray Douglas hoped so too, but she had seen too many charming, normally intelligent young men make idiotic and even disastrous marriages to feel very hopeful. All she could do, as they gathered up the rug and burberry and started slowly homewards, was to talk cheerfully about the time, only a few weeks ahead, when Lucy would have all her family with her, or at least close at hand.

CHAPTER TWO

1

"OH, LUCY! So the new carpet has come in time, after all! How in the world did you manage to inveigle Davie Dunlop into laying it? It *does* look nice!" Gray Douglas, arriving at Woodside to have supper with the Lorimers on an evening towards the end of June, a night or two before the first contingent of the family was due, stopped in the drawing-room doorway to admire the effect.

"I'm so glad you like it, Gray. You are a great comfort," said Mrs. Lorimer, squeezing her friend's arm affectionately.

"Like it? Of course I like it. Who doesn't?" Gray asked, and indeed the soft green which covered the drawing-room floor was extremely handsome and showed up the chintzes of sofa and chairs, the sheen of the old mahogany display cabinet, to perfection.

"My dear! You have no idea, no idea at all, how Jack has been going on ever since it came," said Lucy. "He has prophesied every possible harm that can come to it, from moth and spilt ink to the boys' shoes and Nan's hoovering!"

Gray laughed. "That's quite customary, isn't it?"

"Yes, but he has never been so bad about anything new that I've bought for the house. Never," replied Lucy impressively. "Here he comes. Now you will get it all at first hand."

The Colonel entered, shook hands with his wife's friend in his usual courteous fashion, fixed her with a piercing eye, and demanded: "What do you think of Lucy's new carpet?"

"I think it's beautiful. And I'm sure it will wear well," said Gray, and received a look of gratitude from Mrs. Lorimer.

The Colonel shook his head gloomily. "I hope you're right, Gray, but I doubt if it will get a chance to wear well. As I said to

Lucy, it is a sheer waste of money to put down a new carpet in this house."

"Why?" asked Miss Douglas.

"Oh, Gray, don't encourage him!" murmured Mrs. Lorimer, knowing well that Gray never could resist doing so.

"Why?" cried the Colonel. "Why?" he repeated on a slightly lower note. "Do you remember the old carpet. Gray?"

"Yes, of course I do. It was a very nice carpet but it had got badly worn."

"Ah!" said the Colonel. "'It had got badly worn,' you say. Quite so. Quite so. And that's what will happen to this one, mark my words."

"But, Jack, it will be *ages* before this one gets worn to that degree," said the bewildered Gray, on whom the repetition of the words 'Carpet' and 'Worn' was beginning to have the effect of heavy breakers battering a cliff, all sound and no sense.

"Ah, well! I don't suppose it will survive the boots and shoes trampling over it when the family come," said the Colonel, registering resignation. "And the children dribbling milk on it and treading jam into it, and the cigarette ash that will be sprayed everywhere—Ah, well, I must go and wash my hands for supper." He made a fine exit on these words, rather spoiled by his reappearance a few seconds later to say: "I can't think why, if you had to have a new carpet at all, you didn't wait until these hordes had left!"

"Because I wanted to have it before they came," said Mrs. Lorimer. "Do go and wash, Jack!"

He vanished, leaving the door open. A stunned silence fell upon the room.

"I must say," said Miss Douglas at last, with an air of critical admiration, "that I have seldom if ever heard Jack in such form."

"Really," Lucy answered, "life is too short and difficult to get in a fever over a carpet. There's the gong. Come to supper."

One of the reasons why Gray had come to supper this evening was so that she and Mrs. Lorimer might discuss the final arrangements for the housing and feeding of those members of the Lorimer family who were to sleep at Thimblefield Cottage.

"The trouble is that I can't tell you exactly when Thomas and Mary will be here," said Lucy, rummaging in a large wicker market-basket which she found a convenient receptacle for her more immediate papers. "Here is Thomas's letter. He says they are coming by car, and Mary will let you know the probable time. But I don't suppose she will ever remember. And I've had no word from Guy yet."

This was awkward, since Gray herself had had a short but friendly letter from Lieutenant Guy Lorimer, R.N., in which he announced that he expected to come to Threipford by road, some time on Saturday evening. She could guess the reason for his writing to her quite easily; he could simply thank her for giving him a bed and did not need to go into details about his young woman or his own feelings—or to omit them—one of which he would have had to do in a letter to his mother. It struck Gray as very sinister, but she would have to tell Lucy, sinister or no.

As carelessly as she could, she said, "Oh, I've had a note from Guy. He's coming by road too, and will turn up some time late-ish on Saturday. I suppose he didn't have time to write you a proper letter, Lucy, and wanted to let me know because he's sleeping at Thimblefield."

"I suppose so," said Lucy dubiously, but without much conviction. "It's not *like* him, Gray! There's something wrong. Oh dear! Sometimes I wish children didn't have to grow up. One can do quite a lot for them while they *are* children, but now—It's hard to have to sit back and watch them hurting themselves."

"It must be," Gray said. "But as long as you have the sense to sit back and not interfere, you will at least have the satisfaction of knowing that they'll probably come to you for comfort sooner or later."

"It isn't much satisfaction," Lucy said sadly, and Gray could think of no reply to this disagreeable truth.

2

Everyone knows that horrible feeling of impending doom which occasionally casts a dark shadow on their waking moments. To Lucy Lorimer it was no stranger, especially during the wars, in the first of which her husband, and in the second two sons, a daughter and a son-in-law had been in constant danger. But it was in a way even more horrible, because it was so unnatural, to trace this feeling to its cause on a fine Saturday morning at the end of June, and find it was due to her younger son's expected arrival. With deep and growing distress she realized that the reserve on which, privately, she had always prided herself, was going to stand between her and Guy. Nor could she hope to move this barrier by allowing the affection and anxiety in her heart to appear in her manner; any unwonted demonstrativeness would only seem to threaten his own reserve, inherited from her, and do more harm than good. Remembering, while she looked unhappily out at the sun-washed hillsides, the serious small boy with the scratched and grubby knees who had brought all his perplexities to her, Mrs. Lorimer, that quiet woman, so unsentimental that she had sometimes been condemned as cold and unfeeling, shed a few of the slow bitter tears of middle age.

But it is impossible to lie in bed and weep, however much one may wish to do so, when morning tea is cooling by one's side, when the gong will sound presently, and the family gather for breakfast. A face showing the traces of tears is liable to cause comment, or at least to make everyone else wonder what is the matter, and with Alice and Vivian already in the house, with the voices of their children chirping like the birds but a great deal louder, downstairs, Mrs. Lorimer had to deny herself this indulgence. She dried her tears, drank her tea, and prepared to face the day's demands.

Once involved in the daily round Mrs. Lorimer had no time to sit and brood over Guy's possible troubles, and though they were present at the back of her mind, her remaining brain power was fully occupied. Alice had to be invited, without hurting her feelings, to keep her children out of Colonel Lorimer's way, weekend meals for the large household had to be discussed with Nan, who was inclined to show very little interest in them, her burning wish being to tell Mrs. Lorimer with great frankness what a low opinion she had of Alice's Nannie, coupled with the hope that Phillis's nurse would prove less stuck-up. Vivian wanted a round of golf if someone could be found to play with him, the flowers had to be done. By the time she had gone to the town, where the shops were filled with the usual Saturday morning crowd, swelled by visitors who had nothing to do but dawdle in and out obstructing the housewives intent on filling their shopping baskets, or formed solid blocks of humanity on the narrow pavements, Mrs. Lorimer was conscious only of a longing for lunch to be over so that she could retire for an hour to lie down before evening brought the rest of the family to Woodside.

3

At Thimblefield Miss Douglas, who very rarely indulged in an afternoon rest because she did not feel the need of one, decided that she must mow the lawn before her visitors came, while she had a little spare time. Backwards and forwards she went to the accompaniment of the mower's metallic voice, a shower of green fragments and daisy-heads, and the delicious smell of fresh-cut grass. The lawn was behind the house and separated from it by a large half-moon shaped herbaceous border, at present full of lupins of all colours in full bloom, red pyrethrums and the tall spires of delphiniums. Every now and then she paused to look at them with great pleasure, and at the sloping roof, on three levels, of the house, with its odd little gables jutting out in unexpected places. Thimblefield, an old cottage, had been built on to at different times; one owner had added a room, another had put in a dormer window, and the result, though highly irregular, was attractive and harmonious. Miss Douglas loved her funny little house and was happy in it, and knew that she was happy, an enviable state which is rarer than one would suppose. She had reached that half-way stage in life when there seems to be a pause before starting down the far side of the hill to that unknown valley where death is waiting, and the dark river that has to be crossed. Youth with its fevers and unrest, its terrible miseries and lovely ecstasy, was behind her, gone for ever. She knew it was a loss, but an unavoidable one, and very sensibly seldom looked back over her shoulder.

But this afternoon the rhythmic soothing job, varied by journeys to empty her box of grass-cuttings in the corner behind the large leaves of a row of rhubarb, had given her time to think, and she deliberately glanced at her own youth, remembering it, wondering if by doing so she could perhaps find there something that might help Guy Lorimer—if he needed help. Because she had not married, she felt that she probably knew more about men than her dear Lucy, or knew them from a different angle. It seemed to her that by marrying young, by seeing one man at such close quarters, a woman lost her sense of perspective where men as a whole were concerned. Gray had heard her married friends discussing husbands, and had frequently wondered if such discussions did not betray as much ignorance as knowledge of those queer complex creatures, men.

"But I may be quite wrong, of course," she added aloud, banging the box back on the lawn-mower and pushing back the hair from her hot brow with her wrist so that she transferred a quantity of bits of grass to her face. "After all, being married must teach you a lot that otherwise you can never know. Love affairs aren't the same at all."

A young man who had wheeled his dusty motor-bicycle in at the gate unheard, come quietly round the house and now stood watching her, smiled involuntarily.

"Still talking out loud to yourself, Gray?" he said. "It's a sign of madness, you know. Or so they say."

"Good heavens, Guy!" exclaimed Gray crossly. "Fancy coming creeping in on me like that! It's enough to make anyone go mad.

And here I am, as red as a beetroot and covered with grass, I suppose—"

"Yes, love. Covered—at least, your face is. And I must say that your welcome is original if nothing else."

Gray laughed. "I'm sorry. I really am very glad to see you, Guy. Did you come straight here—to Thimblefield, I mean?"

He nodded. "I thought I might as well dump my gear before going home," he said. "Would there be a cup of tea going? I'm dying of thirst."

"Bed and breakfast were the terms of my agreement," said Miss Douglas severely. "What will your mother think if you don't go and see her at once?"

"Oh—well—she's probably still resting, isn't she?" Guy said, adding persuasively, "So what about a nice cup of tea?"

"Oh, all right. I'll go and put the kettle on." Gray realized that in her sympathy with Lucy's feelings she was not playing her part of hostess very well. "It won't take long."

"I'll finish the grass for you!" he shouted after her as she went into the house, and the sound of the lawn-mower in action drowned the rush of water into the kettle.

"He ought to be putting his things in his room, I suppose, so that he can go on to Woodside as soon as he has had his tea," thought Gray, setting cups and saucers on the tray, and getting out a large gingerbread, its top generously sprinkled with almonds, from a tin. "But he'll probably find mowing soothing. He's being violent enough about it to take his mind off anything!"

She glanced from the kitchen window at him, noticing, when he turned and the light caught his face, how thin it had grown, surprising on it a look of misery that distressed her greatly.

As if he could feel her eyes on him, Guy stopped. "What are you snooping for?" he called.

"Can't a woman look out of her own kitchen window if she wants to?" Gray called back. "I'm watching to see if you're making a good job of it."

"Oh!" was all his reply, but she thought there was relief as well as amusement in the exclamation.

Just as she had made the tea he came to the window. "Operation Daisy completed," he announced. "Coming to inspect?"

"All right," said his hostess. "You come in, though, and after you've washed your filthy paws and dried them on the towel provided, *not* on the dishcloth, you can carry the tray into the drawing-room."

"Anyone'd think I was twelve years old," he grumbled, coming in by the back door and bringing a large quantity of grass-cuttings with him which proceeded to fall all over the floor.

"You were twelve when I first met you," observed Miss Douglas, unmoved. "And you look every bit as dirty now as you did then."

Guy flung his arms round her and squeezed her until she shrieked for mercy. "I like a nice armful," he said as he released her, breathless and untidy and covered with grass. "Perhaps that'll larn you to be more civil to an officer of His Britannic Majesty's Navy."

"This is all very undignified," said Gray, and made her escape to the garden, where she found the lawn mown to her satisfaction and the mower put neatly away in the tool-shed.

"Tidy creature," she thought approvingly. "He's like Lucy in that too."

"Tea is served, and my tongue is blackening with thirst!" shouted Guy, so she went in and poured it out, filling a large cup which held almost half a pint for her guest.

"What a sensible woman you are," he said, drinking it to the dregs and holding it out for more with a horrid collection of tea-leaves all up the inside. "None of your fiddling little things like egg-cups, but a real CUP. May I have a refill?"

"I suppose so. You've emptied the tea-pot already, and what a disgusting trail of tea-leaves you've sucked all up the side of your cup," said Gray inhospitably. "But as soon as you've drunk it you must go to Woodside. Have some gingerbread? It's good. I made it."

"No, thanks. I'm not hungry," said Guy. "I suppose I must push on home in a few minutes."

"You certainly must," replied Miss Douglas, handing him the replenished cup.

He took it, set it carefully on a little table at his elbow, leaned forward and said: "Gray! I'm in the very devil of a mess!"

"So it's come!" thought Gray Douglas. "Help me to say the right thing!" she implored inwardly. Aloud she said quietly: "Money?"

"I'm on the rocks, but that's the least part of it. I can get over *that* all right," he answered, staring at her as if he did not see her at all.

"Do you want to tell me, or am I just to say I'm sorry?" asked Gray.

"I don't know what I want!" he said, stirring restlessly so that he knocked against the table and made the tea in his cup pour over into the saucer and splash to the carpet. This clumsiness in Guy, usually so neat of movement, and his entire disregard of the tea dripping from the table's edge, showed Gray more plainly than any words what his state of mind must be. Then he went on, speaking fast and low, the whole thing tumbling out in broken sentences as if he could not stop them. "By heaven, I *do* know what I want, though! I want Iris—Iris—she's so lovely, Gray! I thought she would marry me, it was just about settled when I went off on the Spring cruise. I got back to find her engaged to the Surgeon Commander. They were married yesterday—arch of swords, garland rigged, and all—and I was one of the arch of swords! Laugh that off! I've come straight from their wedding, after changing. What a joke, isn't it?"

There seemed to be nothing to say, so Gray remained silent.

"Don't tell me there are as good fish in the sea, for heaven's sake!" he begged.

"I wasn't going to. It isn't much use, when your heart is set on one particular fish."

"And you know, I thought she was as fond of me as I am of her," he said in a voice of complete astonishment. "Why are women like that?"

"All women aren't," said Gray.

He did not appear to have heard her. "I feel as if I were filled with red-hot coke," he said. "All the way here I could see her face a little way ahead of me—that lovely face! I kept on trying to catch up with her—oh, what's the use? I can't explain."

"You don't need to." Gray knew that madness in the blood, remembered it with a stab of pain. While it lasted there was nothing more terrible, and it was no good telling Guy that it passed; after a long time or a short, it did pass . . .

"Did you come all the way here without stopping?" she asked, wondering how, in his present state, he had avoided an accident.

"Oh, I stopped for cups of tea or coffee at those long-distance lorry drivers' dives," he said listlessly. "There didn't seem much point in stopping for the night anywhere so I just came on. The trouble is, I don't know how I can face Ma."

"It won't be easy. And yet you will have to," Gray said quietly.

"You're being uncommonly decent to me about this," he said suddenly, looking at her again, but this time seeing her. "You must think I'm the world's greatest fool—"

"When you're in love you can't help being a fool," said Miss Douglas.

"How d'you know that?" His voice showed a faint curiosity which she was thankful to hear. Uncomplimentary though it was, it did at least betoken a return towards normality.

"Perhaps that womanly intuition one reads about," she said, remembering that to the young it was almost indecent to suggest that their elders had ever known these shattering experiences.

He sighed. "It sounded more as if you *knew*," was all he said. Then his glance fell on the cup lying on its side, and the dark stain on the old red carpet. "Good Lord! Did I do that? I say, Gray, I'm sorry! What a clumsy brute I am!" he exclaimed, getting up. "Look here, we ought to do something about it or it will leave a mark. I'll fetch a cloth and a pail of water."

Gray did not stop him, tired though he was; and the careful rubbing and mopping which he proceeded to do seemed to restore his balance.

He rose and stretched himself. "I'll put these away and then I'll go on home," he said. "I feel—a bit more like a human being and less like a mad dog."

"Good. Lucy is worrying about you. She guessed something was wrong."

"She was bound to, I suppose. My letters have been pretty scrappy lately. But the great thing about Ma is that she keeps calm," he said. "She never makes a fuss."

He got on to his motor-bike and chugged away.

Miss Douglas, feeling as if she had been put through a mangle and then run over by a traction-engine, went to wash up the tea-things.

CHAPTER THREE

1

WHEN Guy came to the cross-roads where he should turn north for Woodside, he stopped again, and still straddling his motor-bike, wondered once more how he was going to face the family, and especially his mother.

"If I play the clown it will be worse than being just plain gloomy," he thought. "Why did I come at all? I'd have been far better to stay away."

But the instinctive longing for the familiar places where he had been happy had not led him astray. As he sat there with the noisy engine switched off, the sights and sounds and scents of the countryside began to work their gentle magic on him.

Unconsciously Guy was drawing in strength as he breathed. He was wretchedly unhappy, with a gritty burning misery which made him feel, as he had said to Gray Douglas, that he was filled with red-hot coke, but he seemed better able to bear it here. At last he started up the bike again and roared off towards his home.

The solid Victorian house, which had no claim to beauty, sat down so comfortably above its sloping garden, among its sheltering beeches, its stone walk and slate roof were so well suited to the landscape, that it always succeeded in conveying an impression of good looks. First and foremost, it was a home, a house where people lived happy, useful lives, where a certain standard of conduct and thought obtained, where money was assessed at its proper value because it had been earned, but was never allowed to usurp too high a position. It was always a servant, a useful servant, never a master. Mrs. Lorimer set the standard by which the household at Woodside was ruled; her quiet personality irradiated its every activity.

It would be quite untrue to say that thoughts like these were in Guy Lorimer's mind as he pushed his vehicle up the steep hill, for his thoughts were a jumble of what shall I say to Ma when I see her? Iris—Iris—Why on earth the parents picked a house at the top of a precipice beats me—and Iris again. He simply felt in every nerve and muscle of his tired body that this was home and everything that home should be.

The garage, formerly a coach-house, filled one end of the cobbled yard at the back of Woodside, and here Guy, wheeling his horrible bike in at the open double doors, discovered his brother-in-law George Gordon, Phillis's husband, subjecting his car to a passionate scrutiny.

"Well, my boy!" said George, straightening himself and giving the motor-bike a glance of contemptuous tolerance. "So you've fetched up here all right."

Guy liked George, apart from his habit of greeting people far too often with "Well, my boy," a trick which he was popularly supposed to have adopted from an Engineer Admiral whom he much admired. So he responded: "Well, my boy to you. Yes, I've got here. Why not?"

"Wonder you trust yourself to that infernal stink-box of yours," said George.

"Well, you trusted not only yourself but Philly and the brats to your rattle-trap. The marvel to me is that *you* got here. Where's everybody?"

"Somewhere about. It's just on tea-time," said George absent-mindedly. Then his eyes lighted with the fire of the single-minded enthusiast: "The old car's a blooming wonder, Guy. She came here like a bird. There's nothing to beat these pre-war engines."

"They're not so good when they are attached to a body like Noah's ark. I wonder you didn't *marry* an internal combustion engine," said Guy. "It beats me how Philly stands it."

"Philly's all right. She's got the children," murmured George with his head inside the bonnet.

"Well, if this is matrimony—"

"You don't know a thing about it," George mumbled.

"Nor I do," answered Guy, reminded of his misery. "I'll go in, I think." And he walked off round the corner of the house. A confused noise which he had been conscious of vaguely while he talked to George became deafening and resolved itself into the babble of voices, the clatter of china, and children shouting. As he reached the door, Colonel Lorimer came out, wearing an expression of acute disgust, and carrying a cup of tea.

"My dear boy!" he exclaimed. "How are you? Fit, I hope? I'm glad to see you, extremely glad. That is," he added, "I should be glad if I were able to feel glad about anything at the moment."

"What's wrong, Father?" asked Guy. "And what's all the noise?"

"The noise," said Colonel Lorimer in a voice of restrained fury, "is my grandchildren. Your nephews and nieces, Guy. With the idea of giving them a treat, they are all having tea with us today. A *treat*! My boy, the dining-room is Bedlam. Sheer Bedlam. I've been driven out to drink my tea in comparative peace." He took a large gulp of tea and continued: "Even poor old June can't stand it. Look at her, Guy!"

Indeed, June, creeping disconsolately about the gravel with a large pink ribbon tied round her shrinking neck, was a deplorable spectacle. Guy began to laugh as she turned her mournful eyes on him. "Here, then, June, old lady," he said, and when she advanced, ripped the adornment off. "She'll feel better now, Father."

"Thank you, my boy, thank you. I only noticed it on the poor creature after I had picked up my cup. It was Alice's twins who did it, or their nurse—a terrible woman, Guy. I don't know how we are going to survive this visit," said his father. He groaned. "And it has only begun. We have to endure a week of it, I understand."

"Well, Father, I've got a fortnight's leave," said Guy. "Are you going to turn me out after a week, or what?"

"My dear boy! Of course not!" cried the Colonel, horrified. "Though as it is, you have been turned out to make room for these young children who would be far better in their own homes. I don't know how your mother can stand it, upon my word, I don't. There she is, a delicate woman, easily tired, sitting in the middle of that frightful din pouring out tea—"

"Good heavens, so she is. I'll go in. I want to see her, and I'd like some tea," said Guy. "I say, Father!" he called, as he went into the house. "Don't forget to give *June* her tea! She looks as if she could do with it."

The hall was cool and dark after the sunlight outside, but it was neither as empty nor as tidy as usual. Before Guy's eyes had accustomed themselves to its mild gloom, he had blundered into a large obstacle and barked his shins. Pushing it away with a hearty curse, he saw that it was a perambulator. The oak chest was littered with small cardigans and sun-bonnets, and a headless doll lay on the rug. At the dining-room door he walked on something soft which squeaked, and recoiled in horror, only to find that what he had trodden on was a peculiarly hideous woollen animal. With a good deal of sympathy for his father, Guy kicked it aside, opened the door, and walked in.

The big oval table was surrounded by Alice and Vivian, Phillis, and a collection of children, all of whom appeared to him to be disagreeably coated about the face with cake crumbs and jam. At the far end, with her back to the windows, behind the tea-tray, sat his mother, wielding an enormous tea-pot. She set it down with a crash and rose.

"Guy dear!" she said in her soft voice.

"Here I am, Ma, all in one piece," he said, giving her two kisses, one on each cheek, and a third "for luck" as he had always said from his preparatory school days.

The meeting, so greatly dreaded, was over; in a minute he was sitting beside her, squeezed in between her and Phillis, and drinking tea as if he had never been away from home except to school.

2

No sooner was tea over than Phillis, who had jumped up three or four times while it was in progress to attend to her small boys' wants, said abruptly, "Coming for a walk, Guy?"

"Oh, not now, Philly! Have a heart. I've only just got here. It's hot, too, let's sit on the lawn," he said.

"What, the whole mob of us? It's like being in the parrot house at a zoo," said Phillis.

"Two of the parrots are your own," he pointed out. "I'm tired, Philly. If you're so set on walking, why not get George to go with you?"

"George?" Phillis laughed. "You don't imagine that anyone is going to tear George away from that horrible box on wheels that he calls a car until it's time to dress for dinner, do you?" Her tone and her laugh had a sharpness which Guy had not heard before in his sister. He guessed, from Mrs. Lorimer's quick turn of the head, that she had noticed it too, but her voice when she spoke was composed and quiet.

"Don't all go rushing away. I'd like to have a look at you, and Thomas and Mary ought to be here soon, then we'll all be together."

"All except George. I suppose you've forgotten him," retorted Phillis. "And I can't say I blame you. I often forget him myself!"

"Philly, you fool!" This was Alice, coming to take her younger sister by the arm, "Ma didn't mean that. You know she didn't. And look at Martin. He's got hold of the jam-spoon!"

The warning came a trifle late. Even as Phillis with an exasperated cry sprang at him, three-year-old Martin, who liked the taste of strawberry jam, withdrew the spoon from his mouth, dipped it into the jam-dish again, and tried to insert its overflowing richness into his mouth once more. Phillis seized his arm, Martin raised the wail of a baffled gourmand, and the spoonful of jam was distributed between his own clean jersey and the table.

"Little pig!" cried Phillis, shaking him, though not urgently.

"Fetch a damp cloth, Alice dear," said Mrs. Lorimer. "It's all right, Martin. Don't cry. Gan will wipe it up."

Vivian Fraser, who had remained an interested spectator, now hazarded the opinion that Martin was howling not because of the mess but because he had been deprived of his prize. The Fraser twins watched with quiet disapproval, and Martin's younger brother, raging helplessly in the confines of a high chair, added his roars to the general turmoil.

"Stop it at once, all of you!" suddenly said Mrs. Lorimer in her deepest voice, which so fascinated her grandchildren that a complete silence fell like balm on the dining-room.

Then Alice's Nannie entered, with Phillis's young nurse-maid in her wake, and the entire brood was swept away, leaving their elders, a little dazed, to betake themselves to chairs and cushions on the lawn.

If Mrs. Lorimer felt that she really preferred children brought up according to more old-fashioned methods, she did not say so, but Guy suffered from no inhibitions on the subject.

"What they all need," he remarked in a general way, throwing himself down on the short dry turf, "is to be beaten."

He had spoken idly, to keep his mind from the hidden pain to which it returned, like the constant biting on an aching tooth, but he was amused to notice the various reactions of his hearers to what, after all, was a perfectly sensible theory.

Mrs. Lorimer smiled faintly, raised her eyebrows, and said nothing. Vivian Fraser also smiled, but sardonically. Phillis turned on her brother in a sudden fury.

"Oh, you brute!" she exclaimed. "I pity *your* children, if you ever have any."

Gentle Alice was looking distressed. "But Guy, you didn't mean it, my dear! It would break their poor little spirits," she began in a worried tone.

"But Alice," said Guy, mocking her kindly, "you surely don't believe that anything short of a sledge-hammer could break those infants' spirits?"

"Children, children," said Mrs. Lorimer, and at once they were carried back to the years when their youthful bickerings could be quelled by that quiet voice.

They all laughed, though Phillis was half-indignant still, and Alice said, "Oh, I *knew* I had something to tell you! It's about Harperslea—you did know it had been bought, Ma, didn't you?"

"Yes, I knew," said Mrs. Lorimer, suppressing a very small sigh as she thought of her own overcrowded house.

"But *have* you heard the name of the man who's bought it?" asked Alice.

"Ramsbottom," and "Huggins," said Guy and Phillis simultaneously.

"*Far* worse. It's Smellie," Alice said.

"I daresay it is, though I can't quite see how a name can be smelly," said Phillis with interest. "But what *is* it, Lal?"

"I've just told you. Smellie."

There was a short pause of complete non-comprehension, and then Mrs. Lorimer said in pitying tones: "Poor things! You mean their *name* is Smellie?"

"Yes, Ma. That's what I said," Alice replied patiently.

A great light broke on the others. "Fancy being called Smellie! How simply frightful," said Phillis.

"Of course one sees it in telephone directories and obituary columns and things," Mrs. Lorimer observed, with the air of one trying to be reasonable. "So there must *be* people called Smellie. But I have never met any of them yet."

"Are you going to call, Ma?" asked Phillis.

"Oh, dear! Do you think I need? Of course they are quite near neighbours, but such a dreadful name," murmured Mrs. Lorimer.

"The girl looks quite a nice little thing," observed Vivian suddenly through a cloud of smoke from his pipe.

"You old satyr! How do you know?" demanded Guy. "You haven't been twenty-four hours in the place and you've smelt out a girl already—no pun intended," he added hastily, as his sisters cried out in indignation.

"She was at the Dunnes' playing tennis. While Mrs. Dunne and Lal were talking, Dunne took me round the place to look at a bull he's bought," explained Vivian. "And we passed the tennis court and I saw her."

"Is she any good?" asked Phillis. "It will be an agreeable change to have someone who can play. I wonder if she's joined the Club?"

"As to the Club, of course, I can't tell you," said Vivian placidly. "She seemed to be banging the balls over the net pretty heartily."

No one else was particularly interested in a strange girl with an unfortunate name who seemed to be good at tennis, but Phillis pursued the subject.

"I wonder if I could ring her up and find out if she is a Club member," she said. "I'd like a game or two, and singles are good practice."

"Good heavens, Philly, you can't ring up a total stranger like that," said Guy, scandalized. "It isn't even as if you lived here now."

"Oh, can't I? Well, I'm going to." Phillis jumped up and went into the house.

"How restless Philly is," murmured Alice.

"Irritable too," added Guy.

Mrs. Lorimer said nothing, but she wished that Phillis were as tranquil and content as Alice. It seemed to her that Guy was not the only one of her children who needed help.

3

Thomas Lorimer, M.B., Ch.B., F.R.C.S., who had never been called Tom even as a very small child, because he had looked grown up and like Thomas from birth, according to his mother—Thomas and his wife Mary had decided to go straight to Woodside and dress for dinner there.

"You did remember to write and tell Miss Douglas that we wouldn't be with her until late in the evening, Mary, didn't you?" he asked, with a quick sidelong glance at her dreamy face.

She was driving, and he saw it in profile, her chin a little lifted, so that the beautiful line of her long neck and the curve where it melted into her narrow shoulder were seen at their loveliest. No one ever called Mary Lorimer pretty, she lacked the colour and life for that, but she had a roe-deer-like elegance which made her noticeable among more beautiful women. She did not turn her head when her husband spoke, but answered in a moment:

"Yes. I'm sure I did."

"I hope you really did, my sweet. It would be a bit rude if you didn't. Gray Douglas might be kept hanging about waiting for us to come."

Thomas was a worrier. He resembled his father in this; but whereas the Colonel's wife was a woman who never forgot the small conventional things which add a graciousness to life, no matter how much she might be engrossed in her writing, Thomas her son had married a vague dreamy creature with her head in the clouds and an impatience of all forms and ceremonies.

Mary's housekeeping was a perpetual round of small muddles, of unordered rations, unmended clothes, unpaid bills, unpunctual meals. It was an uncomfortable life for a surgeon of all men, and Thomas was thin and looked older than his years. But through it all he loved his wife and found solace and mental ease in her, in spite of holes in his socks and last minute discoveries that there was nothing in the house for breakfast. He still worried, however, over her refusal to answer necessary letters, and her constant offending of touchy persons by neglecting small politenesses, and though he knew it was useless, he tried to reform her. It was rather like trying to catch a waterfall and hold it, he thought, as he looked at her now. The water slipped through one's hands and poured on, bright and beautiful and heedless.

Mary spoke again. "Even if I didn't remember to send her a postcard, I don't believe Miss Douglas will bother. She always strikes me as a very sensible person."

Thomas gave it up. He leaned back in his seat and prepared to enjoy his short holiday. He had left no urgent cases, and if there were an emergency he hoped his young partner would be able to deal with it. How pleasant it was to leave cares behind, to be speeding through the warm fresh air towards the place which Thomas, significantly, still considered home. He thought with deep contentment of the well-ordered house, which his mother ran so quietly, so easily, that she appeared to take no trouble at all. He anticipated the hot water, the appetizing meals, the shining silver, all the things which he had taken for granted until he married. And yet he knew that if he had been given the chance to go back five years and choose again, he would not have chosen differently, he would still want to marry Mary.

It was extraordinary, he thought idly, watching her slim, small-boned hands light on the wheel, that she should drive so well. Anyone as vague and dreamy as Mary ought by rights to be a menace in charge of a car, but she was not, she was an excellent driver. All the powers of concentration that she possessed seemed to be given to this mechanical art, for it was an art. Sometimes Thomas wondered why she had married him, unless it was that his own passionate love had moved her, just for once, from her dreaming calm. She had been a member of the A.T.A. during the war, had ferried planes of every make from factory to airfield all over the country in all kinds of foul or fair weather. The air still seemed her proper element. Thomas had simply captured her somehow between flights, and, incredibly, married her. Would she have been different, more earthbound, if she had been able to bear a child, he wondered? He did not know, he would never know; but he loved her and she made him happy in a strange way.

Suddenly he said to her: "Are you happy, Mary?"

Her eyes still on the road ahead, she answered quite seriously, "Do you mean at the moment, or generally?"

"Well—both, I suppose."

She considered this, while the car covered another stretch of the winding road. "At the moment, certainly I am. And I think, generally, yes, Thomas. I don't think I was ever cut out to be a wife, but I rather like being yours."

"Oh, good," he said, oddly relieved, oddly touched.

The road ran round a great shallow depression in the hills, then rose to curl up through a cleft. The hollow was brimful of golden afternoon light, and the car sailed out of it, over the rise, and dipped like a swallow in flight down the long valley. Far below and ahead of them the smoke of Threipford hung blue against the heavy summer foliage of the woods which surrounded the little town. Threip Water ran, clear and low, in the bottom of the valley beside them. It was a perfect day to be coming home, Thomas thought, and the pinnacle of that perfection was reached when Mary brought the car effortlessly up the last steep hill to Woodside, and there they were, the family, sitting about the lawn, with drinks in their hands, and his mother, rising from her wicker-chair, coming to meet them.

"Dear Thomas! Dear Mary!" she said. "How lovely to see you both. Come and have something to drink before you change."

CHAPTER FOUR

1

THOMAS kissed his mother and his sister Alice, nodded to Vivian, and threw himself down beside Guy, where he could see Mary, who was lying back in a low chair, her hands linked behind her head.

"Where's Philly?" he said. "We saw George's back-view as we came in. His head was stuck into the car's innards as usual."

"Philly? Telephoning—no, here she comes," Guy said, and Phillis came out of the house. She was wearing brief white shorts and an open-necked shirt of bright blue cotton, and carried her tennis-racquet.

"Good Lord, Philly! You don't mean to say you really did ring that girl up?" said Guy.

"Certainly I did," answered Phillis coolly. "I'm going down to the courts to meet her now and have a singles. Don't wait dinner for me, Ma. I'll quite probably be late."

The challenging tone, the mulish look, were familiar danger-signals to her mother. Mrs. Lorimer knew that to ignore them was the best treatment, so instead of allowing herself the satisfaction of telling her daughter how tiresome she was, she only said calmly, "No, we won't wait for you, Philly. But try not to be too late, it does worry Father so. Dinner isn't until eight."

Phillis turned scarlet, just as she had done as a child, when it had looked as if the actual waves of hot colour under her fair skin had forced angry tears to her eyes. There were no tears now, but the sullen voice was the same, muttering: "Oh, all right. I'll be back if I can. She's probably rotten anyway and I won't want to stay long."

"Hi, Philly! Aren't you going to say 'how d'you do' to us?" called Thomas, scrambling to his feet and following her down the path. Phillis halted reluctantly; as they all knew, she had seen Thomas and Mary and was deliberately ignoring them. It was the sort of thing she always had done in her frequent rages. But Thomas was her favourite. She allowed him to take her arm and shake her gently, though she kept her head obstinately turned away, so that he could only see the forward fall of her soft brown hair against her flushed cheek. Presently he went on with her through the screening bushes, and the creak of the gate at the bottom of the garden was heard by the others, who had remained silent, watching the scene.

"Thomas has a very calming influence on people. I'm sure that is partly why he is such a good surgeon," murmured Mary, her voice stealing into the silence so smoothly that it hardly seemed to break it.

"Philly's a bit like her own offspring. She could do with a beating," remarked Guy.

"You really mean that the other way round," Vivian said lazily, puffing at his pipe. "It's because the children take after Phillis that they need beating—if they do need beating," he added, as he caught his wife's reproachful eyes.

"No, I don't think that *is* what I mean," said Guy.

"The person I sometimes think I should like to beat is George," said Mrs. Lorimer suddenly and clearly. "And now let us talk about something less annoying."

"That sort of remark, Ma, kills conversation dead," said Guy. "No one can think of a word to say except on the forbidden subject."

The others all laughed and agreed with him. Mrs. Lorimer rose. "Well, I have one or two things to see to, so I'll leave you to discuss it—though I think it would be better not to. That remark I made was one of the things that should have been left unsaid. I suppose," she ended, with an air of slight surprise, "I must have been thinking aloud—a very bad habit."

She wandered off up the bank, saying to herself, "I wonder any man alive will ever rear a daughter!—or any woman, if it comes to that. And as for sons! Thomas is terribly thin and pale. I'm sure Mary doesn't see that he gets enough to eat. But at least he looks happy enough . . ." In the rather dark little corner of the hall where the telephone lived in the middle of a grove of waterproofs, she lifted the receiver and asked for Miss Douglas's number. When Gray answered it, Mrs. Lorimer said, "Thomas and Mary seem to have come straight here, Gray, and I didn't know if they had told you they were going to. They didn't? I'm so sorry, my dear. You know what they are, Mary so vague and Thomas so busy. We are expecting you a little before eight. Yes, of course we want you. *I* do, most certainly. How did you think Guy was looking?" The telephone clucked as Miss Douglas, at the other end, made a carefully noncommittal reply. "Oh, he is cheerful when he's talking, but he looks wretched. Until a quarter to eight, then."

She hung up, glanced with distaste at the waterproofs, which the Colonel insisted on hanging there instead of in a perfectly suitable cupboard a little nearer the kitchen, and went into the dining-room to see how the table looked.

The bowl of roses glowed in the center of the shining oval, silver and glass glittered, and her new table-mats were really very attractive. Nan had remembered to salt the almonds she had managed to find in the town, and put several little silver bonbon dishes full of them at various points. It would do very well, she decided, and went on to the kitchen to tell Nan how nice the whole effect was, hoping that Nannie had not upset her cook in any way.

"And how awkward it is, having a Nannie in the house as well as a Nan," she thought. "Even the names make it difficult!"

When she entered the kitchen, however, she found that it was not Nannie who was making difficulties at the moment. Colonel Lorimer was standing at the table in the middle of the room, slowly and methodically preparing June's evening meal; June herself sat beside him drooling gently with greed, and round them both dodged Nan, obviously in a simmering state of fury, her face like fire.

"'Thunderclouds rend the air,'" thought Mrs. Lorimer dismally. Aloud she said: "Will you be long, Jack? The family are outside, and I'm sure they are wondering where you are. Thomas and Mary have arrived. If you went out now you would have time for a quiet talk before dinner."

Her husband gave her a reproachful look. "I must feed my poor old dog before I do anything else," he said. June crept nearer to him, doing her fat best to look like a famine-stricken pariah, and Nan, passing, tripped over her. June uttered a lamentable yelp.

"Poor dumb beast," said the Colonel sadly. "She has had a wretched day. Wretched. Where's that knife I had by me just now, Nan? I was cutting up her meat with it, and I am sure I laid it down here."

"It's my vegetable knife. I'm just after taking it to scrape the potatoes," Nan said with ominous calm.

"But these new potatoes need nothing but scrubbing, and the skin comes off them quite easily!" cried the Colonel. "To scrape them is a waste of time and—"

"Jack, do give poor June her supper," said Mrs. Lorimer, fearing an explosion and wishing that she could scream or throw a few plates on the floor to relieve her feelings. It might do them all good, she thought revengefully, if I made a scene for once. But it is very difficult to make a scene when one's whole nature abhors them, so she only added: "Poor old June, then."

Her husband, stung, picked up the enamel dish in which he had been mixing a nasty mash of brown bread and scraps of meat and vegetables, and strode off towards the back premises with June in even closer attendance than usual. Mrs. Lorimer turned to Nan, and before she could speak, said easily: "I came to say how very nicely you have done the table, Nan. It really looks beautiful."

Nan hurriedly opened the oven door, and to an obbligato of crackling and a delicious smell of roasting chicken, mumbled something that sounded like "Glad you're pleased."

Nan always took praise in this ungracious manner, but Mrs. Lorimer knew that she was gratified.

"It was splendid that you managed to find time to salt the almonds," she continued, addressing her cook's humped back-view, for Nan was still basting the chickens. "Mr. Guy is so fond of them."

Nan, apparently speaking to the contents of the oven, said, "It beats me how anybody can eat the nasty things."

"I hope the chickens are good ones?" said Mrs. Lorimer, aware that she was gradually talking Nan into good humour, but rather weary of the necessity.

"What can you expect these days?" countered Nan. "But they're not bad," she finished grudgingly.

"As Mrs. Pringle is coming in to wash up, I hope you will be able to get out for a little after dinner," said Mrs. Lorimer.

Nan shut the oven door, straightened herself and turned. "I'm not heeding for myself," she said in a self-sacrificing manner. "But I thought I might as well take yon Doreen, Miss Phillis's nurse, down to m'mother's. She's quite a nice wee thing, an' fair terrified o' that Nannie o' Miss Alice's."

Privately Mrs. Lorimer thought that the unfortunate Doreen might be a great deal more terrified of Nan's mother, old Mrs. Gibson, but she said, "That would be very kind of you, Nan," and left the kitchen before she could be involved in any discussion of Nannie's shortcomings.

2

"How are things going?" asked Miss Douglas when she arrived for dinner and was taking off her coat in her friend's bedroom. "You look a little harassed. Is it the grandchildren?"

"Jack would say it was the grandchildren," replied Mrs. Lorimer. "They are a little turbulent, poor things. But I don't find them nearly so worrying as their parents and uncles and aunts."

Gray drew a comb through her thick silvery hair, looked coldly at the result in the mirror, and nodded. "Guy is a bit off-colour," she observed lightly.

"But being very good about it," said his mother. "One can't help noticing of course, but he is trying to be quite his normal self. I don't think the others have been given any food for speculation. I wish I could say the same for Phillis! She is really behaving just as she used to when she was out of temper."

"Any reason for it?" asked Miss Douglas.

"Well, no, unless you can call having a husband whose entire interest seems to be centred in his horrible old car a reason—" Mrs. Lorimer said with a rueful smile.

"I daresay it's a good enough reason for Phillis. And I gather that Mary is as absent-minded as ever—"

"Yes. And Thomas is as thin—if not thinner. He is all bones and beak," said his mother.

"Poor Lucy. Your children do worry you! But I can safely bet on Alice and Vivian, I suppose? *They* are all right?"

"Oh, Lal and Viv are still the ideal married pair, cooing away like two doves." Mrs. Lorimer sounded a little irritated. "Of course I am glad that they should be like that, but dear me, how dull they are getting! That is ungrateful of me, Gray. I would be thankful to see all the others showing some of that kind of dullness. Come down to the drawing-room and see them all."

But there was no one in the drawing-room except Guy, hunched in a chair turning over the pages of a book which he was obviously not reading, and George, prowling to and fro across the new carpet.

"Do you know where Phillis is?" he demanded of his mother-in-law after greeting Miss Douglas.

"Playing tennis at the Club, I believe," said Mrs. Lorimer.

"I've told him that twice," said Guy from behind his book.

"I can't think why she dashed off like that, our first evening on leave, too, without saying anything to me." George sounded aggrieved.

"You were so busy with the car, George dear," murmured Mrs. Lorimer. "I think Phillis perhaps felt a little neglected." She spoke quite quietly and without a hint of reproach, but George's fair skin reddened and his face assumed a sullen expression. "Amazing how alike George and Philly are when they are in a temper," thought Mrs. Lorimer.

"The car's old. She needs to be overhauled after a long trip like that," George said defensively. "A big load for her too—Philly and me and the children and Doreen, and all our gear. You can't travel light with a family."

"Of course. I quite understand. Philly will feel all the better for a little hard exercise," Mrs. Lorimer said. "Where is everyone else, Guy, do you know?"

"Holding a meeting of the Children's Admiration Society," said Guy with a grin, and threw his book away, so that it fell in a whirl of open leaves, on the sofa. "Oh, I was invited, as an uncle, to be present, but I refused."

Mrs. Lorimer picked up the ill-treated book, smoothed its pages and restored it to a book-case.

"I'd better go up and say good night to the infants," said George, with the air of a deserted husband and father. "They will be wondering why Philly hasn't been in to see them."

"Yes, do, George dear," said his mother-in-law.

"Old George doing the heavy father is a bit oppressive," remarked Guy. "I say, Ma, is it anywhere near dinner time? I'm starving, and there's the most gorgeous smell coming from the kitchen."

"Only another five minutes," Mrs. Lorimer said. "It's an extraordinary thing about this family," she went on to Miss Douglas, "that as soon as any meal-time approaches, they vanish."

"They're all here, though. They will come down whenever the gong goes."

"All except Phillis."

"You aren't going to wait for *her*?" Guy asked in alarm. "She said not to—and there's the gong! Good old Nan! Come on, Gray love, we'll lead the way!"

Voices were heard on the stairs, and as Mrs. Lorimer followed Gray and her younger son into the hall, the others came down. Colonel Lorimer led the procession with Alice on one arm and Mary on the other, the three younger men behind them. All four gentlemen were in dinner-jackets, a trifle old-fashioned, and the Colonel's at least smelling of mothballs, but their white shirt-fronts gleamed, and they made an impressive spectacle. Nan, standing beside the gong, with its stick still in her hand, looked at them with pride, and muttered to Guy as he passed her, "It's a pity you're not dressed right too!"

Alice in blue, Mary in cloudy grey, also met with her approval, though privately Nan, who liked gay colours, considered that they might have been "a bit brighter, like," and as for Mrs. Lorimer and Miss Douglas, who both wore black, she dismissed them without a second glance.

The party seated itself, after a certain amount of rather noisy sorting-out and Mrs. Lorimer could see that her husband was about to ask where Phillis was, when Phillis herself appeared, flushed and defiantly smiling, and dragging a strange girl after her by the hand. The girl was evidently most reluctant to be dragged, and Mrs. Lorimer thought with irritation, "Too bad of Philly, bringing in a stranger to the family party!" But of course nothing could be said or done about it, not only for the strange girls sake but because it would make Phillis feel a martyr, which was exactly what she would like in her present mood.

So Mrs. Lorimer rose, shook hands with her unwanted and obviously unwilling guest, asked Guy to move up and make room for her at table, told Nan to set a place for her, all with smiling composure. If she noticed the looks exchanged between members of the family, eloquent of their disapproval of Phillis, she paid no attention. But she realized with gratitude that it was on these difficult occasions that her dear but often trying husband was at his best. Colonel Lorimer's courtesy to a guest never failed him or his wife. He had risen now, was welcoming Miss Smellie—and he took the name in his stride, like a gallant hunter at a bad jump, which he somewhat resembled—as a new neighbour, professed himself delighted to see her at their family gathering, laughed away her diffident murmurs of apology.

Phillis having waved her as a flag of defiance, now figuratively threw her away, took her own seat between Thomas and Vivian and began to chatter to them with great animation. George, sitting almost opposite her between Alice and Mary, she ignored as if his chair had been unoccupied.

"Come and sit here beside me," said Mrs. Lorimer. "This is my younger son Guy. The others can be properly introduced after dinner."

The girl, still murmuring thanks and apologies, sat down. She was an ordinary-looking little creature, except for waving hair of a curiously lovely colour like dark honey, with the same almost greenish glint in it which some honey shows, and eyes that were green also.

"Did you have a good game?" Guy asked politely, under cover of the babel which now rose all round the table.

"Your sister is a bit too strong for me," said the girl. "But I enjoyed it."

"Phillis can be a terror when she likes," said Guy. "And I don't mean only at tennis." He felt sorry for her, poor little mouse-like thing, pitched headlong into a party of total strangers, and not even dressed for the occasion either, because of course she was wearing a very short white tennis frock and no stockings. It was really a bit steep, even for Philly, he thought.

"I feel *awful*," said the small voice beside him while he was still promising himself the pleasure of telling Phillis what he thought of her behaviour.

"I say, I'm sorry about that. Are you going to be sick?" asked Guy in some anxiety. Her face certainly was very pale.

"No, of course not. I don't mean I'm *ill*. I just feel awful about being here," said the girl.

"Oh, I shouldn't let that worry you. It isn't your fault anyhow. We all know that. It's nice to have you," said Guy with careless kindness, and turned to speak to Alice on his right.

As Mrs. Lorimer happened at the moment to be talking to Thomas on her left, the stranger flung into the midst of this family party was left to her own devices. She took the opportunity to glance quickly round the table at these good-looking Lorimers. They all seemed to have inherited their father the Colonel's straight clean-cut nose, and their mothers broad forehead and smoky blue eyes, deep-set below well-marked black eyebrows. Phillis was the fairest of them, and had more colour in her cheeks; Alice had a beautifully serene face. Their husbands were good-looking too, in totally different ways. Lieutenant-Commander Gordon was big, square, and blond, Vivian Fraser very dark with brilliant hazel eyes. She had got so far in her observations when Mrs. Lorimer spoke to her.

"Do you and your father like Harperslea, Miss Smellie? Have you settled in quite happily?" she said. "It is a beautiful house."

"Yes, it is beautiful," said the girl. "But I don't feel as if it would ever belong to us, or we to it."

Mrs. Lorimer had felt the same, but naturally did not say so. She merely looked inquiringly at her guest.

"Well, think of it. People with a terrible name like ours! We belong in a villa on the outskirts of a town, really. That's what we have always lived in, a suburb, but Papa had set his heart on buying a place like Harperslea, and I couldn't bear to spoil his fun," said Miss Smellie, her green eyes very earnest. "It was to be a surprise for me—and it was!"

"Well, now that you are here, you must enjoy it," said Mrs. Lorimer. "Have you got a good housekeeper?"

"Oh, no. I keep house for Papa. I have since I was seventeen, when Mother died. The cook came with us, and I have got a country girl as house-table maid. She is really very willing, and I get a woman from Threipford when I need her," said Miss Smellie.

She spoke as if housekeeping held no terrors for her and Mrs. Lorimer realized that though shy, she was not a non-entity.

"Now that you have found your way to Woodside, I hope you will consider us as friends," she said kindly. "And come and see us as often as you like. Though the young people are very seldom here. This is a most unusual treat, to have them all at home together. But I hope you will come to see me."

"That is *very* kind of you, Mrs. Lorimer," Miss Smellie hesitated, then went on in a rush: "I know it is too soon, and that you don't know me, but if you would be even kinder, and please not call me Miss Smellie! It is *such* an ugly name. My Christian names aren't much better, in fact I hate them both, but nothing could be worse than Smellie!"

"You're wrong," broke in Guy, who had been listening-in to the last part of this conversation. "I know one worse."

"What?" said Miss Smellie incredulously.

"Smelt," said Guy solemnly. "I once knew a fellow called Michael Smelt. Just say it once or twice aloud and you'll see what I mean."

"I don't think it is any worse than Nesta Rowena Smellie," retorted the unlucky owner of these names.

"Nesta Rowena! They did saddle you with something when they christened you," said Thomas from across the table.

"Couldn't you add a bit of each of them together and make something you didn't mind so much?" This was Alice, from beyond Guy, for one of those lulls had occurred, during which everyone at the table listened to two people talking.

"Well, I did try, but all I got was Nero," announced Miss Nesta Rowena Smellie, suddenly producing a dimple as she smiled for the first time. "And Papa didn't seem to care for it. He *likes* Nesta Rowena."

Hubbub then arose, everyone speaking at once, suggesting various abbreviations, all of them either clumsy or ridiculous, or both, until Mary's quiet voice was heard, murmuring vaguely, "Rona is nice, I think."

"Then we'll all call her Rona," said Phillis, as if naming a doll or a puppy.

"Only if she says we may," Mrs. Lorimer said so firmly that her younger daughter pouted.

"May we?" asked Guy, turning to the girl with a smile.

"Oh, I do hope you will," exclaimed the newly re-named Rona. "I like it *awfully*."

Dinner now progressed in a very lively way, and Mrs. Lorimer, though still annoyed with her daughter Phillis, felt grateful to Rona ("As I suppose I will have to call her now, though I dislike Christian names except when they belong to old friends" she thought) as the unconscious cause of dispelling the rather thundery tension which had hung over the family party earlier.

3

As Mrs. Lorimer had never tried to force confidences from her children, but had waited for them to come to her, she could not now break the habit of years, much though she wished to. So she possessed her soul in patience, moved quietly through the weekend following the arrival of her family, admiring her grandchildren and telling them not to when she thought it necessary, and saw that the congested household was as comfortable as she could make it, which was very comfortable indeed.

Guy was taking his trouble, whatever it was, very quietly. It was Phillis who kept on disturbing the harmony of the gathering, as her mother noticed with concealed annoyance. All Sunday morning she fretted because she could find no one to play tennis with her, though she might have remembered, Mrs. Lorimer thought, that in Threipford very few people cared to play tennis on the Sabbath even in this enlightened year of 1951. To all her entreaties her brothers and sister turned a deaf ear, or told her to wait until Monday and they would make up a four. Vivian did not play at all, "and as for Mary," Phillis said petulantly, "she'd probably forget which end of the racquet to hold."

She made this remark in the drawing-room, where Mrs. Lorimer was rapidly finishing a letter to her publishers, and finding her younger daughter's gloomy restless presence a great hindrance. Now she put down her pen, took off her spectacles, and turning round from her desk, said, "That is really unnecessarily rude, I think, Philly. Surely you can manage for one day without tennis?"

"Well, what else am I to do?" muttered Phillis, tying knots in a blind-cord and looking like a sulky small girl instead of a married woman with two children.

"Take George for a walk, or if he doesn't want to go, I'm sure some of the others will. They were talking of going to the top of Wuddy Hill—"

"George!" cried Phillis, suddenly exploding. "*George!* He doesn't care a hoot for anything except that vile car! He pays no attention to me or the children! We might as well be dead, and

I'm sure I wish I were!" Here she gave the blind-cord a violent tug, broke it, and burst into tears. "Now look what I've done!" she wailed loudly.

"Well, it's very tiresome of you, but one of the boys can mend it. Now stop making all that noise, Philly, and try to tell me what has gone wrong," said Mrs. Lorimer, adding, "If you were twenty years younger I'd give you a dose of syrup of figs."

Phillis's sobs redoubled, and Mrs. Lorimer was thankful that the drawing-room door was shut and most of the family either at church or in the garden. "Syrup of figs!" howled Phillis. "All I want is a little s-sympathy and you s-say I need s-syrup of figs!"

Mrs. Lorimer rose, went across to the window, and took her child in her arms. "Now tell me all about it," she said, giving Phillis her own handkerchief.

It was a wild and garbled plaint which Phillis poured out between her snuffles and catchings of the breath, but it all seemed to center around George's single-hearted devotion to his old car. There was no other woman involved. The car, and again the car, was all her cry. When she had sobbed herself to a full stop she appeared to be greatly comforted.

"If *you* would speak to George, perhaps he'd listen," Phillis ended, giving her eyes a final mop with her mother's handkerchief. "Oh dear, I feel better now. Thank you, Ma, you are an angel. I must look a perfect fright. I'll have to go and do my face." She handed back the soaking handkerchief to its reluctant owner and made for the door. There she paused a moment. "You *will* speak to him, won't you, Ma?"

"I'll have a word with George," Mrs. Lorimer promised, and Phillis, with a watery smile, disappeared. She would spend half an hour carefully making up her pretty face, and not improving it in her mother's estimation, and would reappear, consoled and restored, a new woman.

Mrs. Lorimer sank exhausted upon the sofa. A scene with Philly, she thought, invariably left her in much the same condition as the handkerchief which she now threw aside in disgust. Not for the first time she wondered if Phillis's marriage had been a mistake. She had met George at a dance in Portsmouth five years earlier, when she had been just twenty, they had fallen madly in love and married after a whirlwind engagement lasting five or six weeks. It had been quite impossible to stop them, and indeed, apart from their having known each other such a short time, there had been no real reason to stop them. To suggestions that they should wait for a few months both had refused to listen, and until now they had apparently been quite happy. Phillis enjoyed the rather haphazard existence of a Naval wife, her children had been born with the minimum of discomfort, and Mrs. Lorimer had been able to settle enough money on her daughter to give her an adequate allowance and make life easy and pleasant.

"It would be absurd if their marriage should come to grief over a car," said Mrs. Lorimer aloud. "I really *must* speak to George, if it's only to hear his side of it—and how I don't want to!"

"Are you talking to yourself, Ma? You are as bad as Gray!" said Guy's voice, startling her so that she almost shrieked. He had thrust his head and shoulders in at the open window and was grinning at her impudently. "And did you know one of the blind-cords is broken and trailing on the deck? If Father sees it he'll be convinced that the house is falling to pieces and go about muttering Rack and Ruin."

"Come and mend it, then, instead of frightening me to the skirling, as Nan would say," retorted his mother.

"All right, I will. Where are the steps?"

"In the cupboard under the stairs where they always are," said Mrs. Lorimer.

He vanished, there was a crashing sound in the hall, and presently he came in by the door, carrying a small pair of steps, which he proceeded to set up at the window.

"Don't fall, Guy," his mother entreated as he mounted to the top and balanced there precariously. It was only a formal protest, he knew, and he gave it no more attention than it deserved.

"There," he said, descending again.

"Please put the steps away before your Father sees them and begins to ask questions," said Mrs. Lorimer.

Guy did so, with a good deal of clatter, and coming in once more, remarked, "You've dropped your hankie—heavens, it's sopping!" he added, as he picked it up. He looked at her suspiciously. "I say, Ma, you—you haven't been *crying*, have you?"

He sounded so horror-struck that Mrs. Lorimer laughed. "No. Philly has been doing one of her weeps," she said. "Put the horrid thing in my desk, Guy. I'll take it upstairs when I go to tidy for lunch."

"I don't know what Philly's got to cry about," he observed, throwing himself into a chair so that its springs groaned protestingly.

"You'll break that chair," said his mother automatically. "Philly will be all right now that she has relieved her feelings."

"And left you washed-out. I know," he said. "Have a cigarette. Very soothing to the nerves. I wish I could cry like Philly and feel better afterwards."

"I'm sorry you should need to," said Mrs. Lorimer sadly.

"Oh—well. I may as well tell you, Ma," he said suddenly. "That business with Iris—I wrote quite a bit about her, didn't I? Forget it. She—it was all a mistake—she's married to someone else. That's all."

His deliberately light tone did not deceive Mrs. Lorimer, who looked at his shadowed eyes and the nervous twitching movement of his hand as he flicked ash off his cigarette.

"I'm sorry, Guy dear," was all she could say. Unlike Phillis, Guy could not bear a scene.

He got up, threw the cigarette into the empty fireplace, where Colonel Lorimer would be certain to see it and deplore its presence there, and came over to her. "Anyway, it's better here at home," he said, dropping a kiss on the top of her head. "I think I'll go for a long tramp by myself this afternoon. Walk it off, you know." And he left the drawing-room in his turn.

Mrs. Lorimer put her head back against a cushion, wondering what use a mother was, when she could do nothing for her children, and did not, in this case, even dare to speak a word of comfort to them in their distress.

CHAPTER FIVE

1

GUY succeeded in evading the other would-be walkers by leaving the house quietly immediately after lunch was over, instead of sitting about smoking and reading one another's horoscopes in the Sunday papers and saying at intervals that they really *must* go and put on their thick shoes if they meant to walk at all before tea. He felt he had to have some hard exercise and enough fresh air to make him so tired that he could not help sleeping when he got to bed. The open hillside was what he needed, and this afternoon he intended to get to the top of Maidenleap, the higher crest behind the Wuddy. Though he and Thomas had frequently made plans to climb Maidenleap, neither of them had ever done it yet for one reason or another, usually weather. It was a fool's game to attempt it in mist, of course, and Maidenleap was more often than not shrouded.

But today, as he took the first easy slopes with a long slow stride, he could see the top, shimmering in a heat haze, far ahead of him, far above him. Presently he would lose sight of it, only to see it again when he was breasting the last steep stretch. Larks rose all about him in a madness of song, curlews called as they sailed overhead, and he put up a covey of grouse, the young ones strong on the wing, the old cock shouting: "Go-back! Go-back!" at him.

"I'm not going back, old boy," Guy said aloud. "But I'll stop for a breather to oblige you."

He turned and looked away down the long slope towards the south. There was not another human being in sight. Almost without his knowing it the wide spaces round him, the loneliness so terrifying to city-bred people, comforted him. For the first time since Iris's wedding he felt as if blood ran in his veins instead of the red-hot coke which had been burning inside him.

Two hours later, breathless and leg-weary but exultant, he reached the cairn on top of Maidenleap. It was cold up there, and the wind sang loudly in his ears, drying the sweat on his brow with its chill strong breath.

He did not want to leave this lonely place, eerie though it was even in the sunshine, but it was too cold to linger. So he went downhill again in great headlong strides, pausing every now and then to glance back at the cairn he had left standing gaunt against the sky until he had dropped too far below it to see it any longer.

He was already late for tea, so he decided to give it a miss altogether and take the longer way home by Wallace's Well, a place which he had loved as a boy, when Wallace had been his greatest hero.

When he came, suddenly, as one always did, owing to a bend in the path through the glen, in sight of the Well, he realized to his great though unreasonable indignation, that he was not going to be able to enjoy it alone. There was a figure sitting on one of the big flat stones beside the spring, and to make matters worse, it was a female figure. Guy halted and muttered "Darn!" wondering if he should turn back, when the female figure looked up, and he recognized the honey-coloured hair of the girl whom his family had taken upon themselves to call Rona.

She did not give him a particularly welcoming look, he noticed, but when he had reached her a smile curled the corners of her mouth.

"Oh, it's you," she said. "I was afraid it was someone. I hope I didn't look very cross?"

"Merely a trifle indignant—which was how I was feeling myself," said Guy. "Because when I saw you first, I thought *you* were someone."

"Are any of the others with you?" asked Rona.

"No. I'm on my own. I've been up on Maidenleap, and I thought I'd have a look at Wallace's Well on the way home. Have you been here before?"

"No," said Rona. "This is the first time. I read about it in a guide book, but it isn't a bit like what I expected."

"What did you expect?" asked Guy, sitting down on another stone.

"I was afraid there might be tourists, or at least a lot of people. You know—picnics and a mouth-organ or even a portable wireless," she explained. "But it's beautiful, and so still. You feel you oughtn't to talk out loud at all."

"That's the effect of being on fairy ground," Guy said seriously.

"Oh, is it a fairy well? I thought it was Wallace's."

"I think the fairies must have given Wallace a lease of it," said Guy. "It's theirs really. Have you drunk and wished yet?"

She shook her head. "No, but I will." She went to kneel beside the rough stone basin, made a cup of her hands, bent her head and drank from them with serious simplicity. "What lovely water!" she said as she rose. "Aren't you going to wish too?"

Guy shrugged his shoulders. "I'll have a drink for old time's sake, but I won't wish. Nothing to wish for," he added, but more to himself than her.

"Fancy having nothing to wish for," murmured Rona.

"Well, what was *your* wish?"

She coloured a little. "It sounds terribly silly," she began. "But I'll tell you, just to pay myself out. I always wish the same, when I see the new moon, or the first star at night—I wish I could have another name. I do *hate* mine so."

"As you'll get rid of it whenever you marry, I should have thought it would have been easier to wish for a husband right away," Guy said. He was a trifle bored. How all these girls' minds were set on marriage, even this child's, who could not be more than twenty, he thought from the height of his own twenty-nine years.

Now she would probably blush and protest that she didn't mean that at all, and he was being dreadful . . . But she was speaking quite earnestly, and he could see that her flush was caused by that earnestness and not by coyness.

"No, I'll never do that. It seems too much like leaving marrying to chance, and you see, I'm *determined* to marry," she said.

"The devil you are!" exclaimed Guy, taken aback by her coolness.

"Most girls want to be married," she said, voicing his own thought of a minute before but in a matter-of-fact tone. "But you see, I'm so terribly handicapped by my name. It's enough to put any man off, and it isn't even as if I were very pretty."

"You're very young still. I shouldn't worry," said Guy, at a loss to know exactly what he ought to say. "Some fellow will come along and fall in love with you, and you'll fall in love with him. And that will be that."

She shook her head. "Far too chancy. I mightn't like him, or I might like him and he mightn't like me. No," said Miss Smellie with complete composure. "I am going to make a marriage of convenience as they do on the Continent. I think it is a much more sensible arrangement."

"That's all very well, but it's the parents who do the arranging on the Continent."

"I know," she said mournfully. "But if I waited until Papa did anything about it I should never get married at all. I see quite plainly that I must look out for myself."

"And pick out a man with a name you like? Is that the idea?" asked Guy, who was feeling mildly interested and mildly amused by now.

"Yes," she said. "He *must* have a pretty name, or it would be no use at all. That's where falling in love would be so awkward. One might fall madly in love with a man called Buggins."

"I see your point," said Guy. "By the way, do you like my name? This isn't a proposal, of course, merely a question."

"Yes, I do. I think Guy Lorimer sounds just right," she said, and added with an absurd, somehow pathetic little air of dignity, "You understand that this—this discussion isn't personal, don't you? I wasn't considering you as a man at all. It was purely—purely—you know the word I mean."

"Purely academic," he agreed gravely. "Though I don't quite care for not being considered as a man. What am I supposed to represent? A confidante?"

"Like in Racine or Corneille?" asked Rona. "Yes, I believe that was the way I was thinking of you."

Guy was conscious of feeling slightly nettled. It was a bit much, he thought, to be accepted calmly as a sexless creature, or possibly an elderly greybeard tottering towards his grave, by this young woman.

"We'd better be getting home—at least, I must," he said, rising and stretching. "And you too, or you'll be frightfully late for dinner or supper or whatever you have on Sunday evenings."

"Dinner," she said absently, "Papa hates cold Sunday supper." She had risen too, and taken a few steps away from the Well. "You know," she said suddenly and rather incoherently, as they were walking down through the long narrow glen. "I didn't mean it the way you think—about not thinking of you as a man, I mean."

"Didn't you? What *did* you mean?"

"Well, I would never have talked to you as I did just now, if I hadn't known that you were out of the running where marriage is concerned," she said surprisingly.

"How the deuce could you know that?" asked Guy, too amazed to be angry.

"There's a sort of look—I had a brother—he was killed in Normandy—he was quite a lot older than me, and I got to know when he had—had—"

"When he had taken a toss over some girl, I suppose you mean?"

"Yes. He used to tell me. I was too young to matter, you see, and I think it helped him a little," she said simply.

"I see. And I look like that?"

"Yes, I think you do. I don't suppose other people would notice it. I wouldn't have if it hadn't been for Roy," she said. "I hope you aren't angry?"

"No, I'm not angry," Guy said thoughtfully. "Only surprised. You are rather a surprising young woman."

"Oh, am I? D'you think perhaps men would find me interesting?" she demanded.

They had reached a grass-grown track between dry-stone dykes, once a road, now only used occasionally by cows or farm-carts. Harperslea stood among its woods of oak and beech not far off, with a small gate opening from the grounds on to the track. By one accord they had stopped there, and she turned her face, vivid with curiosity, her green eyes sparkling in the sunlight, to look at him.

"Yes, I think they might, quite easily," said Guy. "Is this where you turn off?"

She nodded. "Thank you for not laughing at me," she said. "Goodbye."

"Goodbye for now, Rona," said Guy, and watched her until she had shut the gate behind her and disappeared into the trees. Then he walked thoughtfully home.

2

"That was Mrs. Young ringing up," said Mrs. Lorimer, re-entering the drawing-room after a prolonged conversation on the telephone. Dinner was over—for at Woodside the family had not been given a cold supper either, though it was normally Nan's evening out every Sunday—and all the Lorimers were sitting about in attitudes of lazy comfort.

"What did she want this time?" asked the Colonel apprehensively.

"As all our young people are at Woodside, she hopes that some of them will go round to Netherton tomorrow for sherry, about six o'clock," said Mrs. Lorimer. "You and I are invited as well, of course, Jack."

"You know, Lucy, that I never go to sherry parties," began the Colonel in a great hurry. "Owing to the condition of my inside I am unable to drink sherry any longer."

"Yes, Jack, I do know that, and so I made your apologies to Mrs. Young," said his wife. She looked at her family, all ostentatiously absorbed in books or knitting. "Some of you will have to go," she said.

"Oh, Ma! Why should we have to?" cried Phillis. "I want to play tennis tomorrow—"

"You can play tennis earlier, surely?" said Mrs. Lorimer. "Lally, will you and Viv come with me? I really couldn't think up an excuse that sounded authentic for everyone."

"We'll come, Ma Lorry," said Vivian. "You'll be there to protect us from our hostess, won't you?"

"Oh, yes, I shall have to go," agreed Mrs. Lorimer. "Now, who else? George?"

"Well, I rather wanted to go over the car again tomorrow and perhaps try her out on a short run," said George slowly.

Phillis uttered a disagreeable laugh, and Guy said, "I'll be a victim, Ma, if you like. And I don't see why your short run shouldn't be to Netherton, taking us with you, George my boy."

"All right. But don't blame me if she breaks down half-way there," said George.

"It won't be anything new if she does," muttered Phillis. "What about Thomas and Mary, Ma, if you're so keen on taking a whole bunch?"

"I think Thomas ought to rest in the garden. He looks a little tired," said Mrs. Lorimer firmly. "And probably Mary would like to stay with him."

"No, I'll come, Mrs. Lorimer," Mary said. "Then Phillis can play tennis. We shall be six without her, won't we?" she added vaguely, counting on her long slender fingers, while she murmured: "Guy and Alice and Vivian, that's three, you of course, Mrs. Lorimer, and me—is that five? And George—"

"Oh, I don't think I'll come if Phillis isn't going," put in George.

"How touching!" said Phillis. "Or rather, how touching, if I weren't going to be playing tennis and you weren't going to be playing with your blessed car!"

"Philly," said Mrs. Lorimer warningly, and her younger daughter subsided scowling. Then she turned to George. "If you are going to drive us to Netherton as Guy suggested, George, it will be very pleasant," she said.

George looked up from the motor magazine in which he was apparently engrossed, and met her clear gaze. There was no reproach in the rather tired eyes, but he reddened slightly and mumbled, "Oh, very well, Ma, if you want me to take you, of course I will."

"I suppose she means well, but how much kinder it would be to leave us alone," said Alice. "However, if we go tomorrow, it means that we'll have got it over, and that will be a mercy. Oh, bother, I've dropped a stitch!" She poked frantically at her knitting with a needle already laden with stitches, and several more fell off.

"Let me," said her husband, taking it from her and securing the runaway stitches with practiced ease. "There you are, but for goodness' sake don't lose them again."

"That is very accomplished of you, Vivian," Mrs. Lorimer remarked admiringly.

"Good eyesight and a steady hand," he said complacently. "And I'm keen to see that jersey finished. Alice has promised me faithfully to knit me a pullover next, and not before time. She's so occupied in covering her young that she lets her husband go in rags."

"Back and side go bare, go bare," remarked Guy.

"Oh, Viv!" said Alice, her soft eyes darkening with distress. "You know I'd love to be knitting your pullover, darling, but the children seem to wear their woolies out so much faster than you do. And then they're growing and of course you aren't."

"This is the moment for you to play a man's part, Viv," said Guy, who had been listening with some amusement to his elder sister and her husband. "Tell her that in order to regain her wifely attentions you will tear all your knitted garments to shreds at once."

"My dear Guy, if I thought it would be the slightest use, I'd do it like a shot," Vivian answered. "But I know it isn't. The woman is a MOTHER first and foremost, and I am merely her husband. True, Nannie is continually knitting for the young, and I am half responsible for them, but I think Alice has forgotten both those facts."

Alice looked at him so meltingly that he at once recanted, to Guy's increased amusement and Phillis's open disgust. "No, Lal darling, I didn't mean it," he said. "You are a perfect wife as well as a doting mother. I take it all back."

Mrs. Lorimer, listening, wondered why this eminently satisfactory married couple should make such fatuous remarks. Perhaps happiness killed good conversation? But then Phillis, who was unhappy just now at least, made remarks quite as dull and a good deal less pleasant. It was all rather a muddle, she thought. There was Thomas. He seemed quite happy, and he was not dull, and she would much rather that Guy were a bit duller, if he could be happy as well . . .

"But Thomas isn't nearly as comfortable as Vivian, you see," suddenly murmured the voice of her daughter-in-law Mary, who was sharing the sofa with her.

"Was I thinking out loud again?" said Mrs. Lorimer guiltily.

Mary shook her dark head, with the wings of smooth straight hair sleeked back to a loose knot on the nape of her neck. "No, but I knew what you were thinking. You were looking from one to another of your family," she said.

"It is rather alarming to find oneself an open book to the daughter-in-law whom everyone calls 'so vague,'" said Mrs. Lorimer. "But as you are perfectly right, Mary dear, do tell me if you meant what you said just now? That Vivian is rather dull because he is so comfortable, and Thomas isn't?"

"Yes, I meant it, of course," Mary said. "I do think that after a certain standard of cushioned ease has been reached, one's mind rather goes to sleep. Vivian has—or had—quite a sense of humour, and a pleasant wit, but he is losing it."

"Is that why you prefer not to make Thomas too comfortable? Bodily, I mean. He is comfortable mentally," said Mrs. Lorimer.

Again Mary shook her head. "I wish I could say Yes, but it wouldn't be true. Poor dear Thomas is without his bodily comfort simply because I am such an abominably bad housekeeper."

Not for the first time it struck Mrs. Lorimer how much more she had in common with Mary than with either of her own dearly loved daughters. "You are very honest, Mary," she said. "And I'll be honest with you. I do think Thomas is happy, but I should like to see him looking a little less thin and tired. Surely he could safely be more comfortable without becoming fat and lazy in his mind?"

"Yes, he could," Mary agreed, looking gravely at the unconscious Thomas, who was trying to do Ximenes' crossword in the Observer and making heavy weather of it. "And I could promise to be a better housekeeper, Mrs. Lorimer, and see that he had more appetizing meals, but it would be no good. I just can't keep my mind on it, somehow. And don't tell me that it might have been different if I could have had children, because it wouldn't. Things would have been far worse. The children would have been even more neglected than Thomas."

Mrs. Lorimer did not argue the point. Instead she asked: "What sort of a cook have you got just now?"

"Well, the last one found the brandy that I keep in the medicine chest," said Mary. "And Thomas came home and found *her* just after she had finished it, and as she seemed rather homicidal he dismissed her on the spot. There is a new one coming the day we go home, but she seems to be a good one so she won't stay. The good ones never do," she ended sadly. "They get so discouraged because I don't take enough interest and forget to order things for them to cook."

"If you won't think me interfering, I believe I could suggest a solution," said Mrs. Lorimer, whose mind had been working at express speed during the telling of this tale of woe.

"Of course I won't! You must be the most uninterfering mother-in-law in existence," said Mary, smiling at her. "Tell me, Mrs. Lorimer."

"Instead of being apologetic about your absent-mindedness you must turn it into an asset," said Mrs. Lorimer impressively. "You must be an eccentric, that's all. It will work beautifully. Eccentrics always seem to be well served. Thomas must explain to the new cook that you were flying all through the war, and that you are not to be bothered with household affairs. The explanation will come better from him—"

"I am to have a mind above housekeeping, in fact?"

"Well, you do seem to, don't you, Mary dear? I mean, your head is always up in the sky," said her mother-in-law, but very kindly. "If your new cook really *is* a good one, she will be pleased to have the responsibility. Once she understands that you are something out of the ordinary, she will run the house for you, do the ordering of the food and cook it, so you and Thomas ought to be quite comfortable and well fed. It isn't as if you can't afford to pay a staff, after all."

"It sounds wonderful," said Mary. "But what surprises me is that a good housekeeper like you should understand my failings and find a way out instead of trying to reform me."

"I never waste my time and efforts on useless endeavour," said Mrs. Lorimer. "And I do understand, because when I am writing Nan takes over the housekeeping for me. She thinks I am a little mad at those times, but she is rather proud of me. I don't see why your cook shouldn't be the same."

"Mother-in-law, you are a jewel beyond price," said Mary. "As long as she doesn't make us so comfortable that we both become dull."

"I think you and Thomas are fairly safe on that score. It would take a great deal of soft living to make either of you dull," said Mrs. Lorimer. She felt rather pleased with herself. Unless she was greatly mistaken in her estimate of human nature, her plan should succeed in making Thomas look a little less thin in the future;

and Mary could be absent-minded with a clear conscience—which might possibly result in her being less so, for that was human nature again.

3

Monday was passing, but up to the time of departure to drink Mrs. Young's sherry Mrs. Lorimer had not found a suitable opportunity of speaking to George. This would not have troubled her, since she believed in waiting for the right moment to reveal itself, but Phillis's continual glances, appealing or sulky, had begun to get on her nerves.

"It's no use your going on looking at me like that, Philly," she was finally goaded into saying shortly after tea, when her younger daughter, dressed for tennis and looking absurdly young, pretty and cross, waylaid her in the drawing-room. "I can't just hold a pistol to George's head. It would be worse than useless. In fact, I doubt if I ought to speak to him at all about this. I am sure that he really does care for you, and is only sulking over something."

Phillis muttered what sounded like, "You'd do it fast enough if it was for Thomas or Guy."

Mrs. Lorimer's detractors—they were not many, but they existed—were fond of saying that she greatly preferred her sons to her daughters. It was rather more than the truth; but Mrs. Lorimer unconsciously expected her daughters to show as much sense as she herself did, while the boys, as belonging to the so-called stronger sex, required more attention. She knew that she was accused of favouritism, and thought very little about it as a rule, but when Phillis said the same thing, the grain of truth in her sulky muttering stung her mother.

"That is ridiculous and unjust, Philly," she said, sharply for her. "I am very willing to help you all if I can, but in your case I can't help feeling that you must be in the wrong as well as George, and that if he thinks I am taking your part he will know that you have been complaining to me, and resent it. It really does seem silly to be jealous of a car, Philly dear, when you must know in your heart that George would set fire to it for your sake if need be."

"That's where you're wrong, Ma," said Phillis stubbornly. "If it came to choosing between that car and me, George would choose the car every time."

"Oh, Philly," said her mother in exasperated despair.

"I can't argue with you in your present mood. I'll do my best to help, but you must leave it to my discretion. Now go and have your tennis. Who are you playing with?"

"The Camerons and the Smellie girl," said Phillis. She suddenly smiled enchantingly. "I'm sorry to be such a pest, Ma," she said, gave her mother a swift glancing kiss and flew out of the house in a flash of white.

Mrs. Lorimer sighed and went to put on a hat suitable for a sherry party at Mrs. Young's. She felt certain that if Phillis gave George a smile and a kiss like that, he would be quite ready to forget the car; but how to get Phillis to see it?

The family was gathering outside the house when Colonel Lorimer appeared from the direction of the garage. "Lucy, I have just told George that he can't possibly take you and the girls to Netherton in that car of his," he announced. "It's filthy. Filthy. Covered with oil and mud. You would ruin your clothes. Better to walk."

"Oh dear, Jack, I hope you haven't hurt George's feelings," said Mrs. Lorimer apprehensively.

"What have George's feelings got to do with it? I told him the car was a disgrace and he'd better clean it," said the Colonel. "Ah, here he is. George, I've just been telling them they would be better to walk to Netherton. And you too. You don't want to spoil that suit of yours. It's a good suit. Fits you well. Sets off your figure."

George, who had followed his father-in-law with a slight scowl on his face, was obviously torn between gratification at the compliment to his suit and his own looks, and rage over the insult to his car. Before he could speak, however, Alice said, "You *do* look nice, George! I wish Viv had a suit like that."

"Gieve's," said George, preening himself. "And not paid for yet, either. I'm glad you like it." He turned to Mrs. Lorimer. "The car *is* a bit dirty, Ma," he said. "I'm sorry. Do you mind walking?"

"Not in the least. And if I really wanted to, I could always take my own car," said Mrs. Lorimer.

"The place is stiff with cars," said Guy. "But as it's less than a quarter of a mile to Netherton and a lovely afternoon, I can't see why we need any of them. Let's walk."

They set off in a procession, and as they approached Netherton, the subdued roar which tells of a sherry party could be heard issuing from its open windows.

The large room which they entered was already so full of people that it was impossible to see their hostess, but presently her loud voice could be heard above the noise, and Mrs. Lorimer slowly made her way towards it, much impeded by her acquaintances in the throng, who bawled greetings as if she and they had become totally deaf.

Mrs. Young had allowed herself to be hemmed into a corner—a fatal thing for a hostess—where she stood with a sherry decanter in one hand, talking if possible more loudly than anyone else in the room. At sight of Mrs. Lorimer she broke relentlessly through the crowd.

"So here you are!" she shouted. "Thought you were never coming. Have you brought your young people with you? I don't see them."

"I've brought most of them. They are somewhere about the room, at the other end, I think. Jack sends his apologies and hopes you will forgive him for not coming, Margaret, but you know he never does come to sherry parties," said Mrs. Lorimer.

"Never goes to anything except the British Legion and the Show. He's a regular stick-in-the-mud. You've trained him badly," said Mrs. Young. "Oh, by the way, there's a man here—says he's an old friend of yours. The Dunnes brought him. He's staying with them. Now I wonder where he's got to? Must find him for you, Lucy. Old friend, ha ha! I believe he's an old flame, if the truth were told—"

Mrs. Lorimer would have liked to repudiate the "old flame," a form of expression which she actively disliked when used by Mrs. Young, but she was aware that by doing so she would lay herself open to loud cries of disbelief and probably a dig in the ribs from Margaret's bony fingers. So she only said: "What is his name?"

"Haven't the foggiest idea! I suppose he must have been introduced to me, but you know how it is, one never hears names at a crush like this. Never mind, when I find him I expect you will know him all right. Now I'd better go and talk to some of these other bores." With this final remark, also uttered at the top of her voice, Mrs. Young barged away, leaving her friend Lucy Lorimer to wonder how many of her hearers had taken umbrage. Judging by their faces, quite a number had. It was a pity Margaret Young was so tactless, when she was not being downright rude. In the meantime, Lucy was still empty-handed, a dismal state of affairs at such a party, when to hold a glass, even if it is empty, gives one a feeling of self-confidence.

As usual, in a big noisy crowd, largely composed of people whom she hardly knew or did not know at all—for her acquaintances all seemed to be at the farthest possible part of the room—Mrs. Lorimer felt herself becoming more and more reserved, less and less convivial.

"Good evening, Lucy. What a job I've had to get to you. Why are you stuck in this distant corner?" It was Gray Douglas's voice, and Mrs. Lorimer turned thankfully to her, with a real smile of welcome.

"Gray dear! How nice. I didn't know you were here," she said warmly.

"No, it *is* a little surprising," agreed Miss Douglas. "But I suppose Mrs. Young felt it might be rather too pointed, even for her, if she didn't ask me. I should think everyone for miles round has been gathered in."

"Everyone but Jack," said Mrs. Lorimer.

"I can't imagine anything more improbable than finding Jack at a party like this—but Lucy, aren't you going to have anything to drink? Or to eat? There are some lovely small eats," said Gray, suddenly realizing Mrs. Lorimer's unencumbered condition. "Don't you want *anything*?"

"I haven't been given the chance of having anything yet," began Mrs. Lorimer. Miss Douglas put her cigarette hastily into a convenient ash-tray, and seized the arm of a stalwart young man who was standing with his back to them. He turned. It was George Gordon.

"Oh, George!" said Miss Douglas. "Thank goodness it's you. Look here, Lucy is being neglected. She hasn't had anything to drink or eat or smoke. Can you do something about it?"

"Yes, of course," he said. "Just stay here and don't get lost and I'll be back in a minute. Sherry, is it, Ma? Right."

He was gone, cleaving a way through the people without bumping into any of them in a neat fashion which roused Miss Douglas's admiration.

"I must say there is something about the Navy!" she murmured. "Prompt action is not what one would expect from George, because his brain works slowly. It must be the training."

"I wish he could be trained to pay more attention to his wife and less to his car," said Mrs. Lorimer, suddenly overcome with weariness.

Miss Douglas gave her a quick understanding glance, but said lightly enough, "Well, he can't bring the car into the middle of a sherry-party with him! And I must say he's a great deal nicer without it."

"Yes, he is. Unfortunately Philly isn't here to benefit by it. She wouldn't come. She is playing tennis," Mrs. Lorimer said, adding: "Tiresome child."

"Never the time and the place, And the loved one all together!" said Gray. "Sorry to be obvious, but the occasion seemed to demand it. And here comes the Rescue Squad."

Not only George, but Thomas and Guy now appeared, bearing sherry, plates of small savouries and salted almonds.

"How lovely this is. Do stay and talk to us," begged Mrs. Lorimer. "There isn't anyone else here I'd rather meet."

Though they all laughed, including Gray, they obeyed, and Mrs. Lorimer surrounded by those she was fond of, was able to enjoy the party very much and to congratulate her hostess quite truthfully when she took her leave.

"How nice a party is when it's over!" she exclaimed in heartfelt tones when they were out of the crowded room where the flowers in their great bowls and vases were wilting among the drifts of tobacco-smoke and scent. She drew deep breaths of the warm evening air, heedless of the laughter and expostulation of the family. George, who was beside her, pulled her hand through his arm. "Poor Ma, you were being a bit neglected among that howling mob," he said kindly.

Mrs. Lorimer felt a sudden warm glow of affection for him. In spite of all Phillis's complaints, there was nothing much wrong with George at heart. She decided not to say anything to him about the car. Instead, she smiled at him.

"You rescued me so nicely, George, that I really enjoyed myself afterwards," she said. "It was most comforting. I think Philly is very lucky to have a comforting husband."

His arm stiffened a little under her fingers. "Afraid Philly wouldn't agree. She hasn't much use for me these days," he said. "We seem to quarrel about everything, big or little."

Mrs. Lorimer realized that she would have to alter her plans again. It seemed that she must speak to him. "Phillis is jealous of the car," she said baldly.

"Jealous? Of the car?" He sounded incredulous. "You can't be jealous of a *car*!"

"Philly can."

"But I go and tinker with the car just to take my mind off, and to keep out of her way and avoid a scene. I hate scenes," George said miserably.

"So do I. But Philly absolutely revels in them. I don't know where she gets it from, I'm sure. What you ought to do, George, you poor gump," said his mother-in-law, but very kindly, "is to make a bigger and better scene. Roar and stamp at her instead of creeping away to your car. It will bring her to her senses quicker than anything else."

"Well, thanks, Ma," George said. He sounded dubious but hopeful. "I'll see what I can do."

"All I ask is, don't make a scene where your father-in-law can hear you. It will upset him," said Mrs. Lorimer.

George laughed suddenly and squeezed her hand against his side. "You are a wonder, and no mistake," he said.

They had fallen behind the others during this conversation, and now, as they went in by the main gate to Woodside, there was no one in sight. The garage faced them across the yard, its double doors pushed back, to show a gap inside between Mrs. Lorimer's little car and Thomas's bigger one.

"I say!" George stopped, bringing Mrs. Lorimer to a standstill too. "The car's *gone*! Someone's taken her out."

4

His face was so pale, he looked so disturbed, that Mrs. Lorimer felt annoyed with him. The car, it seemed, was more important than he admitted.

"It is not in the least likely that the car has been stolen, George," she said rather coldly. "And Phillis is the only person who would have taken it out."

"Of course it's Philly. That's the whole point, Ma," said George. "She's such a rotten bad driver, poor sweet, and the car needs careful handling. Her steering is very erratic and Philly doesn't know how to humour her."

From this confusion of personal pronouns, feminine gender, third person singular, Mrs. Lorimer gathered, with the hideous dual sensation of sinking stomach and rising dread, that George's concern was for his wife.

"I suppose you have forbidden Phillis to drive it?" she asked hopelessly. "Really, George"—as he nodded. "I don't know which of you is the bigger fool!"

If her son-in-law heard this remark, it was quite evident that it made no impression on his mind. "I'll have to go and look for her," he said. "Guy will have to lend me the motor-bike. It will be faster than any of the cars."

Nan appeared at the back door, every crease in her apron signifying disapproval. "The Colonel's after asking for his dinner," she said. "It's gone eight. You'll not be waiting for Miss Phillis? She's gone out wi' that shandrydan of a car. I told her she'd be late, but she never heeded, just banged out through the gates."

"Which way did she go?" demanded George.

"How should I know?" Nan replied. She turned to Mrs. Lorimer. "Will I sound the gong?" she asked.

"Give me five minutes to tidy, Nan, and then sound it please. You'd better keep some back for Miss Phillis and Lieutenant-Commander Gordon," said Mrs. Lorimer, catching at this prosaic straw to keep her mind off probable accidents. George had vanished; it was no use trying to dissuade him from going to look for his wife, and no doubt he would rather be doing something.

Mrs. Lorimer went slowly upstairs to her room, washed her hands and tidied her hair, and when the gong sounded, went down to face the dinner-table, try to eat, and wonder to herself if Phillis were all right. The cheerfully matter-of-fact attitude of the rest of the family, who apparently felt no doubt as to Phillis's safety, was reassuring, though it struck her as rather callous of them all merely to dismiss it as one of their younger sister's (or sister-in-law's) tiresome escapades.

The telephone rang, and everyone jumped a little. Colonel Lorimer who was nearest, went to answer it, while the others stood listening in the hall.

"Hullo. Hullo. What? Yes, Phillis. Why haven't you come home to dinner? I can't understand this rushing about the country at all hours, and in a filthy car like—what? Speak up. I can't hear a word you say—"

"Oh, dear," said Mrs. Lorimer to Guy. "Don't you think someone else had better speak to Philly? Something must have happened—" She moved towards the telephone, but Guy restrained her.

"Let Father do it, Ma. You'll only confuse the issue if you interfere," he said.

The Colonel, who had been listening with a puzzled expression, now spoke again to the mouthpiece. "You want to be fetched from Heathergill? But you have got the car. What in the world are you doing away out there? All right, all right. Don't shout at me. I can't make it out at all. Heathergill? It's—" He turned to face them. "She's rung off. It sounds quite impossible to me. Something about the car, she said, and she wants to be fetched from Heathergill. I simply cannot understand these young people, Lucy. Taking cars out and then unable to bring them home—"

"It's all right, sir. Alice and I will go and fetch Phillis," said his son-in-law Vivian. "Coming, Lal?"

He nodded reassuringly to Mrs. Lorimer, in whom the relief of knowing that Phillis was at least alive and apparently unhurt, had been succeeded by acute annoyance.

"Thank you, Vivian," she said. And to the others, "Come and have your coffee before it's cold. It is *too* tiresome of Philly."

In a short while, a car was heard at the gate, and Mrs. Lorimer rose. "Here they are," she said, going towards the door. But before she had reached it, Nan opened it from the other side and announced with pleasurable gloom, "It's the Sergeant, to see the Colonel."

Standing aside, she disclosed the bulky figure of the Threipford police sergeant, cap in hand.

"Colonel Lorimer is in the garden, Sergeant," said Mrs. Lorimer. "If you will come with me—"

"Oh, it's all right, Mrs. Lorimer. It was just to tell you Mrs. Gordon's not hurt at all," said the Sergeant. "The car's wrecked, of course, but she escaped without a scratch. I was going to bring her home in the police car but seeing Miss Alice—I should say Mrs. Fraser—and her husband, had arrived on the scene, I left her with them and come on to tell you."

While Mrs. Lorimer was still trying to collect her thoughts sufficiently to put some coherent questions to the Sergeant, Guy's voice broke the silence.

"She's smashed the car, has she? How pleased old George will be!"

"Tell us what happened, Sergeant. We are all in the dark about this," said Thomas, coming to his mother and putting an arm round her. "My sister, Mrs. Gordon, rang up and asked someone to go and fetch her from Heathergill, but none of us had any idea that there had been an accident."

The Sergeant looked down his nose and coughed in a meaning way. "I must say, sirr, it's no thanks to Mrs. Gordon that she's not hurt, for such driving I have neverr seen. Neverr," the Sergeant went on, his feelings betrayed in the reverberating R's. "I was following her, not aware of who she was, the car being a strange one, and meaning to stop her to tell her she was driving with the silencer off her exhaust. But could I get past her? All up that winding road, hell-for-leather, if you'll excuse me, Mrs. Lorimer, and at the sharp bend by Heathergill—as dangerous as any corner in the county—I could see she was never going to take it, and sure enough she didn't. Over she went."

"But Sergeant! What has happened to Mrs. Gordon?" whispered Mrs. Lorimer, only too plainly seeing the horrible drop to the stream far below that sharp corner in the hill road. "Did she—did she—"

"She jumped, ma'am. Jumped like a rabbit, clean out of the car. Lucky for her it was one o' those old-style open tourers," said the Sergeant. "And landed in the soft ground at the roadside. I took her to Heathergill farm myself, and left her to 'phone you while I returned to the scene of the occurrence to see could anything be done about saving the car. But I doubt if there's anything left worth saving, even if ye could get it up from the burn-side. It's just to smithereens."

At the conclusion of this epic tale, he looked at Mrs. Lorimer and saw that she had regained the composure which she had so nearly lost a few minutes before. "So I just come down to let you know the facks," he ended. "Mrs. Gordon's had a bit o' a shock and is a wee thing highsteerical. I thought it was no use letting her in for a lot of questions then."

"It was most kind and considerate of you, Sergeant," said Mrs. Lorimer. "Perhaps you will have a glass of beer or something? Thomas, will you or Guy take the Sergeant into the dining-room and see that he is looked after?"

The Sergeant allowed himself to be persuaded and went away with Guy and Thomas. Mrs. Lorimer looked at Mary.

"I suppose I'd better see that Philly's bed is ready for her?" she said in a rather distraught way. "And don't people with shock require tea and hot-bottles and things? I can't remember properly—"

"I'll look after hot-bottles and Phillis's bed," said Mary, much less vaguely than usual. "And I'll get some tea made. Would you like a cup? Though we've just had coffee—I always think these first-aid remedies are so disagreeable—"

"But *I* haven't had a shock. And I should hate a cup of tea," Mrs. Lorimer said with vigour.

"Of course you've had a shock. You are a most unnatural mother if you haven't," said Guy, suddenly breaking in on them. "And I've brought you a tot of brandy, Ma. Drink it down, because I hear the car coming."

Making a wry face, Mrs. Lorimer swallowed the brandy held out to her so firmly, and then went quickly to the door. There seemed to be a good deal of noise at the garage. She hurried in that direction, arriving in time to see Alice and Phillis emerging from Vivian's car, while at the same moment George, covered, as Guy had foretold, in dust and oil, roared into the yard on the motor-bike.

"Philly!" he cried, flinging himself off and rushing at his wife. "Thank God you're all right! Where have you been? I've hunted all over the place for you."

For answer Philly, who looked wild and dirty, burst into tears. "Oh, George! Oh, George!" she wept. "I've wrecked the car! I'm so-so s-sorry!"

"Forget the car," said George, clutching at her as if she might melt from his grasp. "What the devil does the car matter? Are *you* all right?"

"Yes," wailed Philly. "But you don't understand, George. You don't know what I did! I took the car out on p-pur-pose to annoy you, and now it's in pieces!" She wept on, her face muffled in his coat, while he patted her back and kept on telling her that nothing mattered, *nothing*, as long as she was safe.

Mrs. Lorimer felt that the time had come to put an end to this touching scene. "George," she said. "I think you should take Philly in and see that she goes straight to bed. She can tell you all about it later. Or the Sergeant can," she added, now aware that the Sergeant had added himself to the group of spectators, though discreetly at the back.

"The Sergeant? The police? Good Lord, Philly, what have you been up to?" asked George.

Mrs. Lorimer almost stamped with rage, but restrained herself. "George dear, will you please either take Philly upstairs yourself, or let me? At once, before her father appears and begins to ask all about it."

George roused himself, put an arm round his wife, now hiccuping hysterically, and led her into the house by the back door in the very nick of time, for as they vanished, Colonel Lorimer appeared in the yard.

"Where is everyone?" he demanded. "What's all the noise about? Ah, Sergeant, good evening. Have you come to make an arrest? Hah?"

Mrs. Lorimer gathered Alice and Mary by a quick glance, and the three of them stole silently from the yard, leaving the men in a group round the Sergeant, who was slowly telling Colonel Lorimer the tale of the car-smash in official language.

"I think perhaps I ought to go up and see that Philly is in bed and has all she wants," Mrs. Lorimer said. She went quietly upstairs and approached the half-open door of the girls' old bedroom, in which Phillis and George were sleeping, and heard George saying calmly,

"Well, my sweet, the car's gone, and that's that. It means we'll have to go home by train, and perhaps that will larn you to go smashing the poor old girl up out of spite and jealousy."

"It would serve me right if I had to *walk* to Portsmouth," came the penitent voice of Phillis.

"Pushing the kids in the pram, I suppose. No, the train journey will be quite enough punishment for you, my love," said George. "Doreen will feel sick and be useless and the offspring will behave like devils. You'll be regretting the car before we get to Crewe, my girl."

"Only because you were fond of her. But George, you'll get a new one?" said Phillis.

"Using what for money?" asked her husband.

"Well, there will be insurance, I suppose? That would help," began Phillis rather blankly.

"Think again. She wasn't insured for anyone to drive but me, so that's out. No, we're minus transport now. You can think of that when we have to cadge lifts to and from dances, or go to parties by bus."

Mrs. Lorimer, for the first time in her life an unashamed eavesdropper, thought with critical appreciation that George was handling the situation remarkably well.

"Oh, George darling! What a beast I've been! Do, do forgive me," said Phillis with a pathetic catch in her voice. "I don't mind about the parties—at least, I *do*, but it's my own fault—but now you'll have to go by bus down to the Dockyard. Oh, I *have* been a beast!"

"No, darling, only rather a fool. But I love you just the same," said George.

Mrs. Lorimer tiptoed away as Phillis said, "I love you too, George, I do *really*."

She felt very limp, but Phillis had worked off her ill-humour. For some time to come, Mrs. Lorimer imagined, the young Gordons would live at peace with each other and be happy.

CHAPTER SIX

1

ON TUESDAY mornings Colonel Lorimer was apt to excuse himself to casual callers by announcing that he must go and do the washing. Strangers and new acquaintances naturally pictured the gallant ex-soldier in his shirt-sleeves, deep among soap-suds, with clouds of steam floating round his smoothly-brushed grey head as he toiled at the washtub. Mrs. Lorimer found their expressions of shocked incredulity and disapproval faintly amusing or less faintly irritating, according to how exigent the Colonel had been about the laundry on the Tuesday in question. For in reality his activities, while much less arduous to himself than they sounded, were very trying to the tempers of his wife and Nan.

In fact, Colonel Lorimer's passion for returns and tabulation found an outlet in the weekly laundry lists. He had been appalled by the feminine carelessness shown in marking down the number of sheets and table-napkins—or as the laundry preferred to call them, serviettes—sent and returned. Even more appalling to him was the meekness with which his wife and Nan accepted rents and holes made by the laundry. Their explanation, that all the laundries did it nowadays, seemed to him spineless; Nan, though she grumbled, mended the articles and that was all there was to it. Full of zeal, the Colonel determined to take the matter in hand himself. Mrs. Lorimer gracefully withdrew, thankful that she could relinquish a household task which she found extremely tedious, to someone who really enjoyed it. Nan, she realized, came off worst, but after all, Nan was well paid, and must suffer occasionally.

So every Tuesday the laundry was drilled, marshalled, numbered off, the Colonel entering the items not only on the official lists provided, but in a private register of his own, in which everything had a letter against it denoting its condition when sent and returned. P for perfect (not many of these), G for good, W for worn and so on. It was a slow process, and drove Nan to angry mutterings beneath her breath, but afforded the Colonel immense satisfaction. Almost more enjoyable was the return of the clean linen, when the entire drill was gone through in reverse, everything was counted twice, ticked off on the list, and initialled in the Colonel's book. Each minutest blemish made by the laundry was marked down in the same, and later became the subject of correspondence between Colonel Lorimer and the laundry. That he never won a victory in this warfare did not trouble him at all; he lodged his protest, filed their answers and waited until the next opportunity for attack showed itself, with glee.

Miss Douglas, walking into the cool hall on the morning following Mrs. Young's sherry party, to see how her friend Lucy had weathered the shock of Phillis's escapade with the car, of which she had heard several garbled versions by Threipford grape-vine, met Colonel Lorimer, notebook in hand, and a careworn expression on his handsome face.

"Ah, Gray! Good morning. Good morning," he said. "You will forgive me, I know, for not stopping to talk to you, but I am doing the washing. How do you find the laundry these days? You deal with the Spotless Steam Laundry too, do you not?"

Miss Douglas said Yes, she did, and was most annoyed with them last week for sending back a very much worn and greatly inferior hand-towel in place of a good Irish linen one.

Colonel Lorimer at once forgot his haste, and prepared to discuss this iniquity at length, until Nan emerged from the back regions and said: "If you've not finished with the laundry soon the van'll be here and the washing not ready."

Whereupon, the Colonel, apologizing again to Miss Douglas for having to leave her, hurried away in the wake of Nan's broad back-view.

Mrs. Lorimer put her head round the drawing-room door as soon as he had gone. "Do come in, Gray," she said. "I would have come out and rescued you but Jack does so love explaining his laundry system! I hope you weren't bored?"

"Not a bit. I've heard it all before, of course, and I still don't believe in it," Gray said cheerfully.

After the car smash and its resulting improvement in George's and Phillis's relations with one another had been discussed, Miss Douglas said suddenly:

"By the way, Lucy, *did* you meet a man at Mrs. Young's yesterday who used to know you? He seemed very anxious to meet you again. A little impressive, I thought him."

"I forgot all about him," said Mrs. Lorimer. "But Margaret Young was being rather facetious on the subject, so I was quite relieved not to see him, whoever he was. I should have felt a fool, meeting any old acquaintance of the opposite sex under her malicious eye! I don't remember ever knowing anyone who was impressive, though. I just forgot all about him . . . Did you happen to hear who it was?"

"Names are so difficult at a party," Gray complained. "I know his had something to do with ducks, but that's as far as I got."

"Something to do with *ducks*?" repeated Mrs. Lorimer. "What on earth do you mean? He couldn't have been called Quack—or was his name Donald?"

"No, it wasn't quite so obvious. It's gone completely. I'm sorry, Lucy."

"Oh, never mind. It doesn't matter. Only if he was a brother-officer of Jack's *he* might like to see him again."

"He didn't strike me as having ever been a soldier," said Gray, and added rather severely, "and Jack should go to parties and then he could meet his friends for himself."

Mrs. Lorimer only smiled at this.

"Stop smiling like the sphinx, Lucy," said Miss Douglas. "And attend to me. Are you going to call on the Smellies?"

"Oh dear! I suppose I shall have to, as Phillis has struck up an acquaintance with the daughter, and Harperslea is so near. It is high time this calling racket died out. I'm sure Threipford must be one of the last places in the country where it still persists," Mrs. Lorimer said with a laugh and a groan. "Gray, would you come with me? I shouldn't mind so much if you were there to support me."

"I was going to suggest it," said Gray. "When shall we go?"

"We might as well get it over," said Mrs. Lorimer in a decidedly anti-social tone. "Could you go this afternoon? The family all have arrangements of their own, so I am free. Do, and then you can come back and have tea here?"

"Jack ought to go too, as there isn't a Mrs. Smellie," suggested Gray, after she had accepted the invitation to tea.

"But he won't," said Mrs. Lorimer. "I'll ask him for form's sake, but I know the answer already."

In view of this remark, Miss Douglas had some difficulty in concealing her surprise when Mrs. Lorimer joined her at the gateway of Harperslea that afternoon accompanied by the Colonel. He was wearing his good suit and a respectable hat, and obviously intended calling on his new neighbour.

"Hah, Gray," he greeted her.

"What is the proper answer to 'Hah!' do you suppose?" asked Gray.

"'Hah yourself!' perhaps," said Mrs. Lorimer, while the Colonel looked bewildered. "But that sounds rude, doesn't it?"

"Very," Gray said gravely. She turned to the Colonel. "Hah, Jack!" she said.

Colonel Lorimer looked at her. "Ah, you like to make fun of me," he said, becoming the simple puzzled soldier. "But it is pleasant when it is done in a friendly way, my dear Gray."

Miss Douglas felt a little ashamed of herself, and said hastily, "How good of you to come calling with us, Jack. It will be much nicer with you."

"I feel that as he is a stranger to the whole neighbourhood, I really ought to go and see him," said the Colonel. "But I must admit his name is against him, poor fellow. Smellie, you know. Terrible. And I thought he might be encouraged to take an interest in the Legion, and the Show."

"In other words, Jack is hoping for a subscription or the promise of one," said his wife calmly. "*I* am hoping that they will be out."

But they were evidently not out, though after a flustered country girl had shown Colonel and Mrs. Lorimer and Miss Douglas into the big shadowy drawing-room with its polished floor and white panelled walls, a long pause ensued, during which the Colonel prowled uneasily about the room, wondering audibly what the deuce was keeping the fellow.

"Look here, Lucy," he said at last. "Why shouldn't we just leave our cards and go? I don't believe they *are* at home."

His wife and Miss Douglas stared at him as if they thought he had gone mad. "Cards?" said Mrs. Lorimer faintly. "I don't possess such a thing! I never thought of them. Have *you* got cards, Jack?"

"Certainly. When I do go out calling, I naturally assume that the thing is to be done properly," said Colonel Lorimer, and he drew a neat little pigskin case from one of his pockets and flourished it in an exceedingly complacent way.

"Gray!" said Mrs. Lorimer. "*Don't* tell me that you have brought calling cards?"

"When I was twenty-one," began Miss Douglas dreamily, "— and that is nearer thirty than twenty years ago, I may say—my Mamma insisted on having a die made with my name and our address on it, and she had a hundred cards engraved for me. I have used quite a lot of them for things, in the garden and so on, but I must have over sixty left. They are somewhere in my desk, I suppose. But anyhow, of course they have our old address on them, so they wouldn't be much use," she finished with an air of great common-sense.

Mrs. Lorimer, who had seated herself in a comfortable chair, listened to this conversation, wondering how long her husband would endure Gray's interruptions without becoming slightly peevish.

The situation was quite ridiculous. They had been left here for ten minutes now, and Jack and Gray were too busy talking one another down to have noticed how time had passed. But she herself would have liked to go, to leave this room, which, though it now belonged to a stranger, was not strange to her. Once again she wished—vainly, she knew—that Jack had seen reason about buying this house. She could see her handsome family sitting here and calling it home. They could dance in this long room and still leave one end comfortably set with sofa and chairs for their elders. And to prevent further thinking of the kind, she spoke.

"Jack, I do think we might go. We have been here almost quarter of an hour. I'm sure the girl who showed us in here has forgotten all about us."

"I shall leave my card on the mantelpiece," announced Colonel Lorimer, once more producing his pigskin card-case. He was carefully propping the slip of pasteboard against a large bronze ornament representing a sketchily clad female struggling in the embrace of a warrior mounted on a rampant steed when the door flew open and a little round man with a very red face trotted into the room.

2

"Mrs. Lorimer! And the Colonel! And another lady! I'm verra, verra sorry to have kept ye waiting. That stupit lassie of a maid we have's been looking for me everywhere but the right place!" he exclaimed. Even the top of his head glowed through his thin white hair like an autumn sun shining through morning mist, in his distress and embarrassment.

His accent stamped him unmistakably as a native of Glasgow, and no doubt unkind persons could have called him a common little man without departing from the truth; but there was something genuine about him which made him likeable, and Miss Douglas in her usual rather headlong fashion decided that she liked Mr. Smellie.

Mrs. Lorimer, always more balanced and cautious, said to herself that he might really be a nice little man if one came to know him. The Colonel's amazed attention seemed to be given solely to their host's clothes, a jacket and knickerbockers of such a large check that they made their wearer look almost broader than he was long.

Mrs. Lorimer had risen from her chair and gone forward to take his outstretched hand as he ended his breathless apology. "I'm afraid we have brought you in from the garden," she said. "And you have been hurrying. I am so sorry."

"Not at all! Not at all!" he exclaimed, shaking her hand violently up and down, and apparently unable to make up his mind to drop it.

"This is Miss Douglas, a friend of ours, who came with us to call on you," said Mrs. Lorimer, firmly removing her fingers from his grasp, and turning to Gray.

That lady now found herself being subjected to the same pump-handle treatment, which she endured very well, as she said "How do you do?"

"Fine, thank ye, fine! This place suits me," said Mr. Smellie. "And Colonel Lorimer, it's a real pleasure to see you with the ladies. But dear me, what am I thinking of, keeping you all standing? Will you not sit down?"

He rushed at a chair and pushed it frantically towards Mrs. Lorimer, who accepted it with a smile. As he seemed about to dart away and set another beside it in the center of the room for Gray, she hastily sat down on the sofa behind her, and assured Mr. Smellie that she was most comfortable. She knew that if she had been set beside Lucy like an exhibit, she would have been incapable of restraining the laughter bubbling up inside her, and that might have hurt the little man's feelings, which would be a pity. It was difficult enough, she thought, to look at Mrs. Lorimer planted in lonely splendour with a sea of brightly patterned carpet all round her chair, and a look of resignation on her face, without laughing outright.

Mr. Smellie still appeared to be troubled. "Colonel, will you not take a seat?" he begged, looking wildly round the room as if to pick out a suitable chair.

"Thanks," said Colonel Lorimer, perching himself on the nearest thing available, a chair with a very small wooden seat and a very high narrow back. "This will do me very well. Don't bother—" as Mr. Smellie seemed about to dash off and fetch another.

Having seated his visitors, Mr. Smellie looked more unhappy than ever. "I'm vexed that Nesta Rowena's not in—my dotter, Mrs. Lorimer—for she knows better than me the right thing to do," he said.

Mrs. Lorimer hastened to comfort him. "We liked your daughter so much," she said in her low tranquil voice. "My younger daughter played tennis with her and brought her to dinner."

"My wee girl was telling me all about your kindness, Mrs. Lorimer," answered Mr. Smellie, now dragging forward a chair for himself and sitting so that he faced her. "Anybody that's kind to my Nesta Rowena is doing Matthew Smellie the biggest kindness they can."

It was evident that he had either forgotten his other two callers or did not know how to draw them into conversation. Mrs. Lorimer was rather at a loss how to bring them back to his notice with tact, but Gray resourcefully let her bag fall and spill its contents with a small clatter on the floor. This brought Mr. Smellie to his feet at once.

"Dear me, where are my manners?" he exclaimed. "You'll have to excuse me, Miss Douglas, and you too, Colonel. I'm not used with society ways. If it had been a board meeting, now—! Let me pick up your things for you."

But Colonel Lorimer had already scooped them together, crammed them higgledy-piggledy into the bag, and restored it to its owner.

"You know, Mr. Smellie, we ought to be going," said Mrs. Lorimer. "We have stayed a very long time for a first call."

"But what about yer tea? Surely you'll stay to yer tea? Oh dear me! Maybe I should hae offered it sooner!" Mr. Smellie looked, with his red face all puckered, as if he would burst into tears.

"It is very kind of you, but we really ought to go home," said Mrs. Lorimer. "But I hope you will bring your daughter to Woodside when we have a little more leisure, and do ask us to tea some other day."

Mr. Smellie cheered up. "Indeed I will, and verra pleased. I'm not one for going out much, but that's a real friendly invitation, Mrs. Lorimer. I'm that pleased you've called at Harperslea. There've been one or two callings," he added simply. "But I knew fine it was just subscriptions to this that and the other that brought them. A guinea here, half a guinea there—not that I'm grudging the money, but it's nice when folk are neighbourly like yourselves."

If Mrs. Lorimer's gaze rested for an instant on her husband's somewhat conscious face, no one noticed it; she felt guilty herself, for she had come feeling that Phillis's determination to play tennis with the newcomer had forced it upon her.

They all rose and moved towards the door. In the hall Mr. Smellie halted. "D'you like the way I've had it done up, Mrs. Lorimer?" he asked, and continued before she could reply, "It looks kind of rich, don't you think? I'm fond of red, myself, though Nesta Rowena had her doubts. But it's that cheery, red."

His visitors looked round them at the yards of bright red carpet which covered the floor from wall to wall and stretched up the stairway. A number of red-deer antlers, a large copy of *The Monarch of the Glen* and a stuffed salmon in a glass case formed the principal decorations. It looked like a rather stodgy old-fashioned hotel in the Highlands, Miss Douglas thought, wondering madly how she could possibly express admiration of what Mr. Smellie so evidently and innocently considered the height of good taste. Colonel Lorimer saved the situation.

"You've got some fine heads there," he said. "Are they your own?"

"D'you mean did I shoot them? I never let a gun off in my life," Mr. Smellie said. "I got the lot at an auction. The hall looked bare, but they just finish it off."

It was difficult to get away from Mr. Smellie, who accompanied them half-way to his gate, but at last they were out in the road, and free to discuss the call they had just made.

"That poor house!" said Mrs. Lorimer sadly. "All the red carpet . . . but he really is a *nice* little man."

"I wonder his daughter didn't stop him from putting up those antlers and things," said Miss Douglas. "But perhaps she didn't like to hurt his feelings by interfering with his arrangements."

"Oh, she couldn't, he's so proud of it all," said Mrs. Lorimer. "I like her better for letting him have his way, though of course he has ruined Harperslea."

"Come, now, Lucy, it was very comfortable," said the Colonel. "I wonder if I'll be able to ask him to subscribe to the Show after what he said."

"Now that we have called I'm sure you can ask him another time," his wife said reassuringly. "I'm sorry the girl wasn't there. Poor child, no wonder she liked the idea of being called 'Rona.' Nesta Rowena in full is a little overpowering."

"I wonder where she was," said Miss Douglas. "Is she playing tennis, do you think?"

"If she is, it isn't with Philly, because she and George went out for a tramp together," said Mrs. Lorimer. "We must ask her, Rona, I mean, to Woodside again soon. She may be finding life rather dull at Harperslea."

3

When Mrs. Lorimer and her husband and Miss Douglas returned to Woodside, slightly jaded by their social effort, their ears were greeted by the piping of young voices from behind the dining-room door.

"Lucy!" said the Colonel, shrinking away from the sound. "We are not having tea in *there*, are we?"

"No, Jack, we are not. We are having tea in the drawing-room, in comparative peace," Mrs. Lorimer said, and called: "Nan! We are in. Will you bring the tea, please?"

Nan appeared, carrying a blue china tea-pot of comforting dimensions. "I heard you come in," she said in her blunt way. "The rest wanted theirs, so I just let them have it when they asked for it."

The day I hear Nan call me 'Madam' or even 'Mum,' thought Mrs. Lorimer, I shall get such a shock that it will probably kill me. Aloud she thanked Nan, pulled off her hat and gloves and threw them on a chest in the hall, and ran her fingers through her hair.

"Do take off your hat and be comfortable, Gray," she said. "Just put it down beside mine."

Gray obeyed, while the Colonel ostentatiously hung his own hat carefully on a peg near the telephone.

"When I see Jack being so frightfully and pointedly tidy, I always long to pick up everything in sight and throw it about the floor," observed Miss Douglas, as the two ladies went into the drawing-room. "Don't you?"

"Well, no," said Mrs. Lorimer. "Because if I did, sooner or later I should have to put everything back myself. But I know what you mean."

She sat down and poured out tea.

A pleasant rather sleepy silence fell on the drawing-room. Scents from the garden were blown in through the widely-opened windows, to mingle with the scent of hot tea and cigarette smoke. A bumble-bee blundered into the room, roared round the ceiling once or twice and then found its way out again. The voices of the children, dulled by the intervening walls, sounded almost musical.

"Blessed peace!" said Mrs. Lorimer, who was leaning back in a corner of the sofa with her feet up. "I must say it is delightful not to have the family in for tea today, and not even to know where they are. I do love it when they are all here, Gray, but it has been such a—a *rousing* weekend, what with all their squabbles and difficulties, and the climax of Philly going and crashing the car. I feel as if they had been here about six months."

"At least most of the troubles seem to have been cured," Gray pointed out. "And having got that over, you can enjoy them for the rest of the time, knowing that when they leave they will be getting off to a better start. Thomas and Mary, we hope, to improved housekeeping, and Phillis and George apparently like a honeymoon couple again. Of course Alice and Vivian didn't need any sorting out, did they? And I don't think they ever will. You must have been pretty clever over the weekend, Lucy, to have accomplished so much."

"I didn't do anything really. I just listened and made one or two suggestions, and scolded Philly. But I haven't been able to do anything at all to help Guy," said Mrs. Lorimer. "And I feel he needs it most."

"Guy is much more himself, though, and he is eating, and sleeping well. There isn't anything you can do. Give him time, Lucy. His ailment can't be cured except by time."

Then the door was opened with Nan's customary violence, and their intimate talk was ended. They had no more to say, so that in its way the noisy interruption was a relief.

As she was wheeling the tea-trolley away, Nan said, "I took a message on the 'phone for you. Did you see it? I wrote it down on the block."

"No. I haven't looked yet, Nan. Was it important?" asked Mrs. Lorimer.

"I wouldn't know about important. It was a Mr. Mally-something," said Nan. "I didn't catch the name right. He said he was staying with Mr. and Mrs. Dunne, but he was leaving tonight and he was sorry not to see you, and he might be back to shoot later on and hoped he'd see you then." This, delivered without drawing breath, left Mrs. Lorimer quite bewildered.

"Mr. Mally?" she said. "Who on earth could it be? I don't know anyone—"

"Lucy!" said Gray suddenly. "It's the man who was at Mrs. Young's, the one who said he was an old friend of yours. I *told* you. Malleson. That was his name."

"That's right," Nan broke in. "Mally-son."

"You told me his name had something to do with *ducks*," said Mrs. Lorimer to her friend.

"I must have been thinking of mallard." Miss Douglas was rather pleased with herself. "I wasn't very far out. Mallard— Malleson. You see?"

Mrs. Lorimer was not listening. "It must be Richard Malleson, of course," she murmured. "I haven't seen or heard of him for more than thirty years."

"What a pity you didn't see him while he was here, then," said Gray.

Mrs. Lorimer roused herself, became aware that Nan was still in the room, bursting with interest and curiosity, and only too ready, her employer could see, to take part in the discussion. "Thank you, Nan," she said firmly. "Oh, by the way, the Colonel must have forgotten his tea. He has never come in for it."

"The Colonel's in the kitchen making June's supper, so I just gave him a cup in there," Nan said, and wheeled the trolley from the room. Her back looked disappointed, but that could not be helped, thought Mrs. Lorimer.

"It's extraordinary the way old friends crop up years and years after you have forgotten their existence," Gray remarked casually. She was just as sensitive to the under-currents where Lucy was concerned as Lucy was about her, and now she rose.

"Thank you for my nice tea, Lucy. I really must go back to my neglected home." And Miss Douglas kissed her friend and went away.

CHAPTER SEVEN

1

NO SOONER had she left than Mrs. Lorimer, who had been feeling that what she wanted more than anything was to be alone, realized that solitude was the last thing she desired.

"What an idiot you are!" she said angrily to herself. "Imagine allowing yourself to get all worked up like this over a man you last saw thirty-two years ago!"

The trouble was that Richard was not just "a man"; he was Richard, and thirty-two years ago he had been *the* man, so far as she was concerned. She could feel the colour mounting to her cheeks in an unaccustomed blush, and was angrier than ever.

"Blushing like a girl," she told herself. "And you—a grandmother, with *five* grandchildren! You'd better go and see them now, and be sensible."

An eventful session with her grandchildren drove him completely from her mind, and as a result she was in bed and settling down to read a light novel until she fell asleep before she remembered Richard Malleson.

There was no reason in the world why she should not think about Richard now, except that she didn't want to. She had been happy with Jack for such a very long time, so that even his peculiarities were dear to her, though at times intensely irritating. Richard belonged to a day when she had not even met Jack. The wound he had given her had healed long years ago, she never thought about it, indeed, she would have said quite honestly that she had forgotten it, yet today the sudden unexpected mention of Richard's name, the realization that she had narrowly escaped meeting him had made the old scar throb again. It did not hurt at all now, but she remembered that it had once hurt her so much that she had believed she would never recover from it. She had still been suffering from its effects when Jack had asked her to marry him. For a time she had wondered if she ought to tell him that she was not heart-whole, but she had never done so, and had never regretted her silence. Young as she had been then, and foolish, she had guessed that such a confidence would only have made him uncertain, unhappy, and she had denied herself the luxury of unburdening herself of her secret. But, she thought with a touch of resentment, it was so like Richard to appear, more than thirty years after, and expect her to want to see him! He had walked out of her life without explanation while she was dizzy with a girl's first love for him; no doubt he had grown bored with the affair which to her then had seemed a matter of life and death, and had simply cut short his visit in the neighbourhood of her home and vanished. Now, apparently, he had discovered her, and to satisfy an idle wish, had thought he would like to meet her again. Lucy Lorimer knew that she did not want to meet Richard Malleson again, but her mind shied away from giving the reason for it. Then she began to wonder whether Jack had read the message which Nan had written on the telephone pad. If he had, he would be certain to ask who the owner of a name unknown to him was. She could quite easily say it was someone connected with her writing, and he would be satisfied, but Mrs. Lorimer was not in the habit of telling lies for her own advantage. She could tell them and had done so when she thought it necessary to save other people pain, but to lie to Jack was a meanness she could not contemplate. Perhaps she ought to put on a dressing-gown and go downstairs and tear up the message? It might save needless trouble if she did . . . There was a slight sound from Jacks room next to hers. He was moving about, and presently she heard him come quietly out on to the landing. There was a gentle tap at her door, and into her perturbed brain sprang the thought that he was coming to ask her who Richard was, and in her muddled state she would tell him the whole story, and upset him horribly, and make him distrust her for the rest of their lives, all over something that had ended thirty-two years ago.

All this flashed through her mind between his tap and the careful opening of the door. Jack came in. He was wearing his old camel-hair dressing-gown and carried a glass of milk on a saucer.

"I was heating some milk for myself, Lucy," he said. "On the little spirit-lamp, and I thought you would be the better for a glass. You're tired, you know, with all these noisy children in the house. There are some biscuits too."

He set the milk down on her bedside table, fumbled in his pocket, and produced two digestive biscuits which had broken into several pieces and looked distinctly unappetizing. "Dear me, how can that have happened?" he said in a tone of vexed surprise. "I was most careful with them, too, and there are no more in my room. I will go down and get the tin from the dining-room cupboard."

"No, don't bother, Jack. These will do perfectly," said Mrs. Lorimer, once more mistress of herself. "How clever of you to think of the milk. I'm not sleepy, and this is what I need."

He beamed at her. "Nothing like a glass of hot milk to send you to sleep," he said. "You should drink it and settle down. All that reading in bed only excites your brain, you know. Just sip the milk slowly—don't gulp it or it will curdle in your inside and give you indigestion—sip it, and you'll sleep like a top. Good night."

"Good night, Jack dear," said his wife as he tiptoed from the room. And though there was no drink which Mrs. Lorimer disliked so much as hot milk, especially when it had a nasty skin on top of it, she drank it all—not in slow sips, for that she really could not have endured—and lay back on her pillows. Certainly she could not visualize Richard heating milk and bringing it to his wife to make her sleep! Her lips curved in a smile of affection. Dear, dear Jack! He had chased away the unwanted image of her ex-love, the rival he had never known. And how trim and slim and upright his figure was still, with the dressing-gown tied tightly round his waist by its rather frayed cord.

"I'm sure Richard has a corporation by now," she thought switching off her light. "And he's probably bald as well." And on this comforting thought Mrs. Lorimer fell asleep, forgetting all about the message on the telephone pad, which did not matter, as Nan, having delivered it verbally, had already torn it off and thrown it away to save herself time when dusting the hall before breakfast the next morning.

2

Miss Douglas was less orderly in her mind and habits than her friend Lucy. From time to time she rebelled against the endless round of housework, cooking, washing-up and gardening, and even writing, especially when she was alone. Had there been someone else to do it for, she would have grumbled less about it, but there was not. So when the restless mood came upon her, and it coincided with fine weather, she was apt to turn the key in the lock and walk out of her little house, though as she left all the windows wide open and quite often forgot to lock the back door, the turning of the front door key and putting it in her pocket was a purely ceremonial act.

A day or so after she had paid her call on Mr. Smellie at Harperslea, Miss Douglas paused in the middle of dusting the pieces of old Lowestoft ware which adorned her drawing-room mantelpiece, and looked out of the window. For some time she had been dusting more and more slowly, less and less conscientiously, and now she suddenly exclaimed in ringing tones: "Of all the senseless and unattractive ways of wasting a beautiful morning, this is the worst! I'm not going to dust another *thing*. I am going *out*!"

In spite of the hot July sun, her long strides took her up the first easy slopes at a good pace. Her objective was a ridge, not more than a mile from her house, which commanded a view of Threipford to the west and another higher, wilder valley behind, to the east. There she intended to lie at ease, filling her gaze with the wide prospect on the one side or the little hidden glen between the hills on the other. It was a favourite spot with her, and she had her own special place in the lee of a large flat-topped grey boulder, where the heather grew short and sparse and the ground was dry under it. Once there she threw herself down with a great sigh of relief, free of the domestic round which she so often felt was like a treadmill, as monotonous and as useless.

When she was tired of the sight of Thimblefield, like a doll's house set in a patch of green, and the distant church spires of Threipford rising among the trees, she still had the little valley east of the ridge to look down into. As she watched, Miss Douglas's eyes caught a glimpse of something moving, and presently two figures appeared on the path which wound up the side of the stream, high above the steep bank. Her long sight told her almost immediately who they were: Guy and the Smellie girl.

How extraordinary, thought Gray, remembering the fear expressed by Mrs. Lorimer that these long solitary tramps of Guy's might only make him more unhappy in his present state of mind and heart. Yet why should she, Gray, think it extraordinary? They might have met by chance, indeed, they most likely had; but if not, it was very sensible of Guy to seek the companionship of a girl who must be so different in every way from his lost Iris. There was nothing of the enchantress about Miss Smellie, including her name! In spite of this reasoning, Gray was a little troubled. She hoped that Guy had not deliberately allowed his mother to think that his long walks *were* solitary, and she hoped that he would not rouse the girls feelings, however unwittingly, and leave her hurt as he had been hurt. Then she shook her head impatiently and told herself not to be a fool. It was not her business, and if Guy thought it necessary to tell his mother, no doubt he would do so. In the meantime, she felt uncomfortably like a spy, though an innocent one, so she stood up, where, if they looked towards the ridge they were bound to see her, and after a minute or two, turned and walked down the hill again to Thimblefield.

That evening Guy came back for the night earlier than usual, with a message from Mary that she and Thomas had gone out to play bridge and could Gray please leave the door unlocked for them, as they might be late.

"I was asked too, but I can't be bothered with bridge," said Guy. "I never was very keen, and I'm worse than useless nowadays. Can't concentrate."

"In that case you are better not to try to play," Gray agreed. "No one really cares for you if you revoke. Would you like a drink?" she added rather doubtfully. "There's a siphon of soda in the dining-room, and I've got some brandy in the medicine cupboard. Or there may be some rum left over from last year's Christmas puddings? I'm sorry the supply is so low. It's time I replenished it."

"I'd much rather have tea," said Guy, and carried a tray with the necessary equipment into the drawing-room, where he plugged in the electric kettle and then sat down, stretching his long legs.

"I walked away up a valley I'd never been in before," he said presently. "Nan gave me a packet of sandwiches so I was out most of the day. Rona went with me."

"Rona?" asked Miss Douglas, who had forgotten the name which the Lorimers had given Miss Smellie.

"Yes. The Smellie girl, you know. Lord, how ghastly that sounds, doesn't it? Poor kid, no wonder she hates it," said Guy. "Imagine being called 'the Smellie girl'! You were there at dinner, Gray, when Mary suggested Rona as a shortening for Nesta Rowena, don't you remember?"

"So I was. I'd forgotten. Rona—for I really can't go on calling her the Smellie girl, or even Miss Smellie—seems a nice little thing," said she. "Very young and quiet, of course."

"She *is* very young, but not all that quiet," Guy said. "She talks quite a lot once she gets going. You ought to hear her views on marriage, Gray."

"On marriage? Does she discuss marriage with you?" Gray was astonished, and sounded it. "Whose, if you don't mind my asking?"

"Not a bit," he assured her cheerfully. "We discuss marriage in general and hers in particular. And I must say I have seldom heard such cockeyed opinions as the ones she trots out quite seriously. She is going to marry as soon as she can. But it must be a man with what she calls a pretty name." He dissolved into sudden laughter. "You ought to hear her, Gray. She's going to make a Continental marriage because she thinks their arrangements are so much more sensible than ours."

"Good heavens!" said Miss Douglas. And added, but inwardly, "I wonder if she considers Lorimer a pretty name." Aloud she went on: "I hope she may find this prospective husband with a name she likes. Do you suppose she will simply ask him to marry her?"

Guy laughed again, a laugh which did Miss Douglas good to hear. Rona, for all her 'cockeyed' ideas, had certainly been very good for Guy.

"I wouldn't put it past her, as Nan would say! But you mustn't think she's silly, Gray, because she isn't," said Guy. "She really means it, and though she will find out that she is wrong, that doesn't mean she is *silly*. As a matter of fact, she's a darned decent kid. It's like being out with a nice boy, except that she isn't a boy."

"And *that*, my dear Guy, is where the trouble begins," said Miss Douglas, again to herself. "Are you going for any more tramps with her?" she asked.

"Yes, tomorrow, if it's fine. She wants to look for cloudberry. One of the shepherds told her it grows on the high shoulder of the Black Dod. Why? Do you want to come?"

"No, but because if you are going to go on meeting her and walking with her, it might be just as well to mention it at Woodside," said Miss Douglas. "No, don't interrupt me for a minute, Guy. Someone will see you and tell your mother, and she will be hurt at hearing it that way. Of course you're a man and can do as you like, but one owes a little regard to the feelings of one's parents, and your mother has been—still is—worried about you. She will be delighted to think that you have friendly congenial company on your walks. There. I've done. Now you can blast me for a meddling old maid."

"Old maid be—blowed!" said Guy, and she knew she was forgiven.

"I'll tell Ma tomorrow that Rona and I are going for a walk," he said as he made for the door. "Does that satisfy you?"

"Good boy," was all the reply he got from Miss Douglas, however.

3

Because his Naval career had made him independent at an early age, Guy Lorimer had long ago lost that resentment towards parental interest in his affairs which so many young people suffer from. Until Iris, beautiful and fickle as the rainbow from which she took her name had crossed his path, Guy had not only answered his mother's questions freely, but had sometimes forestalled them with information given unasked. Now he had changed. Not only had he been absolutely silent about Iris, apart from announcing that she was married, but he found himself oddly reluctant to tell his mother that he and Rona had been out walking together more than once, and were going again on the following day. However, he had given his word to Gray, and he would have to keep it.

How easy it had been to talk to Gray about Rona and her absurd yet rather touching ideas! It had been easy, too, telling her about Iris. Why was it so difficult to tell an understanding person like Ma?

He was honest enough to admit even to himself that there was a good deal in what Gray had said about his mother's hearing of his walks with the girl from an outsider. That would be irritating for her, and there was no need for it to happen.

So he asked Nan for sandwiches while Mrs. Lorimer was in the kitchen, and when she said, as he knew she would, "Aren't you going to be in to lunch, then, Guy? I'm sure you can't be getting enough to eat," he was ready.

"Lord, yes, I'm eating plenty, Ma," he said. "Nan gives me so much I can hardly carry it. Rona's meeting me. We're going up on Black Dod today. She wants to look for cloudberry, and it grows there."

"Rona? Oh, yes, of course, the girl from Harperslea," Mrs. Lorimer answered, skilfully avoiding the name of Smellie. "I didn't know she was fond of walking, or of plants."

"She's pretty good at both," Guy said.

"Well, don't tire her out, she's only a slight little creature," said his mother. "Wouldn't you like to bring her in to tea when you come back? I have been meaning to ask her here ever since we called on her father."

"Fine. Thank you, Ma." Guy gave her a hug, took his packet of sandwiches, and went off. He left his mother surprised and very slightly perturbed, though she finished arranging the meals with Nan, a ceremony which had had to stop while Guy's lunch was being made.

When she managed to escape from the kitchen at last, basely remarking that Nan might think of a pudding for that evening herself as a treat and a surprise, Mrs. Lorimer wandered about the house from room to room, putting a picture straight here, and squaring all the small articles which Mrs. Pringle preferred to set back corner-wise when she dusted. She did it quite mechanically, for she was thinking about her younger son, wondering if he had recovered sufficiently from the Iris girl to be interested in another already, then discarding that idea and wondering if to take his mind off and assuage his hurt pride, he was making the little creature from Harperslea interested in *him*. In which case she might be hurt, and while Mrs. Lorimer would not have liked that to happen, because she was a nice little thing, what she really would mind would be her son's causing the hurt.

"Oh dear, oh *dear*," she though in angry dismay. "I wish the sexes could be segregated until they were all safely married! There is something to be said for the purdah system, after all!"

But when Guy brought Rona in at teatime, both of them hot, tired and triumphant, for they had found a quantity of cloudberry where they had gone to look for it, Mrs. Lorimer's greeting was composed and quietly cordial, as was natural.

As she went upstairs with Rona, who wanted to wash, and tidy her unruly hair, Mrs. Lorimer called down to her son, "Oh, Guy, there's an official looking letter for you on the chest. It came by the second post."

"I expect it is his appointment," she added to Rona, as Guy started to rummage among the gloves, papers and letters which always accumulated on the hall chest, no matter how often they were cleared away.

"You mean—to another ship? I don't know anything about the Navy."

"I don't think one ever does, without having someone in it. It is a closed shop," Mrs. Lorimer answered.

A babel arose from below, the family coming in to tea, but not the children. They were having a picnic on the lawn, presided over by Nannie and Doreen, to everyone's great though unspoken relief.

Mrs. Lorimer had been counting on Phillis to make Rona feel at home, for she had been the one to bring the child to the house in the first instance, but Phillis was very offhand, greeted her casually, said it was a pity she hadn't had time to play tennis again, and turned away. Her mother was annoyed. Really, Phillis was much too careless; in consequence her own manner to Rona was warmer than it otherwise need have been. But Rona seemed quite content to sit quietly drinking her tea and listening to the chatter all round her. She was very good at being an onlooker, succeeding in appearing interested and pleased when no one was paying much attention to her, and possessed of a tranquillity rare in so young a woman; both of which Mrs. Lorimer admired in her.

"I say, Ma," said Guy, during a temporary lull. "That letter was my appointment. I'm to stand by the *Rex*, and she's building on the Clyde, so you'll have me here for weekends."

"Oh, Guy, how mouldy!" cried Phillis. "I was counting on you being at Pompey and able to take me to dances when George is on duty!"

"Too bad. You'll have to find another victim," Guy said, unmoved.

Alice, her gentle eyes beaming, began to wonder if he could manage to get to their farm sometimes.

"You might also spare a weekend to visit *us*," Thomas said mildly. "You won't be as comfortable as you will with Lally and Vivian, but we'd like to see you."

During this discussion Mrs. Lorimer had remained as silent as her young guest, and considerably less content. To have Guy coming home for weekends would have been perfect, if it hadn't meant that he would inevitably see more of "the Smellie girl"; and Mrs. Lorimer now knew quite well that she would rather this acquaintance should not become anything more. The girl was pleasant, well-mannered, passably agreeable to look at; but for Guy—no, never! Guy ought to marry someone with good connections, who would be a help to him in his career; or at least, someone who was more of a person than this quiet creature. Perhaps she was making bricks without straw, thought Guy's mother, but propinquity was so terribly insidious! Almost she wished that she had not been so quick to call on Rona's father. At the same time she blamed herself severely for snobbishness, and felt distressed because she was not delighted at the prospect of seeing more of her dear Guy.

CHAPTER EIGHT

1

MONARCH of all he surveyed—at least within the limits of his own grounds—Colonel Lorimer stood on the gravel outside his house and looked with infinite content at a garden and lawn empty of children and their attendants. His old bitch June sat beside him, luxuriously scratching.

Only Guy was still at home, and one single son was nothing after the horde which had filled Woodside to over-flowing for the past ten days.

These were Colonel Lorimer's private thoughts. In theory he was very fond of his family, and while they were at a distance he was a most affectionate parent, but he hoped that it would be a long time before he had to endure another week like the one which had ended this morning. It had not even *been* a week, he remembered indignantly. A week was what Lucy had mentioned to him as the limit of their stay, but it had actually been ten days, for they had come on a Friday, and this was a Tuesday morning! He brooded over his wrongs for a moment, then reminded himself that his trials were ended; or at least, more or less ended. His face clouded again as he remembered the mess they had left behind. "Havoc! Absolute havoc!" he said aloud, thinking of scratched paint and spills inside the house, untidy gravel and footmarks all over the garden beds. He could not understand Lucy's apparent indifference to these blemishes, which put him in a fever of distress and annoyance.

He was pondering over her strangeness in this respect, when she came out and joined him, putting her hand through the crook of his arm.

"I must say it is pleasant to see you looking like the Monarch of the Glen again instead of the Stag at Bay," she said.

"I was thinking," said the Colonel in a dignified voice, and ignoring her remark. "How my mother would have hated all the noise and mess."

"Never mind, Jack," said Mrs. Lorimer, "the house will soon be put to rights again. Nan and Mrs. Pringle are working like beavers now, doing out the bedrooms."

"Hah!" said the Colonel with great satisfaction. "And what are you going to do today, Lucy, my dear?"

"I've just been ringing Gray up. She and I are going out in the car and taking our lunch," said Mrs. Lorimer. "I think we deserve a little holiday. What are your plans?"

"I have to do the washing, and then I must go over the garden with the hoe," began the Colonel. "And the gravel needs to be thoroughly raked. Thoroughly. I thought that Guy might give me a hand. He's probably at a loose end now that the others have gone."

This struck Mrs. Lorimer as exceedingly improbable, but considering quite rightly that Guy could look after himself, she merely said, "Remember that he's on leave, Jack. He may want to do something on his own," and went away to get out her little car.

2

Mrs. Lorimer and Miss Douglas enjoyed their picnic very much. It was delightful to get away from domestic affairs, especially after the rather extra strenuous ten days which both of them had just spent. Sitting on a grassy bank with a young river talking quietly to itself at their feet and a heather-scented breeze drifting overhead, they ate rolls stuffed with fried eggs, and digestive biscuits sandwiched with cheese, and drank coffee with far more appetite than they would have had for the meal which Colonel Lorimer and Guy were eating in the dining-room at Woodside. Secure in the knowledge that there was no one to see what they did but a few anxious sandpipers and a kestrel hovering far above them in the blue of the sky, they paddled like children until their toes were deliciously numbed by the cool running water, and then sat basking in the sun again while their feet dried. Unwillingly at last they collected their few belongings and wandered back upstream to the road where Mrs. Lorimer's car waited to take them home.

"What a lovely day it has been, so peaceful and satisfying," said Miss Douglas as they got in. "I wish we could do it more often, Lucy dear."

"So do I. But perhaps we wouldn't enjoy it so much if we could always escape whenever we liked," said Mrs. Lorimer.

Both ladies were silent on the way home.

As they walked round the house from the garage—for according to custom Miss Douglas was going to drink a cup of tea at Woodside before she went back to her cottage—the steady soothing hum of the vacuum-cleaner came to their ears. Gray looked inquiringly at her friend.

"It's Jack," said Mrs. Lorimer with a smile. "He loves hoovering, and this is the first chance he has had of doing it since the family came. I thought he would be hard at it. He waits until Nan goes out into Threipford, and then hurries to the cupboard and gets it out."

Gray laughed outright. "What an interesting man Jack is! I find out something new about him almost every time I come to Woodside. In all the years I have known you both, Lucy, I never suspected him of hoovering as a hobby. It's really very useful of him—or is it?"

"Well, I don't think it is useful, really," Mrs. Lorimer said thoughtfully. "He does it so slowly and scientifically that it takes a very long time. But it amuses him, and he does clean the Hoover very thoroughly when he has finished, which is more than Nan does. She probably leaves it for him to empty now, and never bothers."

"She doesn't mind his doing it?"

"Oh, dear me, no. It's just 'the Colonel,'" said Mrs. Lorimer. "I daresay she would object if I started using the Hoover—think it a reflection on her housework or Mrs. Pringle's. But as that contingency is never likely to arise, everything is all right. I have no desire to sweep the carpets, not even with a vacuum-cleaner."

The humming note had died away in a whine disagreeably reminiscent of a distant air-raid siren, and Colonel Lorimer began to come downstairs, carrying the body of the Hoover in one hand, and draped in yards of flex, with a long fat snake-like tube coiled over his shoulder and other arm in a Laocoon-like manner.

"Ha, Lucy! Got back from your picnic? Splendid!" he said. "I've just been trying the Hoover. Good afternoon, Gray. Those bedrooms were in a terrible state, Lucy. Terrible. Alice's Nannie and that girl Phillis brought with her can't have touched them. I'll bet you anything you like that this"—he tapped the vacuum-cleaner impressively—"is full of dust and fluff. Full."

And he disappeared towards the back door, bound for the dustbin.

"Dear Jack!" said Gray.

"He really *is* a nice old thing, isn't he?" agreed his wife. Then the two looked at one another, and as they so often did, began to laugh.

"Let's go and see the result of his labour," Mrs. Lorimer suggested when they had stopped laughing. "Nan isn't back yet, so there won't be anyone to disapprove, and it isn't quite teatime."

Miss Douglas agreeing with eagerness, they went round to the courtyard where they found the Colonel, superintended by June, scooping the horrible remnants of furry dust out of the Hoover's interior by hand.

"Jack, how *can* you?" said Mrs. Lorimer in disgust. "Look at your hands!"

"Only way to get the stuff out properly," said the Colonel. "Ah, that's the lot, I think. Just take a look at that dustbin, Lucy, and you too, Gray. It's worth it."

They peered with undisguised horror at the nasty heap of discoloured fluff, and professed suitable astonishment at the amount the Colonel had gathered, and congratulated him heartily.

"And now do put the lid on, in case it blows about, and wash your hands, Jack," urged his wife. "Nan will be in any minute now, and then we will have tea. By the way, where's Guy? Has he gone for a walk?"

"He said he would hoe the vegetable beds for me," said the Colonel, giving a last lingering look at his harvest before imprisoning it with the dustbin lid. "I expect he's still down in the garden. I'll go and give him a shout—"

"No, we'll go. You really *must* wash, you aren't sanitary," said Mrs. Lorimer.

Gray fancied that she sounded pleased and relieved, as indeed she was. She was pleased to know that Guy was safely employed in the garden and not out on the hills with the girl from Harperslea. After this, it was all the more vexatious, as they approached the vegetable beds by way of the shrubbery, to hear a good deal of laughter and conversation, and to find Guy, hoeing busily indeed, but assisted by Rona, who was raking the weeds together into tidy heaps. Both were chattering so hard that they did not hear their elders at all; and Mrs. Lorimer, who suddenly knew that she would like to box Guy's ears and to shake Rona, had to ask the girl to stay to tea. It was all most annoying, and a little more disquiet was added to her maternal anxiety about her younger son.

3

July gave place to August. A large number of the inhabitants of Threipford, who were in the habit of supplementing their incomes by this means, crammed themselves and their families into much too small a space in their houses, and advertised rooms with attendance for summer visitors. The pleasant little park with its clock-golf and the pond where ducks and an occasional swan floated placidly about in undisputed ownership was invaded by noisy hordes who cut up the turf with high heels or hobnails as well as golf clubs, threw stones instead of crumbs at the affronted water fowl, dragged yelling children up and down the quiet paths, and generally turned the park into a first-class imitation of Bedlam. The native population of Threipford and the neighbourhood, weary of being pushed off their own pavements and shouldered aside in the familiar shops, either sent their young, home from school for the holidays, to do their shopping for them, or had recourse to the telephone.

Only absolute necessity took Mrs. Lorimer into the town during this visitors' season, but one morning about the middle of August, the non-arrival of the fish for that day's lunch forced her to drive down in her little car. Main Gate was full of touring buses parked askew all along the middle of the wide street. Their occupants, most of whom wore paper hats on their tousled heads, and were accompanied by musicians performing lustily upon mouth-organs or accordions, added themselves to the idle crowd which trailed up and down, greatly hampering the people who were searching for food.

"Isn't this ghastly?" said a voice in Mrs. Lorimer's ear, and she turned to find Miss Douglas gazing at what the press might describe as the animated scene with open disgust.

"Only man is vile," murmured Mrs. Lorimer, stepping aside to avoid the onrush of a fresh bus-load of trippers, their faces red as boiled lobsters, their arms and necks a painful pink, with which those of them who were female wore colours which clashed loudly and hideously. "And woman too, of course," she added, as the party surged towards a shop window where fancy goods were displayed, and exclaimed over them admiringly in the accents of Lancashire.

"They buy those appalling funny hats," Miss Douglas pointed out, as a stream of persons issued from Melvilles', each adorned with a specimen of the headgear in question. "Good heavens, Lucy! Look at that woman in the pink bonnet with the green streamers!" She burst into uncontrollable laughter, and Mrs. Lorimer, taking her arm, led her firmly away.

"I must get the fish, Gray," she said. "And you can't stand here having hysterics. I suppose they enjoy making fools of themselves, and after all, it's a harmless amusement."

"It isn't harmless to rain the beauty of Main Gate by looking like that," said Miss Douglas, when she had recovered, but she went obediently to the fishmonger's with her friend, and when Mrs. Lorimer had put a large parcel wrapped in damp newspaper and smelling powerfully of fish into her shopping basket, suggested that they had time for a cup of coffee.

"It will be quiet and cool in the lounge of the Tower," she said. "They don't cater for buses."

Mrs. Lorimer decided that she would like some coffee, and they crossed the street and went into the dark hall of the old hotel, once a coaching-inn where the Edinburgh Mail had changed horses. The coffee was hot and good, there were very appetizing crisp home-made shortbread biscuits with it and it was pleasant to sit at the window of the lounge—quiet and cool, as Miss Douglas had said, and empty but for themselves—and look out at the bustle in Main Gate.

The door of the room swung open behind them, but they paid no attention until, "Lucy! What luck to find you here—and Gray as well!" said a woman's pleasant voice, and they found themselves shaking hands with Judith Dunne from up Threip Water.

"My dears, isn't Threipford awful at this time of year?" said Mrs. Dunne, casting herself gracefully into a chintz-covered chair. "I thought I should *never* get the shopping done. Our telephone's out of order, and we had to have the rations, of course, or I should never have come in."

"Are you alone?" asked Gray. She liked Mrs. Dunne and admired her animation and elegant length of limb.

"No. Walter is buying cartridges and binder twine, but he'll be here in a minute, shouting for beer, if I know him," replied Mrs. Dunne. "Oh, and Lucy, we've got—"

Before she could finish her sentence the door swung open again and two men entered. Mrs. Lorimer, her eyes still dazzled from looking at the sunlit street, could not see their faces for a moment, and Judith Dunne went on gaily: "Talk of the devil! I was just saying to Lucy that we had you staying with us!"

And Mrs. Lorimer found her hand in the grasp of Richard Malleson.

"Lucy!" he was saying in the deep voice which had once had the power to stir her to the heart so many years ago.

Now it sounded just a little affected, perhaps because she was used to Jack's light, clipped speech.

"How are you, Richard?" she said. She felt perfectly composed, and was pleased to hear her voice uttering the words in the easy tones of someone greeting an acquaintance.

"The better for seeing you again. You haven't changed at all, Lucy," he said. He still held her hand, and she quietly withdrew it, laughing a little.

"I am sitting with my back to a strong light," she said. "Oh, you don't know Miss Douglas, do you? Gray, let me introduce Mr. Malleson. We knew each other a long time ago."

Gray, who had been talking to the Dunnes, held out her hand to the stranger, and received a perfunctory shake before he immediately turned again towards Mrs. Lorimer. Amused, Miss Douglas looked at him. Handsome in a burly fashion, he might very easily run to fat if he did not take care, she thought unkindly, and his face was that of a man who would show more tenderness for his own shortcomings than those of other people.

"Spoilt and insensitive," she decided. "What a very strange type to be an ex-boy-friend of Lucy's."

"Now that you have met again," Judith was babbling in blissful ignorance of undercurrents, "we *must* arrange a proper meeting, Lucy. Richard was so terribly disappointed not to see you the last time he was here. Weren't you, Richard?"

"I was," he answered, but he spoke to Lucy and not to Judith Dunne. Mrs. Lorimer recognized the old familiar methods, the cutting-out tactics by which Richard had always managed to convey a sense that he and the woman of the moment were alone together even in a crowded room. It seemed to her that the time had come for her to take charge of the situation.

"Suppose, Judith, that you and Walter and Richard dine with us at Woodside one evening next week?" she said. "Gray, you will come too, won't you? It will be fun to have a dinner-party."

Under cover of a lively discussion between the Dunnes as to which day would suit best, Richard Malleson murmured, "I hoped perhaps that you might have dined with me here, Lucy—just you and I. I want to hear all about you. Or would your husband object?"

"Oh, Jack wouldn't mind. Why should he?" responded Mrs. Lorimer briskly. "But you wouldn't enjoy it, Richard. The food at the Tower is not up to your standard by any means. Besides, my younger son may be at home, and I'd like you to see him." And to Judith Dunne she added: "If you could make it the Friday or

Saturday, Judith, Guy would probably be here. He comes home most weekends."

Determinedly she drew the others into the conversation, but it was difficult, with Richard now muttering into her ear how wonderful it was of her to remember that he appreciated good cooking. Mrs. Lorimer could not imagine how some women seemed to find it romantic and exciting, even when they were happily married, to meet an old flame again. She was finding this maddeningly tedious, and it seemed impossible to make Richard understand that, far from being an old flame, he was the deadest of dead ash to her. She remembered that the impact of Richard's personality had always exhausted her even when her youthful vitality had been at its height, and now she felt battered.

Miss Douglas was sitting quietly smoking a cigarette a little apart from the other four, and feeling that she and Lucy had changed places: for once she was silent and Lucy was positively chattering. But Mrs. Lorimer's look of weariness had not failed to catch her attention. "If it were anyone else I should say she had reached screaming-point," thought Gray. She stubbed out her cigarette and rose.

"I really must go home," she said casually. "Pleasant though this coffee-drinking habit is, it takes up far too much time, and it's a long way to Thimblefield. Look in the next time you are passing, Judith. There may not be anything else to drink, but I can always manage a nice cup of tea."

Mrs. Lorimer seized on the chance to escape. "Good heavens! The fish! Nan will be furious, and lunch will be late," she exclaimed. "Gray, I'll give you a lift, dear. And Judith, we'll expect you all three on Saturday week. That will be lovely. Until then, au-revoir, Richard."

"A rividerci," said Richard in his deepest tone. He seemed about to take her hand, and probably, since nothing was too flamboyant for him, raise it to his lips, thought Mrs. Lorimer angrily; but she was grasping her shopping basket and he had to content himself with a look full of meaning as she and Miss Douglas hastily left the lounge.

"Quite a pleasant break in a morning's shopping," said Gray, when they were crossing the street to the car, parked in the shade of a spreading beech. "But I wouldn't like to do it every day, like some people."

Mrs. Lorimer looked sharply at her friend, but Gray's face was innocent and placid.

"I found it a little tiring," she said, and on impulse added, "I think perhaps it is not a good thing to meet people one has known well a long time ago after a lapse of so many years. It is more than thirty since I last saw Richard Malleson. He has changed very much."

Gray was silent for a moment. Then she said rather hesitatingly, "Do you not think that you are the one who has changed, Lucy?"

"Well, yes, of course, I have. I'm a middle-aged woman—almost an elderly woman—now."

"I don't mean grey hair and a few wrinkles," said Gray. "It's just—you have matured and he hasn't. I should think that mentally Mr. Malleson is just about the same age as he was when you last saw him. And of course, you are looking at him with experienced eyes. That's why you think he has changed, Lucy."

"How very penetrating of you, Gray," Mrs. Lorimer said. "You are right, I'm sure. I wish I hadn't seen Richard again—"

"I should have thought," said Gray, "that you would have been pleased. It is usually a good thing when one can lay the ghost of one's past painlessly—it *would* be painlessly, wouldn't it, Lucy?"

In all their years of friendship Gray had never spoken so openly, but the occasion seemed to demand it.

Mrs. Lorimer nodded. "Quite painlessly, except for thinking what a silly little fool one was at twenty-three," she said.

"Most of us were. Some of us still are. It's a safeguard to realize it. Lucy, we *must* hurry. Think of Nan!"

They hastened their lagging steps towards the car, and presently were driving swiftly away from the hot crowded street, out of the little town to the open country beyond. "But somehow," said Mrs. Lorimer with a petulance very rare in her. "I didn't want Richard Malleson mixed up with my life *here*, my nice contented life. It's all wrong."

As things were, she was able to mention him quite casually to Jack when she announced that she had asked the Dunnes to dinner.

"They have a man—Richard Malleson—staying with them whom I used to know," she said.

The Colonel never failed to receive news of an impending dinner-party with horrified loathing. But his scene of despair and disgust, although frequently performed, still held a certain interest for his family, since they could never make up their minds whether he was more dismayed at the prospect of dining out or of having guests at his own table. Up to date opinion was slightly in favour of dining-out, and Mrs. Lorimer wished that one at least of her children were present on this occasion, because she had never heard Jack make such heartfelt protests against having people to dinner, and she was sure that the home supporters (of whom she was the chief) would by now be in the lead. So anguished was he that he showed no curiosity whatever about Richard Malleson, though his interest when a strange name was mentioned was usually extremely lively.

"But Jack, you *like* the Dunnes," said Mrs. Lorimer at last, breaking in on his lamentations when she felt she had listened to them long enough.

"Yes, of course I do. Walter Dunne is a very nice fellow—"

"Then why in the world are you making such a fuss because I've asked them to dinner? If we are never to go there, and they are never to come to us, how are we going to see them at all?"

The Colonel, cornered, muttered that he could always have a chat with Walter Dunne when they met in the town, just as she had had this morning over a cup of coffee.

"If my seeing my friends had to depend on anything so unusual as the chance of meeting them in the town, I might as well be a hermit at once," declared Mrs. Lorimer. "It's all very well for you, Jack. You go down Main Gate practically every day, and can spend as long as you like there, but I—"

"But you want to stay at home and write, Lucy," said the Colonel, most unfairly leaving his defensive position and advancing to the attack.

"Of course I do, when I *am* writing. But I'm not just now, and you know it very well. And anyhow, I have asked the Dunnes, and they are coming, and bringing Richard Malleson with them. And we sound almost as if we were bickering, Jack!"

"Surely not, my dear?" Colonel Lorimer was genuinely surprised and disturbed. "I had no intention of bickering, I assure you. And of course, as you have asked the Dunnes and they have accepted, there is no more to be said."

("As if," thought his wife, "you haven't already said everything you can possibly think of against it!")

The Colonel, pleased with his own reasonable attitude, now demanded: "Who did you say they were bringing with them, Lucy? Anyone I know?"

Mrs. Lorimer shook her head. "No, Jack, as far as I know you have never met Richard Malleson. I knew him a long time ago, when I was a girl."

"Oh!" said Colonel Lorimer rather blankly. Then his face cleared and he chuckled. "An old flame, Lucy?"

An old flame! Mrs. Lorimer remembered that delicate fire which had burned in her young heart so long ago and been so brutally stamped out.

"Yes," she said quietly. "I suppose you could call him that, Jack."

"Hah!" her husband said. "I shall have to look out, then." Another thought struck him. "Lucy, shall I have to put on a dinner-jacket and a boiled shirt?"

"I'm afraid you will, Jack dear. But you look so nice in your dinner-jacket."

"It's wonderful when you think that it's the same I had when we were first married—in fact, *before* we were married," said the Colonel, rising to the bait so often gently dropped for him. He glanced down at his trim, spare figure with pardonable pride. "I don't believe I've put on a pound since I left Sandhurst. My waist-measurement is exactly the same as it was then."

"You're a conceited old thing," said Mrs. Lorimer very affectionately. "And no one would think to look at you that I feed you up on milk and all the eggs I can get, and far more than your share of the butter ration! You still remain as thin as a kipper."

"Good heavens, Lucy! You wouldn't like me to be *fat*, would you?" he exclaimed. "Fat!" In tones of shuddering distaste.

"No. I like you as you are," said Mrs. Lorimer gravely. "I'm a little bit jealous, you see, because I am no longer the slim creature you married."

"You?" The Colonel stared at her as if seeing her for the first time. "Surely you don't call yourself fat, Lucy?"

"Not fat, Jack, but definitely matronly."

"And very nice too. You look just right to me," he said. He gave her a quick, rather embarrassed smile, and glanced at his watch. "Just time to take old June for a little turn before lunch," he announced. "Coming, June? Walkies, old lady!"

As he clattered out of the room, with June panting noisily at his heels, Mrs. Lorimer sighed. Once again, she thought, he was vanishing just when Nan would sound the gong in a few minutes. "All my family have this failing," she said aloud to herself, "and their father is the worst of the lot. All the same," but this she did not say aloud, "all the same, I am certain that Richard can no longer get into any suit he wore over thirty years ago!"

4

Richard Malleson, when he arrived at Woodside with the Dunnes on the appointed Saturday evening, was quite obviously wearing a dinner-jacket made for him recently and cut by a master; and even so, "burly" was the adjective which described him most kindly. Beside him Colonel Lorimer looked like a rapier next to a bludgeon. It was a little unfortunate that, owing to a spell of wet weather which had prevented Nan from airing the Colonel's evening things, they still smelled of mothballs, faint but unmistakable. Nevertheless Mrs. Lorimer felt pleased with her husband and her younger son as they stood with Walter Dunne and Richard in front of the log-fire which the dampness in the air had made necessary. The ladies of the party, tripping now and again over the long skirts which they wore so seldom, clustered as near the solid male phalanx blocking out the cheerful glow as they could without actually crowding them. Sherry had been handed round by Guy, and the whole scene had a leisured appearance reminiscent of less careworn days.

Rona was there at Guy's request, and to make the numbers even as he said, dressed in chiffon of a dull amber shade which made her skin milk-white and showed up her greenish-gold hair. This evening, as Mrs. Lorimer admitted reluctantly to herself, the child looked really very pretty. Richard Malleson had glanced at her more than once, his hostess noticed, and she thought that Guy had noticed it too, for his own glances at Richard were none too friendly. Did the girl herself realize that she had attracted the attention of this extremely personable man, Mrs. Lorimer wondered. It was high time that Richard settled down if he ever intended to, and Rona presumably would have money, since her father was a wealthy man. It would be a good match for her . . . Then Mrs. Lorimer s feelings revolted against this scheming. Knowing what Richard was, completely selfish, considering only his own interests, how could she have let her wishes carry her to the point of sacrificing a girl younger than her own daughters to such a man? It was frightening to think that mother-love, taking the form of anxiety about Guy's future should have led her even to think of such a solution. She looked round at her guests, and encountered the quiet eyes of Gray Douglas fixed on her face with speculative interest.

Mrs. Lorimer felt the blood rush to her neck and cheeks, and moved away from the fireside a little as if too hot. This brought her close to Gray, who said to her gently, "You wouldn't really like that as a way out, Lucy."

Too shaken to show her uneasy astonishment at this reading of her thoughts, Mrs. Lorimer said, "No, I wouldn't. It was a horrible idea. But I knew that even while it came into my mind, Gray."

"Why do you dislike the thought of Guy's being attracted to this particular girl so strongly, Lucy?" asked Miss Douglas under cover of the burst of laughter which greeted some tale of Judith Dunne's.

"Oh, Gray, it seems all *wrong* to me," murmured Mrs. Lorimer. "She isn't nearly good enough for Guy—not in looks or family or *anything*! Even her name is all wrong! Besides, Guy was madly in love with someone else only a short time ago, and I can't believe he is so changeable. If he asks the Harperslea girl to marry him I'm sure it won't be because he loves her—"

"Everyone doesn't marry the person they are madly in love with," said Miss Douglas ungrammatically but firmly. "It isn't always the best kind of marriage. Being caught on the rebound sometimes works out better."

Startled, Mrs. Lorimer glanced at her friend again. Gray might have been speaking of her own marriage to Jack, only she didn't know about it. Gray was really becoming too acute for comfort! But Gray was looking at the group beside the fire, where little Rona was now standing near Richard Malleson, apparently listening to his words with interest.

The gong, beaten by Nan with all the strength of a muscular arm, broke deafeningly on the buzz of small talk.

"I hate to hurry you," said Mrs. Lorimer, reminded of her duties as hostess. "But would you mind bringing your sherry in with you? Nan has made one of her special cheese soufflés as a savoury and I shall get into serious trouble if it falls."

"Dear Lucy, the thought of an enraged Nan and a sunk soufflé is too dreadful!" cried Judith Dunne. "Besides, I love cheese soufflé. Let us go in at once!"

Clutching their glasses, they made their way to the dining-room, where Mrs. Lorimer marshalled them to their places. "Walter on my right, and Richard, will you come on my other side? Then Gray next to Walter, and Rona on Richard's left. Judith, you sit at Jack's right, and I'm very sorry it means two females next one another and Guy beside his father, but eight is such an awkward number. If Jack would only agree to sit between you and Rona, Judith, it would be all right, but he refuses to give up his place at the other end of the table."

Mrs. Lorimer was conscious that she was babbling with most unusual loquacity, and it did not make her any happier to have Richard murmuring in his annoyingly confidential manner: "I read an article about you in a magazine, Lucy, by someone who described you as a very quiet woman. I must say I shouldn't have recognized you—"

"Oh, you can't go by those interviews with reporters. I was probably struck dumb and couldn't think of anything to say on that occasion," answered Mrs. Lorimer, unable to stem the nervous rush of words which was afflicting her.

"You were very quiet as a girl," Richard Malleson continued. "I remember, when I read that article, thinking that you couldn't have changed very much—"

"How absurd! Of course I have changed," said Mrs. Lorimer. "In every way," she ended firmly.

As if to bear witness to the truth of this remark her son Guy, who had been sitting in slightly sulky silence between his father and Miss Douglas, raised his head and said loudly across the intervening diners: "Ma! Do I smell roast grouse?"

"I think it is quite probable," said Mrs. Lorimer, so delighted at the welcome interruption of what Richard was turning into a tête-à-tête that she forbore to frown on Guy for making this observation and sniffing into the bargain. "It always seems to escape from the kitchen—the smell of cooking, I mean."

"Who cares when it's a smell like grouse?" said Guy, sniffing the air, on which a faint delicious aroma certainly was stealing.

"Guy reminds me of a gun-dog I once had, a Springer spaniel," remarked his father. "But *she* looked like that when she smelt kippers." Rona dissolved into laughter. The Dunnes and Gray followed her example, and the Colonel, pleased with the success of his mild witticism, repeated it once or twice aloud to himself.

Mrs. Lorimer said resignedly, "This was meant to be a *real* dinner-party," which only caused more laughter. She looked to her left and found that Richard remained serious.

"Good heavens!" she thought. "What an escape I had. Imagine being married all these years to such a dreary bore!" And aloud she said to him perfunctorily, "I'm afraid we must seem very silly to you, Richard, with our little jokes."

"Not in the least," he replied in a tone which said clearly that they most certainly did seem silly. He bent towards her, his stiff shirt crackling, and murmured, while the general laughter continued: "Do all your family call you 'Ma'?"

"Yes, they do. They always have. Why?"

"It is such an ugly name. I can't, somehow, associate it with *you*," he said deeply.

"Well," Mrs. Lorimer said in a considering way. "Nearly all the names children call their mothers are ugly: Mum, for instance, or Maw—but they are the outcome of affection, so I suppose mothers don't mind them. I don't. If the children ever call me 'Mother' I know that something frightful has happened."

He shook his handsome head, remarking how impossible it was that she should be the mother of a son of Guy's age.

"It's very nice of you, Richard, to pay me such a compliment," said Mrs. Lorimer. "But I assure you that I am Guy's mother. What is more, Alice and Thomas are both older than Guy, and I am a grandmother several times over."

"A grandmother!" he exclaimed in a tone of such horror that she almost laughed in his face; and with that, evidently dismissing her as unworthy of his further notice, he turned to Rona and began to talk to her in his most intimate manner.

But this move, though it greatly relieved Mrs. Lorimer, gave her son Guy no pleasure at all. As dinner progressed, as roast grouse with its appropriate trimmings was eaten and enjoyed, and Nan's feathery cheese soufflé followed it, Guy became steadily gloomier. Gray Douglas, after making one or two unsuccessful attempts to engage him in conversation, gave it up and devoted herself to the excellent results of Nan's cooking, since Walter Dunne, her left-hand neighbour, was talking to his hostess. She felt sorry for Guy, but a little amused by his obvious sulks. For a young man who had been hopelessly in love with another girl a few months before, she thought he was taking an extremely personal interest in Rona's rather absorbed attention to whatever Richard Malleson was saying to her.

It is not easy to continue to look pleasant and intelligent when thus marooned at a dinner-table, and Miss Douglas gave an inward sigh of relief when Mrs. Lorimer rose and swept the ladies out of the room.

"Not that there is any port to leave the men to, poor dears," she said as they gathered round the drawing-room fire again. "But it gives them an illusion of port-drinking and pre-war days if we go out. They will follow us soon enough for coffee, when they have finished what is in their glasses."

"I wonder what they talk about when they are alone," murmured Judith Dunne, pensively admiring her elegant narrow foot as she held it to the blaze. "I've asked Walter, but he never tells me."

"Judging by the bits I hear from Jack sometimes, it is uncommonly dull," said Mrs. Lorimer, and Rona's face fell.

"I thought it would be so interesting," she said disappointedly.

"I'm sure I know what they are talking about this evening, at any rate," was Gray's contribution, and as the others looked at her in surprise, added: "The Show, of course."

"Of course! How stupid of us!" exclaimed Mrs. Dunne. "Dear me, how bored Richard will be!"

Miss Douglas, feeling that her acquaintance with Richard Malleson was too slight to warrant any comment on this statement, remained silent; Mrs. Lorimer merely smiled. But Rona said:

"Will he? I thought he seemed rather an interested sort of person."

"Do you mean interesting?" asked Mrs. Dunne.

"No," said Rona, flushing but sticking to her point. "*Interested.* He was very interested at dinner when we were talking."

Mrs. Lorimer knew that interested manner of Richard's, and, now able to estimate it at its proper value, hoped that the child Rona would not attach too much importance to it.

"Here they come," she said, as a noise of manly voices rose from the hall. "And now we shall *all* have to talk Show, interested or not."

The Threip Water Agricultural Show, which was now only a week or two ahead, dominated the conversation for the rest of the evening, though Richard Malleson showed an annoying tendency to pen Rona into a corner and there talk to her with lowered voice, and Guy barely uttered a word unless addressed directly by name.

"Allowing for a slight moderation of language," said Miss Douglas, when she and Lucy were alone in the drawing-room while the Colonel sped the remainder of the parting guests at the door and Guy had vanished, "I suppose we have had a very fair sample this evening of what men *do* talk about when they are by themselves. At least, we might just as well not have been there for all the notice they took of us."

"And, Lord! How dull it is!" said Mrs. Lorimer.

"No wonder the fashion of the ladies leaving the dining-room after dessert was instituted," agreed Miss Douglas. "Good night, Lucy dear. It has been a lovely party, for all that."

CHAPTER NINE

1

As Miss Douglas walked home sedately alone, going the long way round by the road because it was rather too hazardous to take the cross-country route in the dark and a dinner-dress, she suddenly became aware of voices ahead of her. They were voices not at all in keeping with the beauty of the night, for they sounded quarrelsome. Not only that, but they sounded familiar; they were, in fact, the voices of Lieutenant Guy Lorimer, Royal Navy, and Miss Nesta Rowena Smellie, alias Rona.

"Dear me!" thought Miss Douglas, mildly interested, but not entirely astonished. "So that's where Guy disappeared to. He is taking Rona home to get a chance of squabbling with her. What a noise they are making."

With the kindly intention of warning them that they were not the only persons out on the road this evening, she coughed so loudly that she rasped her throat, uttering at the same time an inward curse at the selfishness of people who chose the public highway to quarrel on.

The voices continued, and she was wondering whether to stand where she was for a little, or simply to walk on as if she had heard nothing, when they rose on a crescendo of indignation, and abruptly ceased. The next moment a large dark figure collided violently with her, muttered "Sorry," in very perfunctory tones in Guy's voice, and proceeded rapidly back towards Woodside.

Reflecting on the folly of youth, Miss Douglas continued on her way, and presently reached the gates of Harperslea, where another figure, less bulky in outline, paler in colour, stood stamping its foot and denouncing the entire race of men with vehemence.

"'A plague o' both their houses,' by all means," said Miss Douglas genially. "But hadn't you better go home? It's getting rather late."

Rona uttered a squeak. "Goodness, how you frightened me, Miss Douglas! I thought it was—" Then she pulled herself together and said in a dignified way, "It's a beautiful night. I was just—just looking at stars."

"Venus, no doubt," said Miss Douglas with a glance at the completely starless heavens. "Well, good night, Rona. It was a very pleasant dinner-party, wasn't it?"

"Oh, yes. Yes, it was extremely. Such nice people," said Rona vaguely. "Good night, Miss Douglas." Evidently she had had enough of the beauty of the night, for she slipped through the gate and went pattering away up the drive to Harperslea.

Miss Douglas, resuming her quiet saunter, pondered over the ostrich-like behaviour of the young. In this case, Guy was the ostrich, and no doubt even after this evening's quarrel, which must have been caused by jealousy on his part, he would continue to delude himself into imagining that his interest in Rona was purely friendly and had nothing to do with love, unless or until something happened to jolt him into awareness. As to Rona herself, Miss Douglas thought it did not matter so much at present. She was a level-headed little creature, but she was very young and unawakened. So she was probably only bewildered and indignant and had no idea at all why Guy had been quarrelling with her; but of course it was bound to make her think about him all the more.

"And there you are!" said Miss Douglas, talking aloud to herself as she far too often did. Her further ruminations, however, were continued in her mind, for they were too involved to put into words. They were to the effect that Guy's affections had taken a natural pendulum swing away from his false love towards this innocent and unspoiled Rona; that as nature abhors a vacuum, Rona was about to fill it; that whatever Lucy might think, Guy would be a great deal happier with Rona than with many other girls; and finally, that Lucy was worrying far too much over her younger son, and it was time she thought about her other children and neglected him a little. This would be an excellent moment for Phillis to cause trouble, for instance, or Thomas to have a slight breakdown through overwork; or failing them, for the Colonel to take a severe summer cold and retire to bed . . .

Even in her unspoken arrangements for one of the Lorimers thus to create a diversion, Miss Douglas never considered Alice, the placid and perfectly contented.

But while she continued towards Thimblefield, thinking these thoughts and at the same time enjoying the quiet dark night and all its half-heard noises, the telephone at Woodside had broken stridently across the bedward movement of Mrs. Lorimer and her husband . . .

"All right, Jack. I'll answer it," said Mrs. Lorimer, who was still in the hall, ostensibly tidying the collection of odd gloves, scarves and hats on the oak chest and really putting off a few minutes more to see if Guy might come in.

She lifted the receiver and spoke, giving the number as she always did, for as she said, "Hullo?" was an idiotic thing to say and frequently misleading.

From far away came a man's voice, tiny with distance, yet clear. "Ma Lorry, is that you? This is Vivian—"

"Viv?" Mrs. Lorimer was astonished and faintly alarmed, for Alice and her husband were not in the habit of ringing up, and certainly not at eleven-thirty p.m. during harvest, when Vivian was out in his fields from dawn till dusk. "I hope the children are all right?"

"It isn't the children. It's Lal. Appendix. We've had to rush her to the hospital at Ludstown for an emergency operation. They're at it now. I am speaking from the hospital."

Mrs. Lorimer stared at the wall in front of her. Alice, the one child of whose safety and well-being she had always felt so assured, Alice, whom in her gentle content her mother had called dull. Alice—

"Are you there, Ma?" came Vivian's voice.

"Yes, Viv, dear." Mrs. Lorimer had pulled herself together. "I'll come, of course, as soon as I can. I was wondering if I could get to Ludstown tonight. Is—Viv, is she—is Alice—very bad?"

"Pretty bad, yes," he said briefly.

"I'll come straight to the hospital," Mrs. Lorimer said. "God bless you all Vivian."

"Thank you, Ma Lorry. We need it," said Vivian's voice, and then she heard him hang up.

Mrs. Lorimer put back the receiver very carefully and turned from the telephone to see Guy coming in at the front door.

"Good heavens, Ma! Still up? I hope you didn't wait up for me?" he remarked with a brusqueness caused by ill-temper.

Mrs. Lorimer noticed nothing about her adored Guy except that she needed him and he was conveniently to hand.

"Will you drive me to Ludstown, Guy?" she demanded. "I'll go and change and pack a bag and tell your Father—"

"But what's up? Has anything gone wrong with Alice's offspring?" said Guy, shaken from his bad humour by sheer surprise. "Surely tomorrow morning would—"

"It's Alice. She's desperately ill," Mrs. Lorimer was already half-way upstairs, pale as death and unnaturally composed. "I must go at once."

"Lally! I say, poor old Viv!" exclaimed Guy. "All right, Ma. You get ready and I'll shift too, and get the car out. We can be on our way in twenty minutes."

While Mrs. Lorimer took off her evening dress and put on a flannel suit, at the same time hurriedly throwing a few necessary garments and toilet articles into a small suitcase, she explained the situation as collectedly as she could to the Colonel, who hovered about her in great distress, getting dreadfully in her way and making a number of not very practical suggestions.

"I feel I ought to dress and come with you," he muttered unhappily—he was already in pyjamas and dressing-gown. "Poor little Alice, poor child—"

"Well, Jack, why don't you? It will be much better for you than staying here alone wondering how she is," said Mrs. Lorimer. "Only be quick—"

He hurried away, but returned at once. "What about telling Nan? We can't all go off like this without telling her, Lucy."

"Oh dear! I suppose not. It seems a shame to wake her after her long day," said Mrs. Lorimer, her composure slipping a little. "Well, I'll tell her, Jack, if you will get dressed."

But Nan was already awake and boiling a kettle in the kitchen, for Guy had seen to this, quietly and purposefully as he had made his other preparations. Three thermos-flasks were on the kitchen table waiting to be filled with tea when the kettle boiled, and Guy with a steady hand and absolute concentration on the job, was pouring whisky from the one cherished bottle which his father had produced for the dinner-party into a flat silver pocket-flask.

"You'll just take a cup of tea before you go, the two of you," Nan said firmly. "There's plenty to fill the thermoses as well."

Wearing a pink wool dressing-gown over which she had tied a large apron, her hair rigid with curling-pins, Nan was an astonishing spectacle, yet how comforting in her solid sturdiness!

"This is very good of you, Nan," said Mrs. Lorimer, gulping down tea which she did not want in the least but dared not refuse. "But I don't think the Colonel will—"

"I've hot milk ready for the Colonel," Nan said more firmly than ever, and poured it out as Colonel Lorimer joined them. "And as for June," she went on before he could speak, "there's no need for you to be worrying yer head over *her*. I'll mind her and she'll do fine."

They were speaking in muted voices as if someone lay asleep upstairs. Asleep or—dead, thought Mrs. Lorimer with a dreadful sinking of heart, and was thankful when Nan said in her normal tones, "Well, you'd better be getting away. The sooner you leave the sooner you'll be there. And you'll be phoning me?" she added to Mrs. Lorimer.

"Yes, Nan, indeed we will," Mrs. Lorimer said, and followed her husband and son out to the yard, where the car was already standing, throwing a steady stream of light over the cobbles, the outbuildings, and the shadowy bushes beyond.

None of them ever forgot that run through the night, but on Guy it made the deepest impression. Faced for the first time by death, not in war, which was to be expected and all in the day's work, but death attacking the sister with whom he had played and quarrelled and made up in nursery days, he sat at the wheel driving the little car at a steady pace, never so fast as he would have liked, over the winding moor roads, which did not make for speed.

Though they were making good time it felt to Guy that they had been going north for hours, that they would never come to the crossroads where at last they could hum off eastwards. When they reached the signpost, standing lonely in the middle of a gaunt moor, Mrs. Lorimer quietly insisted that they should stop for a minute and drink some tea out of the thermos.

"I know you don't want it," she said to Guy. "And I don't either, but I am sure it will do us all good."

She had her way, and Guy pulled into the side, and they drank the scalding tea, Guy wondering how his mother could bear to stop for a moment on such a journey, and not realizing that she had suggested it for his sake and the Colonel's. Certainly Guy felt livelier, more alert, even, in a strange way, more hopeful, when they went on again.

The last climb over the flank of the Lammermoors came quickly, and then the final long run down into the fertile central plain of East Lothian.

Now that they were nearly at Ludstown, the chill apprehension which all had been holding at bay crept over them irresistibly, and Guy knew the cowardly longing to drive more and more slowly to defer the moment when they must arrive at the hospital, and *know*. In consequence he took the last few miles at a speed which shook the Colonel, from the half-doze into which he had fallen, and made the thermos-flasks leap in their basket. It was the dead hour of the night as Guy brought the car as quietly as he could to the doors, and they got silently out.

Crossing the spotless hall with its faint odour of anaesthetics and antiseptics, a night-nurse came to meet them, but before she could speak Vivian emerged from a room on the left.

He took Mrs. Lorimer's two hands in his, and said gently, his grey face creasing into a painful smile, "It's all right so far, Ma Lorry. She's come through the operation. It was touch and go, and still is. They can't say more until morning, and even then if all goes right she won't be out of danger for a day or two, but so far she's all right."

Mrs. Lorimer said rather faintly, "I should like to sit down." She still clung to Vivian's hands for support, but it was the Colonel who came and put his arm round her and led her to a chair.

"There, Lucy," he said. "It is all right, you see. Nothing to cry about." In proof of which, and though Mrs. Lorimer had shown no signs of tears, he blew his nose fiercely.

Guy was conscious of a feeling of vast fatigue, and an overmastering desire to yawn, which somehow seemed indecent. So he stood grinning foolishly at his parents and his brother-in-law, without saying a word.

Vivian took command of the situation. "You three are just about all in after the long run," he said. "Bless you for coming. I think you ought to push off to Hollyrig now, give yourselves a stiff whisky each, and get to bed. I'll ring up as soon as there is any news," he added, as Mrs. Lorimer seemed about to demur.

Guy pulled himself together. He had seen men strung up as Vivian was, apparently unaware of their own exhaustion yet very near breaking-point, and he knew how little more it took to tip the balance.

"Come on, Ma," he said. "We can't all hang about here, the hospital authorities won't like it. What you need is bed—and so do I."

This acted on Mrs. Lorimer's feelings as he had anticipated. She rose, took her husband's arm and said perhaps it would be better if they did go to Hollyrig. The only thing was, it would mean leaving Vivian all alone, and that was not good for him.

"Oh, I'll probably go to sleep myself. There's a jolly good fire in the waiting-room," Vivian said with a jaunty carelessness that deceived no one, and Guy instantly formed an unspoken resolution to see his parents bedded—or on their way to bed—and return himself to share Vivian's watch. With this end in view, he shepherded Colonel and Mrs. Lorimer out to the car, and drove them swiftly over the wide smooth road to Hollyrig.

Lights were shining in several windows of the comfortable old farmhouse, lying among its barns and dovecote at the end of an avenue of tall beeches. Almost before they had stopped, the door was opened and Nannie appeared on the threshold, full of a kind of hushed importance which Mrs. Lorimer found hard to bear.

Even as she expressed her joy and relief at the news that Alice had come through her op so nicely, Nannie somehow had wafted them all indoors, taken Mrs. Lorimer's case and the Colonel's bag from Guy and set them down in the hall, and told them that she had a nice cup of tea all ready for them in the morning-room.

Mrs. Lorimer was just going to say meekly that she liked a little milk and no sugar, thank you, when the Colonel rebelled.

"I think, Nannie," he said gallantly, and Guy, while admiring his courage, suddenly realized that his father looked an old man as a result of the night's nervous strain. "I think, do you know, that we might be better with a little whisky and soda. Tea, you know, is a stimulant, and might keep Mrs. Lorimer awake—"

"Well, I'm sure, sir," began Nannie, a little offended. "I've always understood that hot sweet tea was the Very Best Thing for shock, but of course if you—"

"Ah, yes. Quite right, Nannie. *Sweet* tea," said the Colonel. "But then, you see, none of us can take sugar in our tea, none of us, and without sugar the whole effect is lost. Lost entirely. Now I tell you what. You've been waiting up for us, and suffering a lot of strain. You should drink that tea, a good strong cup, with plenty of sugar, and we'll have our whisky and soda. How about that?"

Like most of the race of nurses, Nannie was highly susceptible where the gentlemen were concerned. So flattered was she by the Colonel's kind thought for her that she almost simpered as she agreed that it had been a very trying time, and perhaps, as he and madam and Mr. Guy didn't take sugar, they might just as well drink whisky. She went to fetch it without further ado, and Guy, only waiting to whisper, "Well done, Father," followed her to help with the glasses and siphon.

"I say, Nannie," he said, stopping her in the dining-room on her way back, "—let me carry the tray, won't you? I say, do you think you can get them off to bed pretty soon? I thought I'd nip back to the hospital and keep Mr. Fraser company, poor chap, but I don't want a lot of fuss and explaining."

"Just you leave it to me, Mr. Guy," said Nannie, delighted, and surrendering the tray. "I'll settle it all. Poor Mr. Fraser! It does seem a dreadful thing for a gentleman like him all alone there waiting for news."

Matters arranged themselves very easily. Having won over the tea, Colonel and Mrs. Lorimer, who were really worn out, gave in without a murmur to Nannie's calm certainty that they would want to go to their rooms now and lie down, and retreated upstairs behind her as if they were really her charges of tender years.

Guy kissed his mother, patted his father awkwardly on the shoulder, and, waiting until he heard their doors shut, crept out to the car and drove away towards Ludstown again, hoping that they had not heard him go, and hoping too that Vivian would not consider his return a piece of insufferable interference. But when he opened the door of the hospital waiting-room and saw his brother-in-law sitting huddled together in a chair over the last embers of a small sulky fire he was glad he had come.

Vivian only said, "Hullo, Guy. Got your parents safely delivered to Nannie?" and displayed no surprise at seeing him back.

Guy nodded. "It's cold in here," he said. "Don't you feel it, Viv?"

"I don't know. I hadn't thought about it," Vivian said vaguely.

Without saying more, Guy found a coal-scuttle and quietly mended the fire with a few small pieces. "That will burn up in a minute," he said at last. "Look here, Viv, have a nip of whisky? I've got my flask here—brought it in case any of us needed it on the way." He pulled out the flask from his pocket and handed it over.

Vivian looked at it uncertainly.

"Go on, take a pull. You'll be the better for it," urged Guy, and then Vivian unscrewed the cap and took a mouthful. The neat spirit ran burning down his throat, and revived and wanned him. Handing back the flask, he realized for the first time that he was utterly exhausted; but to feel anything at all was better than the awful numbness which had frozen him ever since the doctor had reached Hollyrig and ordered Alice's immediate removal to hospital.

"Any more news?" Guy asked.

"Not yet. There can't be for a bit, you know—"

They sat on by the fire in a silence broken only by the scrape of a match as one or the other lighted a fresh cigarette. Guy wondered if he ought to talk, to try to take Vivian's mind off—things, as he put it to himself, but decided against it. Why worry him to make stupid conversation? Better just stand by and hope that his presence might help a little.

It was amazing how, without a word or a look, Vivian's immobile figure conveyed that if he lost Alice his life would lose almost its whole meaning and purpose. Guy found himself thinking, for human nature cannot help being selfish, "Suppose I were in Viv's shoes, and it was Iris whose life was in danger?" But he could not picture it at all. "If we'd been married, though?" he thought, and shook his head. The realization broke on him again that he had never looked so far ahead as marriage with Iris, that, in fact, his feeling for her had never been the kind that lasts. "Surely," he thought restlessly, "I'm capable of loving *someone* as Viv loves Alice?" And on that, in a blinding flash like sudden lightning, he knew with absolute certainty that if it had been Rona who lay upstairs in the white hospital bed, he would be enduring the same silent anguish as Vivian Fraser was now enduring . . .

The quiet closing of the door brought his head up with a jerk, and he glanced across at his brother-in-law fearfully.

Vivian nodded. "Her pulse is better. They—they say she has a good chance now." Then he smiled a little. "Poor old Guy. What a night you've put in," he said. "Do you know it's six o'clock?"

3

That overworked saying Time and Tide wait for no man, never seems truer than after people have passed through a period of crisis. The clock ticks on, the sea rolls in and washes away all the footprints in the sand, the commonplace activities of daily life proceed on their round, all as if nothing had happened. So the family party which gathered for lunch round the table at Hollyrig, deeply engaged in argument and discussion about the Colonel's return to Threipford, and whether Guy should take him there before going back to his job on the Clyde, looked and sounded quite normal except for shadowed eyes in rather drawn faces, and gentler voices than usual.

At least, Mrs. Lorimer thought, this rather unnecessary manufacturing of transport difficulties prevented Jack from harping on the subject of Alice, which otherwise he would have done, conducting a court of inquiry into every possible and impossible cause for her appendix to have gone septic without warning, and driving his hearers almost mad.

"Well," said Guy, pouring thick cream provided by Vivian's cows over a handsome helping of plum tart. "If you start fairly soon after lunch, I can come with you and drive as far as the Junction. Then I can catch the 5:43 to Glasgow and you can go on home, Father."

This was much too easy a solution to suit the Colonel. "But your mother, my boy," he said in a quiet reproachful tone. "If we take the car, how is she to get home?"

"She could hitch-hike, couldn't you, Ma?" said Guy, grinning at her.

"Oh, of course. What is it I do? Thumb a lift, or whatever it is called," agreed Mrs. Lorimer, at which bland suggestion, and the look of horrified disgust on his father-in-law's face, Vivian laughed and felt much the better for it.

"But seriously, sir," he said, when the children, who had also laughed uproariously without knowing why, had been quietened. "Guy could get the afternoon train to Edinburgh and catch a connection to Glasgow, and you can wait and go home with Ma Lorry tomorrow or the next day, or when you like."

"Thank you, Vivian, thank you," cried the Colonel, trying to conceal his dismay at this invitation. "But I couldn't think of trespassing on your hospitality in this way and to such an extent. The household is bound to be disorganized and everyone extra means more work. Naturally I came with my wife and Guy, and of course Alice's mother will wish to stay on until she can see her, but now that we know the dear girl is doing so well, I really feel my place is at home." He relapsed into vague murmurings of work to be done, things to be seen to, Nan alone in the house, which finally died away into silence.

Mrs. Lorimer, who knew that he was longing to get home to June and his precious peas for the Show, waited until he had run down, and then announced that Guy's plan was an excellent one and that she herself would go home by train in a few days' time.

"That's settled, then," said Vivian. "Now, you three, run along to the nursery. Lunch is finished."

"But Nannie's going out," objected Simon.

"Oh, so she is. Well—" said Vivian rather helplessly. "I've got to get back to the hospital in half an hour. I don't know—"

"I'll look after them, Vivian," said Mrs. Lorimer. "What is a grandmother for, do you imagine? Simon and Susan and Joanna, will you take Gan for a walk in the garden until tea-time?"

There was a joyful chorus of assent. Vivian said good-bye to his father-in-law and Guy and thanked them for coming in a few stiff words to which they responded equally stiffly, and then hurried away to drive to Ludstown. Colonel Lorimer cleared his throat in an embarrassed manner, and muttered that he hoped Vivian wouldn't drive as fast as he was in the habit of doing, and went to his room to pack his bag.

"You take care of yourself, Ma, and don't overdo it," said Guy.

"*We*'ll take care of Gan," said Susan, clasping Mrs. Lorimer's hand in a sticky paw.

"See you do it properly then, and I'll take you to see my new ship when she's finished building," Guy promised recklessly.

"I suppose you realize that they'll remember this and give no one any peace until they have seen the ship?" said Mrs. Lorimer.

"I'm quite prepared to keep my promise," Guy assured her.

Mrs. Lorimer looked at him, but less keenly than usual. Perhaps it was due to relief that Alice was slowly but surely drawing out of danger, but he seemed more like his old cheerful self than he had been since he had met the horrid girl Iris who had jilted him, and with something added to him, too, a sort of resoluteness, a maturer steadiness. It was difficult to define, his mother thought, but satisfying to see.

For once, however, Guy and his affairs had been pushed to the back of Mrs. Lorimer's mind and heart, where the foreground just now was very fully occupied by Alice. She kissed him fondly, told him to drive carefully, and went off to the garden with the three children.

Guy drove home through the gold and purple afternoon in a dream which the ceaseless running commentary kept up by his father hardly disturbed at all. With his thankfulness that Alice would not die was mingled thankfulness for being freed from Iris's Circe-spell, and plans for his next meeting with Rona. In the events of the past night and day he had completely forgotten that he had parted from her in anger after quarrelling with her. He would not write to her nor ring her up, he decided, nor ask her to come to Glasgow and meet him for lunch as she had done once or twice during the past month. No, he would wait until next weekend, and then he would come down to Threipford and get her to go for a long tramp with him into the hills. Then he would tell her that she needn't bother to wait for an unknown man with a pretty name to turn up. Guy Lorimer was surely a nice enough name to please her? And after that—

"Steady on, Guy! You nearly got that sheep!" said his father's voice, rising from its peaceful conversational monotone to annoyed alarm. "What's wrong with you?"

"Sorry, Father. I was thinking," Guy apologized, as an elderly sheep skipped nimbly away among the deep heather.

"You're too tired to drive, that's what it is," said the Colonel. "Let me take a turn. You'll never be fit for your job tomorrow."

"Lord, yes, I'll be all right. I shall sleep like a log tonight, though my mattress in those Glasgow digs is stuffed with something that feels like a river-bed," Guy assured him. "But we'll stop for a little, we've plenty of time, and eat our tea and have a smoke—"

The Colonel agreed that it would be pleasant to stretch his legs, and Guy drew in to the side of the narrow road and pulled up.

They were deep among the eastern end of the Lammermoors, the softly swelling hills rose all about them, the road, empty of traffic, lay in mounting loops up the slope ahead. The ground, far and near, was covered by the glowing mantle of heather in full bloom, the air was sweet with its honey-scent and loud with the bees busy plundering its sweetness. Above arched the faint blue of the sky, and over all lay the lovely clear champagne-coloured light of afternoon.

Colonel Lorimer, feeling in an inarticulate way that the beauty of the scene, so in tune with their relief over Alice demanded a celebration, filled and lighted one of his rare pipes, and the faint smell of good tobacco rose like incense to join the heather and bog-myrtle scents of the moor. Guy who had smoked himself almost sick during the night and early morning, was content to sit doing nothing but look lazily at the surrounding country, comparing it with the greener hills he knew best, thinking that Rona would like it, and finally simply allowing the colour and scent to flow about him, until with a guilty start he roused himself and got to his feet.

"We'd better push on, Father," he said.

The rest of the journey was made in amicable silence, and at the Junction Guy and his father parted with a brief word.

"You'll be down next weekend?" asked the Colonel, who had moved into the driver's seat.

"Yes, almost certainly, unless I get held up over anything. Oh, I say, Father—" said Guy, sticking his head in at the open window.

Colonel Lorimer was already fidgeting with the gear-lever. "Yes?" he said absently.

"Oh, nothing. So long." Guy's head was withdrawn rather abruptly, and he walked rapidly up the path to the long empty platform of the Junction, where his train was now signalled.

"Good thing I stopped myself in time from asking Pop to tell Rona I'd be coming to take her for a walk," he thought, as he sank back in a corner seat and the train puffed and snorted its way from the station. "He would have wondered, and so would she. I can't think what took me just at that moment. Far better wait and go to see her when I get home on Friday."

4

It is probably a blessing on the whole that thought transference is rare, since a great many thoughts are much better confined to the thinker, but there are times when to know what another person is thinking would save much trouble and unhappiness. To Guy, travelling back to his work full of happy anticipation, it never occurred that he had left Rona without any idea of his feelings towards her, and that his last words to her had been not only disagreeable but almost rude.

Rona, unaware of the events which had caused such alarm and distress at Woodside, waited all Sunday for the telephone to ring, making one excuse after another to her father for not leaving the house in order that she might be at hand to receive Guy's apologies. She intended to accept them kindly but quite coolly, laughing off the long explanations he would try to make, telling him that it did not matter at all, and quite possibly ending up by saying that she had hardly given it a thought.

This fine magnanimous attitude lasted throughout the morning, though by the time Mr. Smellie returned from church, which he had had to attend, to his open dismay, unaccompanied by his daughter, it was turning to rage. Rona was a sweet-tempered person, slow to take offence, and she had been as much surprised as angered by Guy's outburst. He had been most unreasonable, of course, and she had spoken sharply to him, but she remembered her brother Roy had been like that too, at times, so perhaps it was a common male characteristic. Only—Roy had always been sorry, as soon as he had calmed down and thought things over, and she had supposed Guy would have been the same.

"To sulk like this!" she thought angrily as the afternoon wore on, and still she could not bring herself to go even as far as the garden. "It is not only childish, it's really rude. And I may be only Nesta Rowena Smellie with no business to be living in Harperslea because I'm only Glasgow people with money and not county, but I *will* not be treated like this." She glared at the telephone, which remained dumb. "If you ring now," she said threateningly, "I won't answer you!"

The bell rang shrilly. Rona picked up the receiver, controlled her voice to ladylike iciness, and was told that the Exchange had rung her in error, and was sorry she had been troubled.

"And that's that," said Rona, and carefully replaced the receiver.

After the fashion of this annoying but useful instrument, the telephone now seemed determined to make up for its previous silence. It rang again and again. Twice for Mr. Smellie; once for the housemaid, whose mother wanted to know if she could change her day out in order to sit with her younger brothers and sisters while her parents went to a whist drive.

There was a call for Rona at last, after tea. A friend of her early schooldays had just got engaged, and wanted Nesta Rowena to know about it before she put it in the papers. And how was Nesta Rowena? And couldn't she possibly tear herself away from the excitements of country life—much gay girlish laughter—and come and spend a few days and meet Norman? He was really a perfect lamb, and Nesta Rowena would be sure to like him and he was dying to see her.

"Oh, I don't know that I—" began Rona, and then paused. Why shouldn't she go? And why shouldn't she suggest next weekend as a suitable date? Lieutenant Guy Lorimer, R.N., could come back to Threipford and find her not there, and that would be a very good thing.

In a steady voice she asked if it would be convenient for her to come on the following Friday, by the morning train, and stay until the Monday. This being rapturously received, Nesta Rowena, with the sinking feeling that she had burned her boats, hung up and went to tell her father what she had arranged.

"Well, dearie, if you're wanting a wee change, I daresay a weekend at Ena Mackintosh's'll be the very thing," said Mr. Smellie, a little worried by his daughter's flushed cheeks and unusually bright eyes.

"It will all fit in very nicely, for I should have had to go to Glasgow soon in any case, to buy kitchen towels and pillow-cases," said Nesta Rowena. "If prices are going up again, Papa, the sooner I get what we need the better."

"You're a grand wee housekeeper," said Mr. Smellie. "Your Mamaw would be real pleased to see the job you make of managing Harperslea. And if there's any little thing you're wanting for yourself, dearie, I'll give you a check."

"Thank you, Papa dear, but I still have a lot of my last quarter's allowance," said his daughter, and kissed the bald patch among his white hairs with remorseful affection, because she was really so unlike the little Nesta Rowena he imagined her to be.

Indeed, it seemed to her during the days which passed before she set out on her visit, that she was a stranger to herself. There were two people living inside her. One was Nesta Rowena, going quietly about her daily supervising of the household, pouring out her father's tea, listening with apparent interest to the snatches he read to her from the daily paper. The other was Rona, full of hurt and anger, who against Nesta Rowena's will watched anxiously for the post, expecting a letter which never came, or flew to answer the telephone in case it might be the call she still hoped for. Nesta Rowena pottered about the garden, and picked flowers which she arranged with elegance in great bowls and vases, displaying them about the house; but Rona went out and walked the hills until she was almost too tired to drag one foot after the other.

"I don't know what on earth is the matter with me," the poor child thought. "I never used to be like this!"

It had not dawned on her that she was suffering from the same malady she had diagnosed in her brother, and more recently in Guy Lorimer. Feverishly she assured herself that all she needed was a change, that perhaps she had not really settled down to this rather lonely life, that she would be quite all right again when she came back from Ena's.

Only now did she realize how isolated she was. There was not a single house in the whole neighbourhood where she was free to drop in without an invitation, and invitations were very few as yet. In the summer most people were so busy with their gardens and farms, or with visitors staying in the house, that they had no time for their neighbours. Mrs. Lorimer had been kind to her, but Woodside was the one house she wanted to avoid. As for Miss Douglas, that lady, having heard from Colonel Lorimer that Alice, after a bad day or two, was now improving almost hourly, sighed with relief and shut herself up at Thimblefield to finish a book for which her agent was clamouring.

Because of their isolation, Mr. Smellie and his daughter never heard of Alice Fraser's emergency operation and her mother's and father's hurried dash through the night to her, for though it had been talked about freely in Threipford there was no one who thought that "the Harperslea people" might be interested, even if any among them had been on more friendly terms than the exchange of a civil "Good morning" when they passed. Even the kitchen grapevine, usually the most up-to-the-minute distributor of local gossip, failed where Harperslea was concerned, for the cook was a stranger like her employers, and the housemaid a country girl too shy to talk to the butcher or the milk if she saw them at the back door, and spending her off-time out of Threipford.

So Nesta Rowena—for she sternly refused to think of herself as Rona—took the train for Glasgow on the Friday still in ignorance of what she would probably have accepted as an adequate reason for Guy's lack of apology, though, having reached the unreasonable stage of being in love, she might not. It gave her a kind of bitter pleasure, as she watched the flying landscape of hill and little town, wood and valley and the curves of a widening river, to think that in a few hours Guy Lorimer, travelling in the opposite direction, would be looking at it too.

If the trains did not actually pass, Guy reached Threipford not very long after Nesta Rowena had arrived at her friend's house on the southern outskirts of Glasgow. Only his father was at home, though Mrs. Lorimer was talking on the telephone of returning to Woodside soon, Nan told him, as Miss Alice had "got the turn." Guy listened and nodded, drinking the tea which Nan had brought into the drawing-room, and presently he cut into the bulletin of local news to say that he was going out, and that if Colonel Lorimer came in, to tell him that he would be home in good time for dinner.

"It's at half-past seven, mind," Nan warned him. "Fried fish and fried parsley."

"Lovely," Guy said, but a little absently, forgetting to say, "Lots of fried parsley, please," so that Nan looked after him in amazement.

Guy walked off down the path through the garden looking the embodiment of leisured ease, but with a fast-beating heart. Now that he was going to see Rona in a few minutes he felt unaccountably nervous. How had he been so sure that she would feel the same as he did? Then he smiled to himself, for he had a weapon which she herself had put into his hand. She had told him so gravely that she was going to make a sensible marriage in the Continental manner: now he could point out that he was single, reasonably well-paid, and the owner of a name she had already pronounced "pretty." In every respect he fulfilled her requirements. Bless her innocence!

He went quickly up the drive to Harperslea and rang the old-fashioned bell. Standing on the wide stone step looking into the cool dimness of the hall through the open doorway, he was conscious that the house felt empty somehow. There was a want about it, something he felt but could not recognize for the moment. Footsteps crossed the hall, there was a gleam of blue and white, and the young housemaid, nervously fingering her apron, came to the doorway.

"Mr. Smellie's out in the garden," she began doubtfully.

Guy smiled at her honest pink-cheeked face. "Is Miss Smellie at home?" he asked, suddenly confident, suddenly aware that the ugly name didn't either annoy him or strike him as funny, since it was Rona's name.

The girl shook her head. "No—sir. She's away for the weekend."

"Away for the weekend?" Guy repeated blankly. This was something for which he was totally unprepared and in the same instant he knew why he had felt that Harperslea was empty. Woodside felt the same when his mother was not there: the person who made the house home was absent.

"Oh, well—" he said, realizing that the girl was staring at him, and pulling himself together. "Never mind. Thank you very much. Er—you're sure she won't be home by Sunday?" And as she shook her head, repeating, "She's away till Monday, she said," he turned to go.

"Any message, sir?" asked the little housemaid, suddenly remembering the careful lessons she had been given by her mistress and the cook.

"No, I don't think so. No, thank you," said Guy, and walked away, feeling extraordinarily dashed and disappointed, and unreasonably annoyed.

CHAPTER TEN

1

THE following Saturday was, with the possible exception of Hogmanay (Anglicé, New Year's Eve), the most important date of the year to Threipford. To the local farmers, bee-keepers, gardeners and members of the Women's Rural Institutes it certainly was, for it was the day of the Threip-Water Show.

In almost every house from cottage to mansion in that part of the county, competitors were tenderly plucking their choicest specimens of fruit, vegetables and flowers, or hovering over newly baked Victoria sandwiches or fruit-cake; or, if they were farmers' wives, making up pats of fresh, powdered and salt butter and washing eggs. At Woodside the Colonel, having gathered the requisite number of plump pea-pods, and with his own hands scrubbed his finest potatoes, and taken them down to lay them out in the fruit and vegetable tent, was beginning to wonder whether they really *were* his best, or if he had not finer ones still in the garden.

"Well, Jack, you can't change them now, and they looked beautiful," his wife assured him. For Mrs. Lorimer had come home two days earlier, promising to go back to Hollyrig after Alice had been released from hospital and take charge of the household there while her daughter convalesced.

"Do you think so, Lucy?" The Colonel shook his head gloomily. "I don't think they are as good as last year's, you know. Turnbull will beat me this time, mark my words. I said to him only this morning when I met him down at the Show ground. 'Turnbull,' I said, 'it's going to be a walkover for *this* year, and I'll be nowhere. Nowhere.'"

As he was obviously enjoying his gloom, Mrs. Lorimer did not try to cheer him up. Instead she remarked, "Will you be in to lunch at the usual time, Jack, or do you want it early? Guy said when he rang up last night that he would lunch on the train or in Glasgow and come straight to the Show ground."

"Well, Nan will want to go to the Show in the afternoon," said the Colonel, "and the judging ought to be over by midday, so perhaps it might be better to have it early." Then he added: "But what about you, Lucy?"

"Oh, it's useless to try to say when I shall get away from the Industrial Tent," said Mrs. Lorimer. "There are enormous entries in the baking section as usual, and piles of knitting, and they always take ages to judge. I must say there are times when I wish the judges were a little less thorough! Gray and I are both on duty, of course. Margaret Young roped us in months ago. I think the best thing will be to have a cold lunch laid out, so that we can come in when we can and forage."

"Mrs. Young is really rather inconsiderate," began the Colonel. "Why should you not be on duty in relays?"

Mrs. Lorimer, who knew that all the available help was already arranged in relays and that, as usual, there was not enough, only smiled. The telephone saved her from any further argument on the subject, which recurred before every Show, every August, and she went to answer it, Nan having thrust her head round the door with the announcement: "Mrs. Young wants you. She's in a great taking about something."

"What did Mrs. Young want this time?" demanded the Colonel when his wife reappeared after an interval during which she seemed to have been doing a lot of telephoning. "Very inconsiderate of her—"

"Yes, very, Jack, but then Margaret Young *is* inconsiderate, and you can't alter people," said Mrs. Lorimer. "She wanted me to get someone else to help in the afternoon, she's discovered at the last minute that we haven't enough stewards."

"Then why doesn't she ring them up herself?"

"For the simple reason that so many people dislike her that she knows she can't ask them," Mrs. Lorimer said. "You know how rude she is, and how tactless. It's all right, though. I've got the girl from Harperslea. She seemed rather unwilling, but she has agreed to come, and luckily she does seem to be reliable. Now we *must* go, Jack, I've got to be there on the dot of ten."

"Hah! Yes, and I must be on the spot," agreed the Colonel, though Mrs. Lorimer suspected that his presence was merely required by his fellow exhibitors to hang about the tent and talk to them, getting in the way of the judges and obstructing them in their duties. For herself, Mrs. Lorimer knew that an arduous day was before her.

The Show was still held in a wide low-lying meadow near the little town where it had been since the days, two hundred years ago, when it had been one of the big Border Fairs. Early as it was, the ground was already crowded. Men and women darted in and out of the big white marquees like worker bees at a row of hives. Sheep and cattle were being unloaded from floats and herded into the rows of wooden pens which had been set up in one half of the field. The gleaming rails of the jumps awaited the hunters which would compete there during the afternoon, the platform for the dancers was ready in the center of a roped-off ring.

Mrs. Lorimer, most of whose day would be spent inside a marquee full of baking, jams, bottled fruit and butter, paused at the gate to look about her. For once it seemed that the Show was to be blessed with a really fine day. She was still dreamily admiring the spire of the parish church with its glittering weathercock glinting, and the quaint little tower of the Town Hall, when the town clock began to strike ten. With a start like Cinderella surprised at midnight, Mrs. Lorimer awoke to her duties, and hurried through the gateway and across the grass, already poached and trampled, towards the biggest of the marquees. From its interior came the trenchant tones of Mrs. Young exhorting Davie Dunlop the joiner and general handyman to collect his nails and hammers and leave the tent free for the judges. Mrs. Lorimer sighed, pulled herself together, and went in.

Here all was bustle and what looked uncommonly like confusion, as Mrs. Young's organization, owing to her frequent and conflicting orders, too often did. But Miss Douglas was quietly occupied at her own particular job, and though she only raised her head and smiled at her friend, Mrs. Lorimer felt relieved and strengthened.

"Now then, Lucy!" shouted Mrs. Young, marching on her from the farthest corner of the marquee. "Have you got the judges? They should be starting. There's a lot to get through."

Mrs. Lorimer knew that she had never been detailed to fetch the judges, but she instantly felt that she was at fault, a sensation familiar to Mrs. Young's underlings. She began to protest, when a quiet voice from the open flap of the doorway said: "I have brought the judges to the committee tent, Mrs. Young. They are taking off their coats and will be ready in a minute."

Mrs. Young emitted the snorting sound usually written as "Humph!" and added: "All right then, Lucy, you'd better go and see that they have their badges and stewards and all the rest of it. And you, Miss—er—go with Mrs. Lorimer and make yourself useful."

"Miss—er," to Mrs. Lorimer's surprise, was the Harperslea girl, wearing a neat grey flannel suit, her lapel adorned with a cardboard disc with "OFFICIAL" stamped on it in gold.

"I thought you were coming in the afternoon?" she said, as the two left the marquee and made for the committee-tent, a dirty grey bell-tent a few yards away. "Did you make a mistake?"

Nesta Rowena shook her honey-coloured head. "No. But Mrs. Young rang up this morning and said you would need me at 9:30," she replied in an expressionless voice. Then, as Mrs. Lorimer uttered an indignant exclamation, she said, "No, really, it is quite all right. I don't mind a bit if I am to help *you*, Mrs. Lorimer."

"Well, of course that will be splendid, and I shall be very glad of your help," said Mrs. Lorimer, walking very fast in her annoyance at this high-handed disarranging of plans. "But I need you this afternoon, which was when Mrs. Young asked me to get you to come."

"I'll come back in the afternoon as we arranged, of course. I meant to anyway," said Nesta Rowena.

"I suppose you realize that you are simply being victimized," began Mrs. Lorimer.

"Then I shall be able to feel noble," Nesta Rowena said cheerfully, and Mrs. Lorimer found herself laughing as she dived in at the sagging entrance of the bell-tent.

It was no easy matter to sort out the judges, for the ladies who filled the tent to overflowing were all large, and all, apparently, bosom friends of one another. They seemed not to have met for a long time, and were delighted to have this opportunity of exchanging greetings and news, while their stewards hovered distractedly about the doorway, adding to the general noise and confusion. Mrs. Lorimer found the Harperslea girl to be clear-headed and efficient. Her small neat figure moved quietly among the chattering throng, pinning badges on to coats, pressing pencils and paper into unready hands, cutting first one and then another out from between her friends and handing them over to the stewards, and all pleasantly and without fuss. In a remarkably short time they had all been dispatched to their various sections and the committee tent was empty except for Mrs. Lorimer and her assistant. Slightly dazed and very hot, the two stood looking at each other.

"The first thing to do," said Nesta Rowena with energy, "is to get a little air into this stuffy place. It's like the Black Hole of Calcutta!"

"I don't know how one gets more air into a tent," said Mrs. Lorimer, on whom the heat and crowd were beginning to have their usual and unwelcome effect of making her feel a little sick and faint.

"I'll do it. I think you ought to sit down," said Nesta Rowena. "You can look busy. There arc plenty of papers on the table there to be tidied."

She pushed a wooden chair up to the rickety bridge-table which was, as she said, littered with papers, and while Mrs. Lorimer thankfully sat down, proceeded to tie back the tent flaps and then to loop up the dirty brailing, going about it in a business-like way which filled Mrs. Lorimer with admiration.

"That is much better, my dear," she said as air began to circulate through the confined space. "Thank you."

"Now we'll have some coffee," announced the Harperslea girl. She brought a basket from under the table, and poured steaming fragrant coffee from a thermos with a neat little beak into two large cups. "Do you like sugar? I did bring some, in case—"

But Mrs. Lorimer did not like sugar. She sipped the coffee gratefully, lighted a cigarette and felt much revived.

Presently she said reluctantly, "We ought not to stay here. It is time Miss Douglas was relieved, poor dear."

"I could relieve Miss Douglas, and she could come in here and have some coffee," suggested Nesta Rowena. "There's another thermos full, and a clean cup."

"You don't mind being pounced on by Mrs. Young? She is a—a little abrupt at times," said Mrs. Lorimer.

"Oh, no. She won't take any notice of me," said the girl. "I'll just take over from Miss Douglas at a suitable moment, and it will be quite all right, I'm sure."

By this time, Mrs. Lorimer, having seen her assistant riding the storm with perfect composure, was ready to believe that she could weather Mrs. Young, and as she really felt tired and had plenty of papers to attend to, she agreed to the change-over with no further argument. Only when Miss Douglas, pushing back the hair from her heated brow, appeared and sank on to a wooden box, Mrs. Lorimer said a little anxiously, "I hope Margaret Young didn't make a fuss because the Harperslea girl took your place?"

"Not she. She's far too busy harrying the other tent," said Miss Douglas. "That girl—Rona—the Smellie girl, I mean—is a bit of a dark horse, Lucy. I had no idea she was so efficient. She could organize the whole of this—" she waved a hand vaguely in the general direction of the marquees—"a great deal better than Mrs. Young."

"Almost anyone could," Mrs. Lorimer said drily. "You aren't paying Rona much of a compliment."

"No, perhaps not, but you know what I mean. Let's forget the Show for a few minutes, Lucy. Anyhow, this part of it will be dead before next year if it isn't under entirely new management. It's moribund now . . . Tell me, what news of the family? How is Alice?"

2

Nesta Rowena found the morning passing not unpleasantly in the strange greenish light of the marquee which housed all kinds of sewn work and knitting. She was kept busy entering prize winners in a large book, but not so busy that she could not look about her. Snatches of conversation came to her ears, to which she paid no attention until she heard a name she knew.

"Mrs. Lorimer's looking terrible tired," said one of the stewards.

"No wonder if she is," responded the other. "They've been that worried about Mrs. Fraser, her that was Miss Alice Lorimer before she married. I'm sure it's not more than a fortnight since she was at *death's door*"—this with immense satisfaction.

Not only her friend but Miss Nesta Rowena Smellie, sitting quietly at a little table entering names and figures into her book, listened intently for what was to follow.

"It was *just* the fortnight," continued the steward impressively. "Saturday night it was they got word, and Mr. Guy drove both the two o' them, the Colonel and Mrs. Lorimer all the way in the middle o' the night. I know that's right, for next day was Sunday, and I met Mrs. Lorimer's Nan an' she told me all about it."

"But Mrs. Fraser's getting on all right now?" inquired the other steward.

"O ay. Right as rain. Thae surgeons'll cut you open and sew you up and send you home wi' no bother at all!" said the narrator with a carefree laugh. "Still and on, it's bound to have given her a bit of a shake, and Mrs. Lorimer as well."

"Bound to—come away, there's the judges looking for us. They're ready—" and the two hastily returned to their duties.

But Nesta Rowena the competent, whose praises were still being sung by the two ladies in the committee-tent, sat staring at the accumulating heap of little slips of paper in front of her and making no attempt to copy their particulars into her book. So *that* was why Guy had never called or rung up on the Sunday when she had waited in vain and grown angry with waiting! "No wonder he forgot," she thought. "Oh, if only I'd known about Mrs.

Fraser, I would have understood. I wouldn't have rushed away the next weekend to Ena Mackintosh's!" Her face burned with blushes for her own babyish behaviour, so noticeably that a steward bringing yet another sheaf of papers to the table commiserated with her upon the heat. The instinct of self-preservation which is potent in all of us even when it is only a question of saving one's face, came to Nesta Rowena's aid. She agreed that it *was* rather hot but that the judging would soon be over now, and whenever she had entered all the prize winners she could go out.

Then she applied herself to her task with such concentration that the judges came to their last decision and trooped away to be the guests at luncheon at the Tower Hotel of the Show Committee, followed by all the stewards, and she never even noticed that she was alone in the marquee.

Just as she had verified the last winning number and put a neat red tick against the owner's name to denote a first prize, she became aware that someone had come in and was standing beside the table looking down at her.

Automatically murmuring her formula, "I'm afraid this tent isn't open to the public until half-past two," she looked up and saw that it was Guy Lorimer.

For a dizzy instant the tent with its contents whirled round her, a kaleidoscope of knitted jumpers, best-dressed dolls, embroidered teacloths and cushion-covers, garments-for-child-under-one-year and leather shopping bags, while she sat at the center of the vortex trying to keep her feet firmly planted on the grass. She heard Guy saying, "Hullo, Rona! Who let you in for this?" and blinked hard.

Everything steadied, but she was still too much shaken by his sudden appearance to speak.

"What's wrong?" he asked.

"Nothing, of course. It's just—I didn't expect to see you."

"I'm usually here at weekends," he said. "And I didn't want to miss the Show. I like the Show, it's fun. When did you get back?"

"I was only away from Friday to Monday," said Rona—she was Rona now, all of a sudden—in a very small voice.

It sounded like a confession, as it was, of course, and Guy stared at her.

"Do you mean you went so that you'd avoid seeing me?" he said slowly.

"I didn't know until today about your sister being ill," said Rona.

"But look here, what has Alice's being ill got to do with it?" he demanded in bewilderment.

Rona tried to think of some way out which would not give her away completely, but it was no use. She could not tell Guy anything but the truth.

"It was very silly and childish of me," she began. "I was angry with you. I thought—"

"Well, come along, come along! Don't waste any more time dawdling! You will never get that wire-netting up before the crowd comes, and they'll tear the exhibits to rags besides helping themselves to anything they fancy!" shouted a domineering voice, and Mrs. Young erupted into the marquee. She was followed by Davie Dunlop and one of his boys, each carrying a roll of rabbit wire and a large hammer.

"What on earth are you doing in here, Miss—er? Haven't you got those prize winners listed yet?" shouted Mrs. Young as she caught sight of Rona and Guy. "Oh, you *have*"—as Rona made a murmur indicative of assent. "Then for heaven's sake take them across to the Secretary's tent, it's in the middle of the field. And after that I'll find something for you to do. Ah, Guy, the very person! Will you see that Dunlop gets the netting up and give him a hand if he needs it?"

"How d'you do, Mrs. Young?" said Guy politely. "I'm afraid I can't stop now. I came to fetch Miss Smellie and take her to Woodside for some lunch. Are you ready, then?" he added, turning to Rona, who had pulled herself together and picked up her book and papers.

Balked of her prey, Mrs. Young stood for a moment speechless. Guy nodded to the two men. "You'll get on a lot better without an amateur interfering," he observed. "Have a drink to the success of the Show on me."

Coins changed hands, Davie Dunlop and his mate grinned and nodded, and Guy, taking Rona by the arm, walked her out of the marquee.

"That woman," he said, barely waiting until they were out of earshot, "is a female Simon Legree!"

"But she may really need me," Rona expostulated, hanging back. "I am supposed to be helping, and it seems rather awful to go off and leave her toiling away by herself."

"There's no necessity for her to toil, if her organization is what she's so fond of boasting it is," Guy said firmly. "She gets a kick out of running everything, so let her enjoy herself. Forget her. We'll dump these papers of yours on the Show secretary, and then I'm taking you to the Tower for some lunch."

"You told Mrs. Young we were going to Woodside—"

"It's far too late to trudge all that way now. Besides, I want to talk to you, and we won't get a chance at home," said Guy.

Rona decided that argument was a waste of time, and as she found herself unexpectedly tired and hungry, she said no more, but meekly accompanied him, first to the secretary's tent, where that harassed official received her books with very little enthusiasm, and then to the town.

"The Tower will be very full," she suggested, when they were making their way up Main Gate among the crowds of shepherds in their Sunday suits, farmers in breeches and leggings, and women in every sort of outfit from long coats over cotton dresses to well-cut, well-worn tweeds, never to mention the usual sprinkling of little boys getting in everyone's way.

"Bursting, I expect," said Guy cheerfully. "That's why I got Mrs. Richardson to say we might have our lunch in her private parlour. She's a decent old thing."

"She must be," said Rona, who felt that this really was a bit much. She could not have explained the feeling, unless it was that he seemed to be making an occasion out of this lunch which he had put to her so casually as a saving of time and trouble.

"Hullo! You sound a little terse. Don't you like my plans?" Guy asked, giving her a quick look from which she turned her head away.

"You—you're making us so conspicuous, a private room for lunch, in Threipford," complained Rona.

"No need to he conspicuous unless you slink in like Third Murderer or something," he assured her. "Everyone'll be far too busy trying to grab food for themselves to notice anyone else. If the Royal Family arrived unexpectedly for lunch at the Tower on Show Saturday, I believe they'd only be glared at as more strangers trying to shove their way in."

"How absurd!" But she could not help laughing a little as they squeezed their way into the hall of the old-fashioned hotel, where the air today was a rich mixture of harris tweed, tobacco smoke and fried onions. A gong was being beaten somewhere behind the scenes with vigour, and for a moment they stood back while the tide of hungry lunchers poured past them towards the dining-room in answer to its summons. Then Mrs. Richardson emerged from her lair at the back of the hall, spied them, and beckoned to them with a mystery which attracted several people's attention.

"'Third Murderer,' indeed," murmured Rona crossly, as heads turned in their direction. "I might as well be carrying a dagger dripping with blood!"

This remark, intended as a reproof, only made Guy laugh. Mrs. Richardson, ushering them into a stuffy little room, looked at them with approval.

"There, Mr. Guy, you'll have it all to yerselves," she said, beaming. "No need to hurry. I'll send yer lunch in to you in a minute."

She was as good as her word. When Rona came back from washing her hands and powdering her nose, a round table in the window had been laid for two, and plates of beefsteak pie were already waiting to be eaten.

"Are you hungry?" asked Guy, pulling out her chair. "Have some beer?"

"Starving. No beer, thank you. This *does* look good."

The pie was excellent. "I believe Mrs. Richardson makes the pastry herself," Guy informed Rona; and after refusing pudding, which was a choice of jam tart or tapioca, they were supplied with not very good coffee, brought to them by Mrs. Richardson herself, who then withdrew, once more assuring Guy that no one would disturb them, and not to hurry.

"What is all this about not being disturbed?" said Rona.

"Mrs. Richardson scents Romance," Guy said solemnly. "And as a matter of fact, she is perfectly right, Rona. Why did you go away for the weekend?"

"I didn't know about your sister," murmured Rona again, pleating and unpleating the edge of the tablecloth and keeping her eyes fixed on it.

"All right. We'll begin again from there. What had Alice's being ill to do with it?"

"Well, you were so horrible after the dinner-party at your house, and you never came to apologize, and didn't even ring up, and I didn't know about your sister until this morning, so I thought I wouldn't be at home when you came last weekend," Rona explained incoherently.

"I was horrible to you?" began Guy, and then suddenly he remembered it all: that revolting type Malleson, Rona so pleased, or appearing so pleased with him, and the quarrel at Harperslea gates ending with himself rushing furiously home and being greeted with the news of Alice's illness.

"Lord!" he exclaimed. "Good Lord! I'd forgotten all about it!"

"Yes. Well, of course I know that *now*. I mean, I know that's what must have happened," said Rona, still pleating industriously. "I told you it was very babyish of me—"

"Come to that, I was pretty babyish myself that night," said Guy. "But Rona, never mind all that now. What I want to say is you can stop looking for that fellow with the pretty name you told me about—"

"What fellow?" Rona was completely bewildered.

"Have you forgotten that you told me you were going to look out for a man with what you called a pretty name and then marry him?"

"Oh!" Warm colour poured into her small, usually pale face, dyeing it from throat to brow. "Oh!"

"He's found. It's me," Guy said, and now his hand came out and took hers into a firm hold. "Won't Lorimer suit you? You said yourself that you liked it—"

"You—you didn't think I was *hinting*, Guy?" said Rona piteously, in a tiny thread of a voice.

"My precious silly, of course I didn't. I never thought about it at all until that night at the hospital," said Guy. "I was sitting with poor old Viv, you know, waiting to hear if Alice was going to be all right, and thinking how awful it was for him, and then suddenly I thought: suppose it had been you instead of Alice, I couldn't have borne it, and then I knew."

"Oh Guy!" whispered Rona, to whom this muddled statement made a perfectly reasonable and satisfactory avowal of love. "And I only found out by being so cross with you!" And two large tears rose in her eyes, spilled over and ran down her cheeks to drop on the hand covering her own.

"As long as you *have* found it out, nothing else matters," said Guy. "But don't cry, my darling, or Mrs. Richardson will think I have been unkind to you. Here, have my handkerchief."

He took out a clean white linen one from his pocket, and bending forward, dabbed gently at her cheeks. Then, even more gently, he kissed her, wondering, as his lips met her soft untried ones, at his own feeling of almost remorseful tenderness. It was something quite different from the wild excitement of kissing Iris; and though he knew that he was offering Rona a more lasting love, he regretted that he could not bring her that young rapture which he had lost and would never know again.

So swift is thought that all this had come and gone in his mind before the kiss ended, and Rona would never know why he said, more to himself than her, "I'll take care of you. I'll be good to you—always."

They sat in blissful silence while time passed unnoticed, hurrying as it always does when human beings are at their happiest. The stuffy little room with its dingy red plush curtains and the table still bearing the remains of their meal might have been Piccadilly Circus in the rush hour or a mountain top for all they saw of it. Suddenly Rona said severely, "And still you haven't apologized for being so horrible to me."

"Good heavens, my girl, are you going to turn out a nagger?" asked Guy. "I shall beat you if you nag, and that's a promise. Besides, you had no business to be so occupied with that fellow Malleson. All the same, because one doesn't get engaged every day, I will apologize."

He rose, carefully pulled up his trousers, fell on his knees before her, folded his hands, and said meekly, "I am very sorry I was rude to you. Nor shall I rise, fairest of maidens, until you have granted me full and free forgiveness."

"Oh, do get up, Guy!" said Rona. "What if someone comes in? Besides it's very bad for your trousers."

"Well, I must say, your method of accepting an apology made on one's knees is refreshingly original," said Guy. "Am I forgiven, or do I stay here? These are my good flannel bags, by the way."

"Yes, yes, of course you're forgiven. I never meant it," said Rona. "Do please get up, Guy darling—"

Guy sprang up in one neat movement. "Say that again—no, not the forgiving bit, I don't care a hang about that! Say 'Guy darling' again, darling."

The door opened and Mrs. Richardson put her head in. "Would you be going to the Show, Mr. Guy, and the young lady?" was her mild inquiry. "It's past three o'clock." Her little sharp eyes were filled with lively curiosity and conjecture, but the two never noticed it.

"Past three!" cried Rona in horror. "How *awful*! I must run, I'm supposed to be helping Mrs. Lorimer—"

"Well, that will be all right," said Guy. "You were very late in getting away this morning. But if we don't hurry we won't see the jumping, and that would be a pity. Mrs. Richardson, I'll come in and settle with you later. Thanks for the lunch, it was grand. Come on, Rona."

Hand in hand they fled down the almost deserted street, towards the Show ground, where the local pipe-band was now in full cry, filling the air with martial music. At the entrance they paused.

"Guy, I'm not coming with you to watch the jumping," Rona said suddenly with determination. "I think I'd rather go straight to the marquee."

"And desert me?"

"I—I don't want everyone to know about us," she confessed. "And they'll guess if they see us together. Don't I look different?"

"Not different. Only nicer, if possible," said Guy.

"Well, then—"

"What about telling the parents?" said Guy. "Shall I come along this evening and ask your father if I may marry you?"

"Oh, Guy! I think I'd better tell him myself first, and you tell your people," said Rona.

"All right. This evening we'll stay with our own parents. Then tomorrow—tomorrow let's go up to Wallace's Well, Rona? I'll come in with you to Harperslea on the way home and see your father—"

Rona nodded. "I'll be at our gate at half-past ten," she promised. "I *must* go now."

"Just wait one minute. This is important." Guy took her hand and held it, heedless of the policeman at the gate. "Tell me: do you love me, Rona? Because I love you."

"Yes, I do, Guy. *Dreadfully!*" said Rona, and with a last quick look at him pulled her hand free and fled. Guy was left standing in a sort of trance of happiness while the policeman watched him with benevolent interest.

3

The afternoon seemed to Mrs. Lorimer to be passing very slowly and heavily. Just at first, when she returned to the Show after having eaten her lunch and hurriedly glanced at the morning papers, it had been agreeable to stroll about the wide field meeting friends, or to squash her way through the marquees admiring winning entries of various kinds, in the comfortable knowledge that she could do so with a clear conscience, since she would not have to be on duty again until after three o'clock. But gradually people began to gather at the tea-tent on one pretext or another—they had lunched early before coming, or they knew that the only way to get tea at all was to find a place before the rush, or they were terribly tired and thirsty and even if the tea was horrible it was hot and wet—Mrs. Lorimer, of course, had lunched late and felt that she would much rather remain thirsty than join the battle in the tea-tent. So while she was watching or pretending to watch several little girls going through the intricate steps of the Highland Fling with more vigour than accuracy, she suddenly realized that she was among strangers, with no one to talk to. She began to wonder why she had not seen Guy. His train had been due at least an hour earlier, and he usually looked for her as soon as he arrived. Of course he might not have been able to get away in time to catch it, she thought—but no, for in that case he would have telephoned. Everyone knows how the feeling of being neglected grows with the speed of a plant in a tropical jungle. Presently Mrs. Lorimer, tired after her busy morning, began to feel not merely neglected but deserted. There were none of her friends in sight, and those of her acquaintance whom she saw as she turned away from the Highland dancing, which showed no signs of ever coming to an end, were not ones she particularly liked. In vain did she tell herself sharply not to be idiotic; the feeling persisted and grew stronger. The Show was no fun at all unless she had at least one of the family with her. Jack did not count on these occasions. At the Show he was an exhibitor of vegetables pure and simple, useless as an escort or company. Even now, she knew, he was in the stuffy marquee where she had left him, among the milling crowd, gloating over his peas, with which, in spite of his forebodings he had taken a First Prize.

And where was Gray? Gray was a good person to walk about with, they found the same things funny or tiresome, and they could exchange views by a mere look, unnoticed by other people. Slowly proceeding across the field in this dejected state, Mrs. Lorimer failed to observe the approach of the neighbourhood's number one female bore, and fell an easy prey to her. Miss Douglas, who, though Mrs. Lorimer had not seen her, was coming to meet her, stopped short.

"Good heavens!" she thought. "What can be the matter with Lucy? She has walked straight into the arms of Diana Leadbitter—I'll wait until she escapes before I join her. Really a dose of Miss Leadbitter on top of an overdose of Mrs. Young would be more than I can take!"

So in a very mean cowardly way she hastily bought a ticket which an importunate small boy was urging upon her, and found herself gazing at a small pen of hurdles enclosing six sheep with numbered labels pinned to their fleeces, of which her ticket entitled her to guess the best animal among them.

While her friend was thus pastorally employed, Mrs. Lorimer was enduring an account of Miss Leadbitter's nieces' summer holidays to date, an account so detailed that it might have been a very dull diary. As she, like most other people, was quite unable to distinguish between the two, who were charmingly named Celia and Rosalind, she was forced to ask Miss Leadbitter if the girls were here this afternoon, only to be rewarded by being told with minute exactness, of all their entries for the Show.

"Dear things, they are so keen you simply wouldn't believe it!" said their aunt with a gay peal of laughter. "I said to them, 'You know, dears, if you go in for so many things we will hardly be able to get your entries down to the Show ground at all!' And Celia said, 'Oh, but aunty, we love it so, we wouldn't miss the Show for *anything*.' And so they both picked wild flowers for the

Best Bunch of Wild Flowers by a Child of School Age, you know, and bunches of heather for the Best Bunch of Heather, and—" At this point Mrs. Lorimer ceased even to try to listen, and let the wave of droning talk pour over her. Suddenly, just when she wondered if it were possible to lose consciousness from sheer boredom, she saw Guy.

"How—how splendid!" she said with false enthusiasm. "Do forgive me, Miss Leadbitter, but I think Guy is looking for me. I do hope the girls will win lots of prizes. Goodbye."

She smiled and walked away before Miss Leadbitter could get going again. In spite of the horror of the last few minutes, her feeling of neglect had gone, and now, as Guy came towards her, the afternoon sun seemed warmer, the pipe-band less deafening.

"Guy dear," she said. "You've had lunch, I hope?"

"Yes, Ma," he answered, taking her hand and pulling it through his arm. How well he was looking, his mother thought suddenly. Well and happy. It was delightful to see him.

"Was it a decent lunch?" she asked. "I always think train food is so unappetizing."

"Train food?" For a moment he seemed a little confused.

"Oh, I didn't have lunch in the train, Ma. I—as a matter of fact I—hullo, there's Gray. What on earth is she doing?"

"Let's go and see," suggested Mrs. Lorimer, and they went up to Miss Douglas, still gazing with puzzled concentration at the six sheep in their pen.

When she had explained, she invited Guy to place them in order of merit. "They all look exactly the same to me," she said plaintively. "I do think, though, that Number Five has a more intelligent face than the others."

"Never mind their faces. It's their fleeces you want to look at," said Guy.

"Shut your eyes and point," said Mrs. Lorimer. "It is just as good a way of judging as any other, and much less trouble."

Gray shut her eyes and pointed, and then allowed the other two to have a turn. It was, as Mrs. Lorimer said, much the easiest method, and gave them quite a lot of innocent amusement, before they wrote out their list and handed it to the small boy in charge, who was deeply disapproving of their levity.

"Where *did* you have lunch, then, Guy?" asked Mrs. Lorimer when they were wandering on again towards the marquees.

"At the Tower," said Guy with patience. Anxiety over her family's nourishment was one of Mrs. Lorimer's proclivities, as they all knew, and it now appeared to her younger son that by telling her that he had taken Rona to lunch he might pave the way for the news he wanted to break to his mother, yet felt oddly shy of doing.

Once again, however, an interruption prevented him. He had only got as far as saying, "I took—" when Mrs. Young hurried up to them, archly wagging a gloved finger.

"Ah ha, young man! So you've got back—at last," she said loudly. "Nothing like giving your girl friend lunch in a private room, eh? Oh, *I* saw you, though you were much too occupied to see *me*!"

"You *would*," muttered Guy under his breath. His mother looked from him to Mrs. Young in blank astonishment.

"Mrs. Richardson gave me lunch once in her own parlour, when I wanted it early because of catching a train," said Miss Douglas placidly. "It's a wonderful Victorian survival, that room, isn't it? All those bobbles and things. I am glad you thought of giving that poor child from Harperslea something to eat, Guy. She must have been very late, and I couldn't help much because I only brought a sandwich for myself."

Mrs. Lorimer was pleased to hear that Guy had remembered her able and willing assistant, but not so pleased that Mrs. Young should have elected to be arch about it.

"You could have brought her home, Guy, there was lots to eat, and all cold," she said.

Mrs. Young gave her noisy laugh again. "That's what he told me he was going to do, but I suppose it wouldn't have been so much fun, Guy!" she said.

"By the time we'd got everything clewed up it was far too late to walk out to Woodside," Guy said. "It was good of you to bother about us, Mrs. Young, when you had so much to see to yourself."

At this piece of impertinence, blandly and politely uttered, his mother and Miss Douglas held their breath, expecting fire from heaven to fall on him and blast him. But Mrs. Young either took the words at their face value or had sufficient sense to appear to do so. She laughed again, rather uncertainly, and announced that if Lucy was ready to go on duty in the baking tent, she herself proposed to go and have a look at the gees jumping. Naturally both other ladies immediately said in a slavish manner that they were ready and willing to take their turn in the marquee, and thankfully parted from their overseer.

"Baking tent it is in more than one sense," said Miss Douglas sadly. "Never to mention being full of wasps."

"Why wasps, I wonder?" murmured Mrs. Lorimer. who was still thinking rather dismally and also rather foolishly, that Guy had been in Threipford since morning and had spent his time with the Harperslea girl instead of at once looking for his mother.

"Because of the jam, of course, Lucy. Every pot had to be opened for the judges to taste it, and the wasps are having a really wonderful time."

Miss Douglas burbled on, and Guy gave her a grateful look. Whether she was doing it on purpose or not he could not tell, but he did not want to talk about Rona until he told his mother that he was going to marry her, and this was hardly the moment.

"Well, unless you want me to come and kill some wasps for you," he said, "I think I ought to go and admire Pop's peas. There's just time before the jumping is due to start."

The two friends, unwilling to leave the warm outer air for the warmer and much less airy marquees, stood for a moment watching Guy walk away to look at the vegetables.

"Guy is looking very well," said Miss Douglas presently.

"Yes, isn't he? He seems to have got over that unfortunate affair with the horrible young woman in Southsea, don't you think?" asked Mrs. Lorimer.

Miss Douglas met her look squarely, with a hint of compassionate amusement in her own eyes. "Yes, Lucy, I do think so," she answered.

"Oh dear—" began Mrs. Lorimer, and then stopped. "No," she went on again in a determined voice. "I am *not* going to make a fuss. I know what you mean, Gray, but you may not be right. But even if you are, I won't complain just because I don't happen to like the idea. Alice's being so ill taught me that I'd been spending far too much time and thought on what seemed to me real troubles and weren't. I've made up my mind not to manufacture mountains out of molehills any longer."

"Dear Lucy," said Gray very affectionately.

"It's just that I am being selfish," Mrs. Lorimer said. "Guy is the only one who isn't married now—"

"We don't know yet that he's thinking of getting married, Lucy."

"No, we don't actually know it, but we can guess it. It's in the *air*," said Mrs. Lorimer solemnly, and gazing at the distance in a sibylline manner. "I know it's going to happen . . . Oh, well! I suppose we had better go and superintend the removal of all those cakes and cardigans and things. Shall I take the baking, or will you?"

"I will," said Miss Douglas nobly. "The wasps know me by this time. If they saw a stranger they would probably be worse than ever. Good luck with your tent, Lucy."

"Back to Bedlam," said Mrs. Lorimer, and they parted, each to the tent of her choice.

4

Mrs. Lorimer was a trifle disconcerted to find the Harperslea girl already in the marquee, standing quietly to one side of the entrance, her hands loosely clasped behind her back. There was a curious radiance about her, as if some inner happiness had deepened the colour of her eyes and added a glint to her bright hair. Yet at the same time there was nothing of the pride of conquest in her demeanor. Her smile as she saw Mrs. Lorimer had a tint of appeal in it which was oddly touching.

Mrs. Lorimer, though she thought half-angrily that any girl lucky enough to have Guy in love with her might well look radiant, could not resist the impulse to smile back. And: "There, you elderly fool," she told herself. "Now you have made the girl think you are delighted with her and that you will welcome her as a daughter-in-law, instead of feeling that Guy is simply throwing himself away on a little nobody! Oh dear, why does one have children at all?"

Then Davie Dunlop came in and started to take down the wire netting, and immediately there was a rush of women to snatch up their entries and make off as if they were taking part in a smash and grab raid. It was most extraordinary how they were all infected in this way, thought Mrs. Lorimer, as she and Rona strove to prevent embroideries from being flung down and trampled underfoot, or jumpers from being pulled apart. The quietest and sanest of housewives became afflicted with a kind of madness that made them push and shove and grab and be exceedingly rude.

"I suppose it's the same sort of thing that makes women fight for bargains at sales and have the clothes torn off their backs," panted Rona during a momentary lull. "Wouldn't it be better just to let them alone until all the things have been claimed? They *must* know their own, surely?"

"Unfortunately they don't," said Mrs. Lorimer quite grimly for her. "We once left them to it, and the result was absolute chaos, and we had repercussions for months afterwards, so many things were missing, taken by the wrong people. Whether accidentally or not, I wouldn't care to say . . . Excuse me, are you sure that is your pair of socks? Have you got your removal card?" she said civilly to a young woman who had just pushed past her and pounced on some knitted socks, sweeping several other pairs off the staging on to the grass as she did so.

"Well, I'm sure! It's a fine thing if a body can't take away her own entries without all this interference!" snapped the young woman. "There's my card, number forty-nine, and I *hope* you're satisfied!"

"Well, no. I'm afraid I'm *not*," said Rona politely but with a crisp firmness which Mrs. Lorimer, falling back with the slightly sick feeling which gratuitous rudeness so often causes, inwardly applauded. "These socks are number forty-seven, as you will see by the label. I think you will find that *this* pair is your own."

And as she spoke she took the socks in question and pressed them into their owner's hands, removing the others at the same time.

"Oh, well done!" said Mrs. Lorimer. "I don't know how you can deal with them. When people are rude like that I just shrivel up."

"Of course you do. Mamma would have been exactly the same," Rona said calmly. "You've never been accustomed to it, but people of my generation grew up in the age of queues and evacuees and rationing that started with the war. I don't think it is nearly such a pleasant age as yours was, but we just have to make do with it. And it looks as if it has come to stay, so we may as well make up our minds that it has."

"How sensible you young things are," said Mrs. Lorimer, struck by Rona's reasonableness towards what she could not alter.

"Yes, I think we are sensible, most of us," the girl agreed. "All the same, we have lost something, you know, Mrs. Lorimer. I can't explain it, but it is true." She darted away to intercept a group of snatchers, took their cards from them and saw that they each had their own rightful belongings, and the conversation was not resumed.

But Mrs. Lorimer to her own surprise, found that she was looking forward to having another talk with Rona. "Though that does *not* mean that I think she is anything like good enough for Guy," she told herself with the obstinacy of extreme tiredness.

She was soon so tired with the heat, the crowd and the noise that she could think only of the moment when at last the marquee would be empty and she could go home. Colonel Lorimer, tenderly carrying a basket in which were his winning peas, his Second Prize potatoes and his unfortunately unplaced turnips, came to look for his wife and was horrified to see how pale she looked.

"You must come home at once, Lucy," he said. "And next year you are not to take on this job. It is far too much for you. Far too much. Ridiculous that you should be kept standing about like this for hours."

To his wife's feeble protests that she hadn't finished yet he turned a deaf ear. "Let someone else finish, then. Where's that wretched woman Mrs. Young? Everyone's gone home by now. I've just said good night to Gray. Get your things and come along."

"I must at least thank Rona—Miss Smellie," said Mrs. Lorimer, and turned to look for her assistant, who was at the far end of the marquee gathering together one or two unclaimed objects. Her head was bent over them, the green gold wave of her hair hid her face, and standing very close to her was Guy.

Mrs. Lorimer was too weary to think any more about Guy. She approached the two and said, "Good night, Rona, and thank you for all your help. You were simply splendid."

"Oh, Ma—" began Guy, when softly but quite distinctly the girl said: "Not now, Guy," and he broke off reluctantly.

"Well," he said. "All right, if you say so."

"I do say so," Rona said. She raised her head and looked at Mrs. Lorimer. "I'm very glad if I was any use," she said. "I'll just take these things across to the Secretary's tent and then go home. No one will be coming for them now. Good night, Mrs. Lorimer and Colonel Lorimer."

Like a shadow she slipped past the three tall Lorimers and vanished.

Guy looked after her for a moment, then gave himself a shake. "Well, Ma," he said. "It's high time you were home. Are you ready?"

With the strange perversity which forces people to do or say what they least want to, Mrs. Lorimer asked:

"Shouldn't you offer to see Rona home, Guy? She must be very tired too."

"Oh, her old man's waiting for her. That's what I came in to tell her," said Guy with a carelessness which did not deceive his mother at all. "I've been dismissed." He did not sound in the least cast down, she noticed, and now she knew that whatever her own feelings were she must be prepared to hear his news with a decent show of gladness.

CHAPTER ELEVEN

1

MR. SMELLIE had rumpled his white hair until it stood up above his distracted red face like a cockatoo's crest.

"I'm not saying anything against yer son, Mrs. Lorimer, mind. He's a fine young man, and I've no doubt you've plenty reason to be proud of him. But it's not what I want for Nesta Rowena, to have her stravaguing hither and yon after him with no proper settled home o' her own. She's all I've got, and I looked to see her marrying somebody more our own kind, if ye take my meaning."

"I do understand, Mr. Smellie, and in a way I agree with you," Mrs. Lorimer said slowly.

This interview which was taking place at Harperslea was a strange one, she thought. Somehow it had never occurred to her that any objections to Guy's marrying his daughter would be raised by Mr. Smellie. Yet here she was, prepared to plead the young people's cause against her own inner conviction that Rona was not good enough for her son; for it appeared now as if Mr. Smellie did not consider Guy a good match for his daughter. The situation had a Gilbertian twist to it and might have been funny if it had not concerned her and her dear Guy so nearly.

When Guy had come home after seeing Mr. Smellie and announced in a flat tone: "The old boy won't hear of my marrying Rona!" Mrs. Lorimer's first feeling had been of relief; but this had been followed at once by distress because Guy was so obviously unhappy, and by indignation against Rona's father. She waited for some days, while Guy of course had returned to Glasgow to his job, wondering whether she ought to do anything, or leave it alone to work itself out, but in the end had decided that she must see Mr. Smellie, if only to hear what he had to say.

It had not been without misgiving that Mrs. Lorimer had rung Mr. Smellie up and asked if she might come and see him, choosing to meet him on his own ground rather than at Woodside, lest she might be at too great an advantage over him. The advantage, however, was all on Mr. Smellie's side. She was not only angry with the little man, but amazed at his point of view, and yet his unhappiness and bewilderment softened her heart.

Gently she said, "So often parents don't really care for the marriages their children make, and in the end come round. And has one as a parent any right to try to stop them? It is not as if you disapprove of Guy, you said so yourself." In spite of her efforts to sound impartial, she could not keep the indignation out of her voice as she said this. Who and what was Mr. Smellie to object to her son?

"Ay. Now I've angered ye. It's not to be wondered at, I suppose. No doubt ye think my Nesta Rowena's not good enough for yer son," he said heavily, his accent broadening in his distress. "But if ye feel that way—and he's not yer only child, Mrs. Lorimer—ye can surely understand my side o' it?"

Mrs. Lorimer murmured, "Indeed, I do." She said it sincerely, and thought she was speaking the truth; but it is hardly possible for a woman to understand the jealousy with which a father of a favourite daughter regards any man whom he suspects of wanting to marry her. The dearer the daughter, the more disagreeable her father to her suitors, for it is not only the Mr. Barretts who behave like this. So Mr. Smellie, while he did not want his Nesta Rowena to be single all her life, and could contemplate marriage for her at some dim future date and to some dim suitable husband, with a degree of equanimity, was quite unable to bear the thought of losing her now, or at any rate quite soon, to this far from nebulous young Naval officer.

It was true that he had nothing against Guy—nothing that he would not have had against anyone who had come and told him that he intended to marry Nesta Rowena. As for Guy's career, and the nomadic life that Nesta Rowena would have to lead as a Naval wife, poor Mr. Smellie had seized on it as a pretext in sheer desperation.

So the two unwilling parents sat there thinking about their troublesome children.

"Ye'll take a cup of tea with me, Mrs. Lorimer?" asked Mr. Smellie suddenly, breaking a silence which was becoming awkward.

Mrs. Lorimer would have preferred to go home, but her host looked so disconsolate that she felt she ought to stay. So she said that tea would be very nice indeed, especially if he didn't ask her to pour out, as she always had to do it at home and enjoyed the change of having her tea poured out for her.

This remark, which she made simply because it was true, put Mr. Smellie much more at his ease with her.

"It's a queer thing," he observed, "you saying that, Mrs. Lorimer. I never gave it a thought, but I suppose ladies do get tired doing all these wee jobs."

When the tea came he poured it out with many inquiries as to how she liked it. "No sugar, I think you said, Mrs. Lorimer? And do you like the milk in first or afterwards? I'm told it's not just the right thing to put the milk in first," he added confidentially. "But it seems to *blend* better that way to my mind."

"I don't see that it matters, as long as you have it the way you like it," said Mrs. Lorimer. "This is delicious, the nicest cup of tea I have had for ages."

"There's nothing beats a good cup of tea," he agreed, sitting back in his crimson chair and taking a deep draught from the cup he held. "If anybody had told me a few hours back that you an' me would be sitting here so cosy drinking tea, I wouldn't have believed him," he suddenly said.

Mrs. Lorimer looked at him in some surprise, but seeing that he had more to say, remained silent.

"Mrs. Lorimer," said Mr. Smellie impressively, "ye'll forgive me for being pairsonal, but you're a verra unusual woman. Verra unusual indeed."

"Oh, I think I am quite ordinary, Mr. Smellie," began Mrs. Lorimer, rather at a loss, but realizing that his intention was to be complimentary.

"Not you. Here was I waiting for you, expecting you to be on about your son being too good for my dotter, putting me in my place, as ye might say. But you've been real friendly. I can think o' the way some of the other ladies in this neighbourhood would have been at me if it had been *their* sons."

"Mr. Smellie," said Mrs. Lorimer. "I will be perfectly honest with you. I can't pretend that I like the idea of this engagement any more than you do. For one thing Guy and Rona—you must forgive me for calling her Rona, it is a pet name my children gave her—Guy and Rona have known one another such a very short time. But I do want Guy to be happy, just as you want your daughter to be, and if being engaged is going to make them happy, what can we do but agree?"

Mr. Smellie did not appear to have heard the last part of this rather involved statement. "'Ilona,'" he was muttering. "Rona. And they gave her a pet name, did they?"

"I do hope you don't mind? You know what these young people are—" Mrs. Lorimer was by now heartily wishing that she had stuck to Your Daughter, or even to the whole of Nesta Rowena.

"Mind? No. I think it was a nice-like thing to do, it shows they like her, and you too. Though she'll always be Nesta Rowena to me . . . But you were saying we want them to be happy, Mrs. Lorimer, and of course that's true. I only bought this place here for Nesta Rowena, for I'm sure I was far more at home in Bearsden. It was for her I did it. Of course I want her to be happy."

"Well, you must have known that when you bought Harperslea and came to live here that Rona and you would make new friends," said Mrs. Lorimer sensibly. "In a way, Mr. Smellie, it is all your fault."

"I can see that now," he said slowly and miserably. "But I never thought. She's still just a wee thing to me, far too young to be thinking of leaving her old Papaw."

Mrs. Lorimer rose. "I think you will really have to give in, just as I shall," she said.

He sighed. "What does the Colonel say to it?" he asked suddenly, as they went across the hall. "He's a sensible man, the Colonel."

"My husband? He hasn't said very much about it at all," said Mrs. Lorimer. "He doesn't interfere, you know, he rather leaves it to me. After all, we can't stop them from marrying, can we? We don't want a runaway marriage, and you can hardly lock Rona in her room and keep her on bread and water—"

Mr. Smellie looked so stunned with horror that she hastened to tell him that she was only joking.

"Oh, I see. For a minute I thought you meant it," he said, and added proudly, "There's no fear of a runaway marriage. Nesta Rowena will never do a thing that she knows I'm against, Mrs. Lorimer."

"That is exactly why you will have to give in. It would be too unfair to trade on her feelings," she exclaimed.

At that he withdrew hastily. "Well, I don't know what I'll do. I'm that upset I can't think right. I'll consider it. That's all I can say," he said, and she went away down the drive leaving him at the door, his round face puckered like an unhappy child's.

2

As she approached Woodside, Mrs. Lorimer saw her husband in the garden picking peas—the same peas which had won First Prize for him at the Show a few days earlier—but though the groaning of the gate as she opened it must have been heard by him, he paid no attention. His back was eloquent of dignified displeasure, and Mrs. Lorimer sighed.

"Now I wonder what has annoyed Jack?" she thought, even while she said aloud and cheerfully, "Are we going to be treated to your prize peas tonight, Jack? I suppose they will be the last dish we shall have this year."

"You weren't in for tea, Lucy," the Colonel said.

"Well, Jack, I am often out for tea."

"Not without letting me know, or at least telling Nan," said the Colonel, and his wife realized that she was in disgrace.

"I'm sorry," she said. "As a matter of fact I meant to be home in time for tea, but I felt I must stay and see if I could bring Mr. Smellie to a more reasonable frame of mind—"

"What's Mr. Smellie—ghastly name, poor fellow!—being unreasonable about?" demanded the Colonel.

"Oh, Jack! Surely you can't have forgotten that Guy wants to marry his daughter, and he won't hear of it," said Mrs. Lorimer, feeling that really her husband was quite as unreasonable in his own way as Mr. Smellie.

"He'll come round if he's given time to think it over. But that's just like you women, you want everything done in such a hurry, like Nan and the hoovering. Must go at it with a rush," said the Colonel.

Mrs. Lorimer considered this unfair and said so. "I told you at lunch that I was going to see Mr. Smellie. Why didn't you say that then, before I went?"

"Well, m'dear, I don't suppose it would have made any difference if I had," said the Colonel. "There, I think that has just about cleared them," he added, showing her a basket pleasantly full of green pods. Then he chuckled. "Good Lord, Lucy, your own father made the same fuss when we wanted to get married, and as for mine—I heard all about the Army being a single man's career for days on end—"

"White hands cling to the tightened rein," murmured Mrs. Lorimer.

"What's that? I never met anyone who changed the subject so quickly as you, Lucy."

"I wasn't really changing the subject, Jack. But I can't imagine why our parents should have objected to our marriage. It was quite a different thing."

"It always is," said the Colonel with an unusual flash of insight.

"Surely you'll admit that ours was more—more suitable, Jack! After all, our people were the same kind, and—" Mrs. Lorimer broke off. She suddenly found that her husband being reasonable was almost more trying than when he was the reverse.

"Yes, yes. Of course, Lucy. I was just saying that our people thought we were very foolish. I can't think how you have forgotten it. Don't you remember your mother saying you were too young and didn't know your own mind? Or perhaps she said that to *me* about you," said the Colonel thoughtfully.

"She must have. I certainly have no recollection of her telling *me* that!"

"There was some other fellow—Good Lord. Good Lord, Lucy! Now I've got it. That fat chap, what's his name, that came to dinner with the Dunnes! Malleson, that's it. Knew I'd heard his name before this summer! Your mother had some idea that you'd quarrelled with him and took me out of—"

"Oh, Jack!" Mrs. Lorimer gazed at him, forgetting Mr. Smellie, Rona, and even Guy in her dismay. Was that old, wretched affair, so long forgotten, going to cause trouble between her and Jack at this late day? "Oh, Jack! How—how *could* Mother have told you that?"

"Oh, I didn't believe her," he said consolingly. "And now I've seen Malleson I know he was never the sort you would care about. I only wish your mother was alive so that I could tell her she was wrong."

"So do I," said Mrs. Lorimer. "She really didn't know as much about us as we did."

"Well, and we don't know as much about Guy and his young woman as they do," the Colonel said, delighted to have scored a point so logically. "Perhaps she—Rona, I mean—isn't what we'd have chosen as far as family goes, but we must move with the times, Lucy. Times have changed, you know."

Jack was becoming so reasonable that it was quite maddening, thought Mrs. Lorimer; and yet, how dreadful it would have been if he had been unreasonable about Richard Malleson, as he well might have, had he not made up his mind that he was not her sort. With a good deal of restraint she replied only, "Unfortunately it is Mr. Smellie who isn't moving with the times, Jack, not you or I."

"Oh, he'll be all right if he's left alone," the Colonel said once more. Then, harking back to his grievance: "I don't see why you had to have tea with him, though, without telling me."

"I didn't know I was going to have tea with him, and really I can't see that it matters so much—"

"There were some telephone calls for you. I had to take them," said the Colonel. "That fellow Malleson rang up, for one—"

"Good gracious, is he *still* with the Dunnes?" exclaimed Mrs. Lorimer indignantly. "Well, that wasn't very important, and I didn't want to speak to him."

"You'll have to. He's going to ring up again." Colonel Lorimer said with some satisfaction. "And your agents rang up. Something about a letter they sent you about serial rights. And there's a letter from Mary. And a telegram from Phillis—"

"What on earth is Philly sending telegrams for? There's nothing wrong, is there? I wish you had told me sooner, Jack—"

"I haven't had a chance. We got on to Guy and Smellie," said the Colonel, but a little guiltily. "No, there's nothing wrong, except that Phillis wants to come here. I'm sure I don't know why. But you'll see for yourself. It's in the hall, I wrote it down and told them to send a confirmatory copy with the post in the morning. Now there's no need to sprain your ankle by running like that, Lucy—"

But Mrs. Lorimer, full of foreboding, was hastening up the path to the house and paid no attention.

"LEAVING GEORGE QUITE IMPOSSIBLE WILL BE WITH YOU IN TIME FOR DINNER PHILLIS."

"Jack, surely this isn't your idea of Phillis wanting to come and stay!" said Mrs. Lorimer, after reading this message several times. "She says she's leaving George!"

"She says leaving George impossible," retorted the Colonel. "Though why she should bother to tell us that beats me."

"No, no. She means that George is impossible and she's leaving him—"

"It strikes me that Phillis is impossible herself," said Phillis's father gloomily. "Well, Lucy, of course she must stay the night here, but she is going back to George tomorrow by the midday train."

It was not often that Colonel Lorimer issued an order in the voice which once had made Orderly Sergeants quake. As Mrs. Lorimer had told Mr. Smellie with truth, he didn't interfere.

"But Jack, you know it's no use trying to force Philly to do anything, it never has been. It only makes her more stubborn than ever," began Mrs. Lorimer.

"I know that you've always *said* it did, Lucy," said the Colonel. "Which is not quite the same thing."

"We can hardly turn her out of her own home if she doesn't want to go."

"This is not her own home now. Her home is with George and her children. Come now, Lucy, be sensible and let me deal with it. I won't have you worried like this by Phillis or any of them. You've been wearing yourself out over Guy and his affairs—though I must say the boy is behaving very well, a lot better than Phillis! But this is too much." The Colonel spoke very firmly indeed.

Mrs. Lorimer, suddenly realizing what an enormous relief it would be not to have to argue with Philly and bear her tears and reproaches, nevertheless said in what she knew was a very feeble way: "You won't be unkind to her, Jack?"

"Unkind? Why should I be unkind?" said the Colonel. "You talk as if I were a brute, Lucy."

"You sound so harsh about her, and I always thought Philly was your favourite," murmured Mrs. Lorimer more feebly than ever, but unable to put an end to this display of maternal imbecility.

Her husband, incensed at the accusation of favouritism, lost his temper. "Upon my word, Lucy, I don't know what has come over you this afternoon. I never heard you talk so foolishly. I haven't got any favourites, as you ought to know, but if I have a favourite at all it is yourself."

And having made this remark in a tone of controlled rage, he stamped out of the room, leaving the door open. June, alarmed by her usually mild master's display of temper, flattened her ears, lowered her tail, and casting at Mrs. Lorimer a look which said plainly: "You *have* been and gone and done it!" crept out after him.

"Men!" said Mrs. Lorimer softly but with great bitterness, and added after a moment's thought: "And women too! Well, luckily there are clean sheets on Guy's bed, so Philly will just have to go in there. I'm *blowed* if Nan and I are going to start getting the spare-room ready for her!" Then she went out to the hall to ring up the Threipford taxi and tell it to meet her tiresome daughter at the Junction. After which she had to go and break the news to Nan that Phillis would be arriving unexpectedly in about an hour.

Nan, however, knew this already. "I could hear the Colonel reading the tellygram back to them," she said calmly. "Indeed, you could have heard him from the foot o' the garden, he was roaring that loud. It's a good thing there's mince for the dinner. I've put a handful of oatmeal in with it to make it go further. An' I put a bottle in Mr. Guy's bed seeing the spare-room bed's not aired."

"Oh thank you, Nan. That's splendid. You have thought of everything."

"Miss Philly—Mrs. Gordon, I should say—fair takes it out of you with her ongoings," Nan remarked. "Just you go and put yer feet up on the sofa for a wee bit."

It was impossible to reprove Nan for her free comments on the family. After all, she had known Philly since she had been a small girl. Mrs. Lorimer therefore merely smiled, said that it would be very pleasant to rest for a little, and withdrew.

As she laid her head back against a cushion, she reflected that far too many things were happening all at once. These emotional disturbances, which acted on some women as a stimulant, she knew, only fretted and tired her. Guy's angry bewilderment at this turn in his affairs . . . Rona's small face looking pinched and wan . . . Mr. Smellie's distress . . . her own worry over these difficulties . . . her annoyance on having Richard Malleson cropping up again . . . Jack's sudden realization that Richard was the man her mother had told him about over thirty years ago . . . Jack's composure and common-sense both with regard to Richard and Mr. Smellie's attitude . . . Phillis's worrying and thoughtless telegram, Jack's determination to deal with Phillis himself . . . and then his sudden amazing spurt of anger and his announcement, uttered so that it sounded like a threat rather than anything: "If I have a favourite at all it is yourself . . . Jack! . . . All these boiled and churned in her brain, and she shut her eyes in the hope that this might help her to think more clearly. The natural result was that a delicious drowsiness began to steal upon Mrs. Lorimer; her thoughts did not become any clearer, but a beautiful carefree feeling took the place of her anxiety as she slid into a light sleep.

3

Phillis's visit, like so many events which are dreaded in anticipation, was much less stormy than her mother expected. She arrived in a very subdued state. Perhaps during the long journey north she had for once taken time to consider what she was doing. Poor Philly, thought Mrs. Lorimer, looking at the pretty face, rather pale this evening, of her troublesome child, she had always been like that, rushing madly into quagmires which a moment's glance might have told her to avoid.

After dinner, when her father invited her to go with him to the smaller sitting-room, which he called his own but which was really much more June's boudoir, full as it was of her rugs and blankets and water-dishes, Phillis made no demur. Her eyes opened a little wider, she gave her mother a quick look, and then meekly went with the Colonel. Of course Mrs. Lorimer, left alone, was unable to settle to anything.

If Mrs. Lorimer had been her friend Miss Douglas she would have gone out and walked hard for an hour, but this did not appeal to her as a safety valve. A calm evening's beauty would have seemed unsympathetic to her present mood and would only have added to her uneasiness. Once more Mrs. Lorimer got up from the chair on which she had just sat down, and went across to her desk. Opening it and idly looking at its neat pigeon-holes, she suddenly thought of the telephone message from her agents about some serial rights, which Phillis's telegram had driven out of her head. Mrs. Lorimer was blessed with a much better business sense than many women who are authors. She sat down at the desk again, pulled out from its appropriate pigeon-hole her agent's last letter on the subject, and proceeded to write an answer. It was a relief to her feelings to put down in clear black characters that on no consideration would she agree to alter the novel which a woman's magazine was prepared to run as a serial. If, wrote Mrs. Lorimer, the editress did not care for the story as it had been written, she must do without it altogether. Quietly though she took her success, she enjoyed being in a position to accept or refuse offers as she wished. Now, as she addressed and stamped an envelope, she suddenly wondered whether Phillis had suffered from having too many of the things she wanted. The others had been old enough, when their mother began to make money by her books, to remember leaner times, but Phillis, the youngest, had only known the years of plenty. In fact, thought Mrs. Lorimer sadly, and once more wondering what was going on between father and daughter, Phillis was spoilt. But before she had time to worry too much, the drawing-room door opened and Phillis came in.

"I'm going home tomorrow, Ma," she said, not defiantly nor sullenly but almost timidly. "I wanted to catch the night train, but Father says I'd better wait until tomorrow—"

"Oh, Philly—" began Mrs. Lorimer, longing to tell her child that this was her home, that she could stay in it as long as she liked, but stopping herself. She could not undermine the Colonel's work. "Oh, Philly! It's lovely to have you here, dear, but—"

"I know, Ma. I've been a fool as usual, and a selfish fool," said Phillis. "I—I hadn't really thought about it properly. I just banged out of the house—you know, a note on the dressing-table and all, in the best tradition! I didn't know Father was so sensible. I wished I'd talked it over with him long ago, because he has been able to show me the man's point of view."

If Mrs. Lorimer felt a pang because Jack had apparently succeeded with ease where she had so long failed, she stifled it instantly. "Do you want to tell me what it was all about?" she asked. Philly usually liked to pour out all her woes in a long involved story.

"Honestly, Ma, I can't even remember now what it was all about," said Phillis slowly. "We quarrelled and I lost my temper—over some stupid little thing, I'm sure."

"Philly, I'm not going to say anything, for your father must have said it all, but I *must* say that I simply cannot understand you. How you can endanger your whole life like this, and George's and the children's, just in a fit of temper passes my comprehension."

"I can't understand myself sometimes, Ma."

"You leave your house and children, never to mention your husband, put us in a fever of anxiety by that ridiculous telegram, and yet you've no idea why you did it!"

"I'll try not to do it again," Phillis said. "I must get it into my head that now I have a home of my own, I must only be a visitor here—I don't mean anything unkind, Ma! But I'm sure it doesn't work if one goes on thinking of one's old home as home. That's what Father was telling me. But I hope I'll always be a welcome visitor, Ma? Because this will be the house I most want to visit."

"Oh, Philly, darling!" said her mother, tears pricking her eyes. "But he is right you know—your father, I mean. By the way, has either of you thought of letting George know that you are going back home tomorrow?"

"Father said he would send a telegram. I wanted to ring George up," explained Phillis. "But Father said a telegram would be best."

It was obvious that she was enjoying her new meekness, thought Mrs. Lorimer resignedly, but then, it wasn't possible to change people's natures. Philly would always dramatize herself. At least this new role might make for a more peaceable married life for her and George! "Well, I think we should go to bed," she said. "You must be tired, and I know I am. Let's go up, Philly."

On the following day Phillis, her luggage increased by a dozen eggs and some sugar which Nan produced from the store-cupboard, kissed her mother lovingly, promised her father to be good, and was driven off to the Junction to catch her train.

"I suppose there will be other occasions like this, though I hope not for a long time," said Mrs. Lorimer as she stood in the doorway, her arm linked in her husband's. "Philly will always be a trouble maker!"

"Philly won't give any more trouble," the Colonel replied firmly. "All she wanted was to have things pointed out to her. Now she sees where she has gone wrong and she won't do it again."

Mrs. Lorimer looked at him, and then looked away again to the far hills, their green faces ruddy in the morning sun where patches of bracken were turning to tarnished copper and bronze. As well expect those hills to alter their shapes, she thought, as to change one person's character! But it seemed a pity to discourage Jack, who had certainly brought Philly to her senses in record time, and in any case it would be useless, for he simply would not believe her.

CHAPTER TWELVE

1

Miss Douglas, seeing the interested glances of everyone who passed, tried to walk on, but in vain.

"Plain as a pikestaff!" Mrs. Young proclaimed. "Oh, there's no need to be so discreet, my dear woman! Everybody's talkin' about it. I must say I don't blame the Lorimers for not wanting Guy to marry a girl like that, but I'm surprised he has given in to them. He's an obstinate young devil. But of course Lucy can do what she likes with him—"

"Mrs. Young," said Gray, "I really don't think we should discuss this, especially not here. In any case it is not my business."

"Not mine either, I suppose you mean? But if you live in a place like Threipford, everyone knows your business and makes it theirs. Place is a hot-bed of gossip."

"And you," said Miss Douglas, but only to herself, "are one of the biggest and most dangerous of the gossips in Threipford!" Aloud she answered, "I think you will find that you are mistaken. Lucy likes the girl—"

"Well, it all seems very queer to me, that's all I can say. The girl's going about lookin' like a ghost and doesn't go near Woodside, and Guy is never here at all."

"I assure you that the Lorimers aren't so stupid as to try to behave like old-fashioned parents. They can't cut Guy off with or without a shilling even if they wanted to, because it wouldn't matter as he is independent. And they can't prevent him from marrying Miss Smellie. Now I really must go and do my shopping. Good morning." She walked away, heedless of Mrs. Young's last muttered "All very fishy!" exclaiming "Odious woman!" with such venom that she surprised herself.

It was true that rumours were floating about Threipford, in which the names of Guy Lorimer and Miss Smellie were murmured. Quite evidently, thought Miss Douglas as she went back to Thimblefield with her laden shopping-basket, it has never occurred to anyone that Mr. Smellie had been the one who objected to the marriage. Rona kept away from Woodside because, as she told Mrs. Lorimer, she felt it was disloyal to her father to go there. And as for saying that Guy was never at home now, Mrs. Young might have remembered that he had a job of work to do and could not get away whenever he wanted to. Lucy Lorimer, Miss Douglas knew, was worried about it all, and was taking it quietly as usual. Lucy could see Mr. Smellie's point of view, though she could not believe that the parent existed who could not approve of Guy as a son-in-law! This was perfectly natural even to Miss Douglas. Lucy, for all her intelligence and outside interests, was a mother first of all. Of course she rated her children, if not as none-suches, at least considerably higher than any other young people. As for what Colonel Lorimer thought of the whole matter, no one knew, or no one stopped to wonder.

Opposite the opening of the small branch road which meandered past Thimblefield and on southward by scattered farms and old toll-houses, was a field gate. As she very often did on reaching this point on her way back from the town, Miss Douglas put down her basket and stood for a rest, looking down the sloping fields to Threip Water.

There is no saying how long she might not have remained there basking in the mild warmth, not thinking of anything in particular, but acutely conscious of the pleasant sappy smell of newly-cut cornstalks and the feel of the warm wood under her arms, if she had not been roused by footsteps on the road. She turned, ready to exchange a greeting and a comment on the fine harvest weather, and found that it was Mr. Smellie, dressed in his usual rather large checks, who was passing.

Gray, though she did not feel any too friendly towards the little man who was causing so much difficulty and distress to her friends, could not ignore him after turning round. She reminded herself that the affair was none of her business and was able to say cheerfully: "What a lovely day, Mr. Smellie."

"Yes, it's a fine day," he answered, raising a cap which matched his suit. "Are you on your way back from the town, Miss Douglas?"

"Yes, and I shouldn't be loitering here," Gray said briskly, picking up her basket. "But it is so beautiful I had to stop and look at it all."

"Would you allow me to carry your basket for you?" he asked rather timidly. "It looks a bit heavy for a lady."

"Oh, but I turn off here, it would be out of your way," said Miss Douglas.

"I'm only taking a wee walk to myself," he said. "I can quite well go round by your house."

He sounded so lonely that Miss Douglas yielded the basket to him without further hesitation. "I'll accept your offer, Mr. Smellie," she said. "But only on condition that you will come in and have a rest when we get to Thimblefield, I have some rather good Michaelmas daisies out just now, that you might care to see."

This was clever of Miss Douglas, who had just remembered that Mr. Smellie was intensely interested in herbaceous borders, and she was pleased with herself for offering the Michaelmas daisies as an inducement. In spite of having just told herself that Guy and Rona were no business of hers, a vague idea that she might be able to drop some word which might shake Mr. Smellie's determination against his daughter's engagement was in her mind. But she also felt sorry for him. He looked so forlorn and miserable that she would have liked to cheer him up a little.

Mr. Smellie trotted at her side, discoursing knowledgeably on Michaelmas daisies and early chrysanthemums, which he regrettably spoke of as chrysanths, and quite soon they were at the gate of Miss Douglas's little house.

"Now what will you have?" she asked him hospitably when she had relieved him of the basket and led him into the cool drawing-room. "It won't take a minute to make tea or coffee, and there is sherry if you would rather have that. You deserve it after carrying my shopping home for me."

Mr. Smellie said that if she had no objections he would like a glass of cold water.

"An excellent drink on a day like this," she said. "I can't think why more people don't indulge in it. I like water better than almost anything, and the water here is so good, don't you think?"

Mr. Smellie took a long pull at the glass which she had put into his hand, its outside, like that of the jug from which she had poured it, misted with the chill of its contents. "Ay, it's fine water," he said. "But there's nothing to my mind beats the water we get in Glasgow. Have you ever drunk Glasgow water, Miss Douglas? Straight from Loch Katrine it comes. There's no water makes a better cup of tea." He might have been speaking of some rare and almost legendary vintage, his hostess thought, but she said gravely that she did like the Glasgow water very much.

Then she led him out to the garden where the Michaelmas daisies stood in all their splendour of blue and rosy mauve and royal purple.

"You've some fine varieties here," Mr. Smellie told her. "And good thriving plants too. I like yon wee yellow one. It's one I've never grown myself."

"I could give you a bit of it when it has finished flowering," said Miss Douglas. "I shall have to separate quite a lot of these plants, so if you will just say what you would like—"

"It's real kind of you, Miss Douglas," Mr. Smellie's eyes brightened with a gardener's greed as he wandered about from clump to clump. Then he sighed. "My! What a bonnie garden I had back at home," he said. "And every plant put in with my own hands. I miss it whiles, and I wonder whether the folk that bought the house look after it."

"But you have such a lovely garden at Harperslea—"

"It's not the same at all. Back at home I could do with just a man coming in for an hour on a Saturday, but here it takes a full-time gardener, and he'd rather have a boy than me helping," Mr. Smellie said mournfully. "It doesn't seem like my own garden, Miss Douglas. I doubt he doesn't like me meddling. Ah well! I bought the place for Nesta Rowena, and here she's wanting to leave me. You'll have heard?"

"Of course I have heard," said Miss Douglas. "Mrs. Lorimer is a great friend of mine and I am very fond of them all, especially Guy. In fact, Mr. Smellie, the whole of Threipford has heard to a greater or less degree."

"I know, I know," he said. "The way folk look at me I can tell they are all talking about it."

Miss Douglas decided to take the bull by the horns. "Do you realize that a great many people think that the Lorimers object to the engagement and that is why it hasn't been announced?" she said. "It really isn't very fair on Mrs. Lorimer and the Colonel, is it?"

"It is *not*," exclaimed Mr. Smellie, horrified. "Nobody could have been kinder about it than Mrs. Lorimer. I don't like to hear this at all, Miss Douglas."

"Nor do I," said Miss Douglas drily. "And I don't suppose it is very pleasant for the Lorimers themselves."

"Surely they'll not have heard that?"

"Of course they've heard. A thing like this always gets back to the people it concerns sooner or later," said Miss Douglas.

"Oh dear me!" he lamented. "I don't like to hear of this! Mrs. Lorimer has been more than once to Harperslea to see me, and never tried to talk me over once she'd put her side of the case to me. I'll have to put this right some way."

"I'm afraid there is only one way to do that, Mr. Smellie."

He looked at her miserably. "Ay. You mean give up Nesta Rowena."

"Yes. Or at least, tell her and Guy that you don't mind their being engaged," Miss Douglas said. "It isn't really giving her up. You are far more likely to lose her by refusing to let her be happy."

"What do *you* know about it?" he cried, forgetting all his careful politeness in his unhappiness. "You that's not married and have no children of your own?"

Miss Douglas said nothing.

"You'll have to forgive me. It was a terrible thing to say, and I don't know what came over me," said Mr. Smellie. "But, oh dear me, Miss Douglas. I'm fair demented. I just don't know what to do."

He stood there among the bright flowers in the sunshine looking as if he might burst into tears.

"It's very hard on you. It is always hard on older people," said Miss Douglas. "Of course you don't want to give your daughter up, and yet, as I see it, it is the only way you can really keep her."

"I've thought that too, in the night when I can't get sleeping," he said, and then broke out: "If the lad was only settled near at hand it wouldn't be so bad! There's times I think if he would leave the Navy and get a place in an office I'd say yes right away. D'ye think I like to see Nesta Rowena going about the way she is? It's enough to break my heart."

"Well, why don't you put it to Guy? I don't know how he would take such a suggestion," said Miss Douglas slowly. "But at least it would show him—it would show them both—that you aren't entirely against them."

"I'll think it over. I'll consider it," he told her, as he had told Mrs. Lorimer in her turn. "I can't say more. And I'd better be getting on my way to Harperslea now."

"I'm afraid I have been very interfering—" began Miss Douglas with compunction.

"Oh, I'm sure ye meant well. It's just that folk don't understand the way I feel," he said drearily, and walked slowly away along the road.

"Poor little man! I do understand, and I am dreadfully sorry for him, in his selfishness and distress!" said Miss Douglas aloud.

2

Mr. Smellie walked slowly, brooding over what Miss Douglas had said. She had spoken straight out, and he appreciated her honesty, even though he felt more battered than before he had met her, and now he was uncertain as well as unhappy. Now he could no longer convince himself that he was acting in Nesta Rowena's own best interests. He began to wonder about the possibility of persuading young Lorimer to give up his career and settle down in an office, say in Glasgow. All right, he decided suddenly. I'll suggest it to Nesta Rowena. If that Miss Douglas is right, it will at least show that I'm not altogether against her. With the thought, his steps quickened.

By the time he reached Harperslea he was almost running in his anxiety to see his daughter and put his proposition to her. It was a grievous disappointment when he hurried into the house to be told that Miss Nesta Rowena was out walking and had not said when she would be home.

"Is she not coming in to lunch?" he demanded.

"I couldna say, sir," said the young housemaid blankly.

All he could discover was that she had not taken sandwiches with her, as she sometimes did when she meant to be out for a long time.

He made a pretence of eating when lunch was served, and ordered that something should be kept hot for Nesta Rowena before retreating to his sanctum to brood again. The afternoon slipped away unnoticed. The sound of a voice in the hall, Guy Lorimer's voice, roused Mr. Smellie at last from his thoughts to the realization that Nesta Rowena had not yet come home. He pulled himself out of his deep chair and went into the hall, blinking like an owl in the rush of sunlight streaming through the open doorway.

"Good afternoon, sir," said Guy. "I had the chance of a long weekend, so I took it, but there wasn't time to let anyone know I'd be down today. Have you any idea where Rona is?" He spoke politely but without warmth.

"Bless me, I'd no idea it was so late," Mr. Smellie said in a worried tone as the grandfather clock half-way up the stairs struck four times with a good deal of wheezing and whirring. "She should have been back, for she took no lunch with her. I suppose she'll have gone on one of these long rambles she's so fond of."

"I've told her she shouldn't go too far on the hills by herself," Guy's voice had lost both its politeness and its chill, it was warm with annoyance that masked uneasiness. "Silly little idiot!"

Mr. Smellie forgot the dread with which he had been looking forward to his first meeting with his would-be son-in-law since the day when Guy had told him that he wanted to marry Nesta Rowena. "What harm could come to her?" he quavered. He looked suddenly very old.

"Oh, probably nothing. But there's always the off-chance that she might sprain her ankle," said Guy. "I have an idea of where she'll have gone, though. I'll go up that way and meet her. Don't worry, sir."

"What's the use of telling me not to worry? Amn't I her father?" cried poor Mr. Smellie, all his pent-up misery coming to a head and rushing out in helpless rage. "Of course I'm worrying!"

And what do you think I'm doing, you silly old so-and-so? thought Guy. Yes, you're her father, and a nice way you look after her after as good as telling me that I'm not capable of it! But he restrained himself, and swallowed the words unspoken.

"Well, try not to worry too much," was all he said. "I'll go up towards Wallace's Well, and I'm pretty certain to meet her. I'll be back with her in no time."

The calm authority in his voice comforted Mr. Smellie, whose brief anger had died down, leaving him feeling that perhaps he had been unfair to the young man. "Well, that's very good of you"—he began, but Guy had had enough of this.

"Not a bit. I hope to marry the girl some day," he said firmly. "So of course I feel responsible for her." And he turned to the door before Mr. Smellie could think of an answer. Perhaps Mr. Smellie did not try very hard; it is not altogether easy to tell a young man who is just setting out to look for a missing daughter that his hopes of marrying her are vain.

Anyhow, Mr. Smellie did not speak, but left Guy with the honours of the last word. He followed him in silence to the door with some vague idea of speeding the parting guest as a host should—if someone who has walked uninvited into the house and is walking out again with equal lack of ceremony can be called a guest.

Guy, marching ahead of him, suddenly stopped, shouted: "Here she is!" and ran out on to the drive; and Mr. Smellie hurrying behind, reached his front steps in time to see his daughter hobbling towards the house before she was swept into Guy's arms.

Panting, Mr. Smellie came up to them. "What's happened to you, Nesta Rowena?" he gasped. "Here were we thinking you were lost!"

"I twisted my ankle, Papa, and it's taken me a long time to get home. Please don't scold me," said Rona, and now he could see that she was pale and in pain.

"Oh deary me, lassie! I'm sure I hope ye haven't broken any bones. Will I get the doctor?"

"No, no! There isn't any need for that," she said.

Guy broke in. "I think it would be a very good idea, sir, if you rang up the doctor and asked him to come and have a look at Rona's ankle."

"What a *fuss*!" said Rona.

"He's perfectly right," said her father. "I'll away and phone as soon as you're into the house."

"And I, though I am no film star he-man," said Guy "am going to carry you in and put you on the drawing-room sofa. Don't argue." He picked her up, remarked that it was a good thing she was a lightweight, and started back towards the house, Mr. Smellie trotting anxiously alongside.

Once they were indoors, Guy took charge without unnecessary bustle. He encouraged Mr. Smellie to go and ring up the doctor, he asked the young housemaid to bring him what he required: two basins, boiling water, cold water, some small towels, a bath towel, several pillows and a pair of scissors.

"And then, if you would make some tea?" he said finally. "Because I am sure Miss Smellie would like a cup, and so should we."

Mary flew on these errands thrilling with excitement and importance. It was a little disappointing to find, when she clattered into the drawing-room with a load of pillows and towels, that the Lieutenant was not bending over Miss Nesta Rowena imprinting a chaste kiss on her marble brow. He was bending over her foot and saying firmly, "I'll try cutting the laces first. If it won't come off then I'll have to cut the leather, that's all."

"Oh, no, Guy! You really mustn't hack those shoes up! It's my hand-made pair!" cried Miss Nesta Rowena, instead of murmuring "My hero," which Mary felt would have been more fitting.

Mr. Smellie, however, had no fault to find with Guy's handling of the situation. He himself fluttered about the room, pathetically useless, constantly asking his daughter how her foot felt now, and gladly if clumsily carrying out the small jobs which Guy found for him out of sheer pity.

Guy had succeeded in easing the shoe from Ilona's foot without having to cut the leather, but he was ruthless about the ankle sock under it, and did some quick work with the scissors before she could protest. Now he had raised the injured foot on pillows protected by a bath-towel, and was laying on it towels wrung out of cold and hot water alternately.

"How does it feel?" he asked after several of these applications.

Rona, looking rather white, smiled and said: "Not too bad now, thank you. The hot and cold helps a lot. But I can't imagine why Mary had to bring you the best hand towels! Any old rag would have done."

"I suppose they were what she laid her hand on first," Guy said, unaware that Mary had carefully picked out the very best as suitable for such a romantic occasion.

They were drinking tea and feeling quite cheerful when Doctor Harrison put his head round the door.

"Ah! Just in time for a cup," he said. "No, Mr. Smellie, I'll look at my patient first and have some tea afterwards. Business before pleasure, you know."

He examined the ankle, approved of Guy's First Aid measures, and announced that there was no fracture. "But you haven't done it any good by walking home on it. You'll have to take care of it. A sprain like that can be just as troublesome as a simple break," he added. "Keep it up. Cold compresses. Better stay in bed, Miss Smellie. Yes, thanks, I'll have that cup of tea now."

Rona looked rebellious. "I *can't* stay in bed," she said. "Won't it do if I stay on the sofa here?"

"It might if you really stayed on it," said Doctor Harrison. "But bed's best really. You don't propose to sleep on the sofa, do you?" He drank his tea and put the cup down. "How are you going to get up and down stairs? I want you to keep that foot up, and I mean *up*, until Monday."

"I'll be here until Sunday afternoon," said Guy. "I can come and carry her up and down till then."

The doctor's bushy eyebrows shot up. "Well, that would certainly be a solution," he said. He hesitated, seemed as if about to say something more, then remarked in his professional voice, "I'll be in to see that ankle on Monday. Until then, keep it up, mind. Now I'll need to be on my way home. Surgery at six." And he marched out of the room, with Mr. Smellie following to see him off.

At the front door Doctor Harrison halted for a moment. "Didn't know if it was in order to offer congratulations or not," he said. "I've been hearing in the town that it isn't a settled thing. Better to say nothing, perhaps? But young Guy Lorimer's a good lad, Mr. Smellie. Your girl might go farther and fare a lot worse. Good day to you." He got into his car, pressed the self-starter with considerable force and roared away.

"Yes, he is a good lad," Mr. Smellie muttered to himself, as he went slowly back to the drawing-room.

He did not find them so much as holding hands, to his relief, though he was illogically rather disappointed as well. Guy was standing at one of the long windows smoking a cigarette and Rona's head was against the pillows, her eyes were shut, and she looked listless and pale.

Mr. Smellie cleared his throat. "I'd like a word with you—er, Lieutenant, if you'll come into my sanctum for a minute."

"Certainly, sir," said Guy, turning from his contemplation of the lawn and the beeches which closed it in.

"His name is Guy, Papa," said Rona. "And if you have anything to say to him that concerns me, I'd rather you said it here."

"But Rona—" and "Now, Nesta Rowena—" said both men together. Guy got in first. "If your father wants to have a talk with me, Rona, it's fair enough that he should have a free hand, and he wouldn't if you were there."

"He's had a talk with you already, when you told him you wanted to marry me," Rona said obstinately. "I'd rather hear what he is going to say this time. If you go away to another room," she added, "I shall get off the sofa and walk after you."

They stared at her, Mr. Smellie in guilty consternation, Guy rather indignantly. It was Guy's look that she answered.

"No, I'm not just being tiresome and obstinate, Guy. I know that Papa is up to something. He's going to say something he doesn't want me to hear, to talk you into something, and I won't have it."

"Oh, verra well, verra well. I'll put it to him now," said Mr. Smellie. "I've been thinking things over," he went on slowly. "And I've made up my mind. You can marry her if you'll give up the Navy and get a decent steady job in an office so that Nesta Rowena'll have a settled home not too far from me. There."

It was Mr. Smellie's turn to be stared at. Guy swallowed hard. Then he said: "That will take some thinking over, you know, sir. I'm not too bad at my own job, which is the Navy, but I have had no training for any other."

Relieved and yet oddly ashamed by his reasonable attitude, Mr. Smellie began, "Oh, I can see that, my boy. But think it over. Take your time, and—"

"No!" cried Rona, sitting bolt upright and jarring her ankle. The sharp pain made her voice sound sharp too as she went on. "I won't have it, Papa! I won't have Guy give up his life like this. If he accepts your terms, I won't marry him at all!"

There was a silence. Rona fought against the tears that threatened to choke her. "Do you think I want a sacrifice like that made for me?" she said at last. "Can't you see, Papa, that it would end in Guy's hating me and my hating you? Don't ever *think* of such a wicked thing again. Promise me you won't—both of you!"

"Well," said Guy. "We seem to be back where we started, don't we?" His tone was determinedly light, but his face was grim. "No, it's all right, Rona my dear. I promise not to think any more about it. Lord knows I am not anxious to leave the Service."

"Oh deary me!" exclaimed Mr. Smellie. "I've made a bad mistake. I see that now. I'll need to think it over again—"

"As long as you aren't entirely throwing me away, sir, it's better than nothing," said Guy. "Now, Rona, what about bed? I'll carry you up, and then I'd better go home to Woodside and let the parents know I am here."

3

The weekend passed without further mention of any settlement. Guy appeared punctually at ten on the Saturday and Sunday mornings to carry Rona downstairs, remained with her a good part of the day, and carried her up again in the evening. On Sunday it had to be earlier, because of his train back to Glasgow, and when he came down he went to Mr. Smellie's sanctum before leaving the house.

"My mother will be coming to see Rona in a day or two," he said. "To bring her some books and so on."

Mr. Smellie cleared his throat. "Did ye—did ye mention that proposition I made about going into business to your Mamma at all?" he asked huskily.

"No, I didn't," answered Guy. "There wasn't any reason to tell her, and it would only have worried her."

"I see. Well, that was good o' you, and I'm much obliged. I wish I'd never suggested it."

"Oh—well—" said Guy, and changed the subject. "Don't let Rona try to walk on that ankle before the doctor says she may, sir. She's an obstinate little thing, you know. Goodbye for now. I expect I'll be down again on Saturday."

He left behind him an even more sorely troubled Mr. Smellie, whose conscience was telling him more and more loudly that selfishness was what was really preventing him from agreeing to his daughter's engagement. He knew now that he wanted to give in, yet his pigheadedness would not allow him to say the words which would make them happy. Guy had spoken of Nesta Rowena as an obstinate little thing; if it was true of her, it was much more true of her father. Mr. Smellie suddenly remembered, so clearly that he almost heard her voice in his ears, his mother saying to him when he was still a boy, "Eh, Matthew! Yer obstinacy will make ye rue, some day."

He was rueing it now as he paced up and down the gravelled sweep before the front door a few mornings later, wondering how he could find a way to give in without seeming to do so. When he saw Mrs. Lorimer's little car coming up the drive he had an idea that he might ask her to tell Nesta Rowena that he had changed his mind; but when she stopped and got out, he found that the words would not come.

"Good morning, Mr. Smellie," Mrs. Lorimer said, in her quiet way, with her gentle smile, and he felt dreadfully guilty that anyone in Threipford should have so misjudged her as to say she would not hear of her son's marrying his daughter.

"Good morning, Mrs. Lorimer. It's verra good of you to come," he said. "Will I take these books for you?"

Mrs. Lorimer handed him an armful of books and turned to rummage in the car again. "I've brought a few eggs," she said. "I don't know if you have plenty, but I thought perhaps Rona would like them. And I hope your cook won't be offended, but Nan insisted on sending one of her special orange creams—at least, Nan thinks they are special."

Between her kindness and his own miserable obstinacy Mr. Smellie was dumb. He took the basket she pulled out of the car, led her into the drawing-room—for the doctor had said that Rona could now hobble down and lie on the sofa all day if she only made the journey once each way during the twenty-four hours—and announced with a show of cheerfulness, "Here's Mrs. Lorimer to see you, deary. Look at the fine books she's brought."

"Oh, Mr. Smellie," said Mrs. Lorimer as he hovered uncertainly by the door. "My husband said he would take a walk down with the dog, and look in to see you and Rona."

"That's real kind of the Colonel. I'll away out and see if I see him coming," said Mr. Smellie and made his escape.

He had not met Colonel Lorimer since the day when Guy had said he wanted to marry Nesta Rowena, and he wondered if the Colonel would be feeling angry with him. It would be almost a relief if he were, Mr. Smellie thought. He could stand up to rage a great deal better than to all the kindness and consideration displayed by his daughter and Guy and Mrs. Lorimer. It was fairly getting him down. Now if there could be a thumping row, so that he might have a chance to roar that they could get married tomorrow for all he cared, that would be fine, thought Mr. Smellie; but at the idea of Mrs. Lorimer taking part in a thumping row his imagination failed him and he shook his head. She was a very quiet lady, Mrs. Lorimer. The Colonel, now, looked as if he might be a bit peppery . . .

The Colonel, swinging up the drive with June hurrying ahead of him, showed no signs of being enraged or even peppery, however.

"Ha, Smellie!" he called, waving his disgraceful old hat. "What a grand morning! I see my wife's got here before me."

Mr. Smellie answered Yes, and asked if the Colonel would like to go into the house.

"No, no, I don't think so. Not just yet. We'll leave the ladies to have a crack. Now I wonder, Smellie, if I might have a look at your shallots? Mine aren't too successful this year, and that man of yours really understands shallots. I'd like to have a word with him if you don't mind."

Mr. Smellie had no objection, and the two walked off down a winding path and entered the walled garden, where that ineffable smell of stored warmth and scent met them like a soft touch as soon as they had opened the door.

But of the gardener there was no sign, and Mr. Smellie, after they had walked all round and shouted once or twice, made a clucking sound of annoyance.

"Tut-tut," he said. "I was forgetting. I told Jamieson he could take a run on his bike this morning to see about a load of manure. I'm sorry, Colonel."

"Oh, never mind. Ill just have a look at the shallots and see how they're shaping," said Colonel Lorimer. He seemed to know by instinct where they were, examined them with absorbed interest and finally, not without satisfaction, pronounced them to be no better than his own. "It must be the season," he said. "But all the same, he's got the garden in fine order. You have a very good garden here at Harperslea, Smellie."

"Oh, it's very good," said Mr. Smellie in depressed accents.

The Colonel looked at him. "Now, you're letting this business of my boy and your girl get you down," he said. "No use doing that, you know."

Mr. Smellie muttered something to the effect that he didn't see how he could help it, but he need not have troubled to say anything, for the Colonel was off on one of his long statements, which neither required nor permitted comment.

"It's this *hustle*," he said, waving his arm as if the peaceful bee-haunted garden were a London railway terminus on Bank holiday. "The curse of the age. Everything must be done in a tearing hurry. Now marriage is a serious business, and ought to be considered thoroughly. As I said to my wife, it's no *good* trying to rush Smellie—no good at all. Give him time to get used to the idea and he'll come round. Just give him *time*. After all, Guy has only known the girl for a few months, and they're both young. They can afford to wait a little. But my wife's like all women, wants everything settled right away. You've nothing against the marriage, I take it?" he added, suddenly breaking off and turning to face Mr. Smellie, who was madly trying to sort out the sense of this speech.

"No, Colonel, I haven't, and that's the truth. But it's just like you say, I need time to get used to the whole idea," he said finally, having grasped the important fact that Colonel Lorimer really saw his point of view.

"Of course you do! And that's what I've been saying all along. When you're ready, you'll tell 'em it's all right and they can go ahead and be engaged—not that either you nor I can stop them if they're set on it," said the Colonel thoughtfully. "They are of age and Guy's independent. But they are both decent youngsters and don't want to upset us if they can help it."

Mr. Smellie hardly heard his last words, for it had dawned on him with the blinding glory of sunshine on snow that here was his opportunity to yield without loss of face. He snatched at it before he could begin to waver. "To tell you the truth, Colonel," he said. "I'm prepared to agree to the engagement *now*. I've seen more of your son—of Guy, as I'll need to start calling him—over the weekend, and I've been verra favourably impressed by him. I see I canna keep my wee lassie to myself, and she's made a good choice. But how to tell her fair beats me, Colonel, for it's no good pretending I'm anxious to lose her. No good at all."

The long years of his army training, of having to deal with men normally inarticulate whose troubles, coming to a head, produced an unwonted fluency of speech, served the Colonel well now. He listened without interruption, only nodding now and then. When he judged that Mr. Smellie had had his say, he walked on for a minute or two along the broad box-edged path in silence, and at last said, "I can see it isn't easy for you, but how would it be if I just go in and see your daughter, as I intended to do in any case, and simply tell her I'm glad it is all settled? That seems to me to meet the case without any bother. And we can ring Guy up this evening or send him a wire, and the whole thing will be fixed."

"If ye would, Colonel, I'd be obliged to you. And if you'll excuse me I'll just potter about here a bit by myself," said Mr. Smellie. "Mrs. Lorimer'll understand I'm not wanting to see anybody for a wee bit, I'm sure."

The Colonel, as he shut the garden door behind him, heard loud trumpeting sounds as of a nose being blown with unrefined violence. "Poor old chap," he thought. "But it has to come to all of us."

And then he walked into the drawing-room and greeted his future daughter-in-law very kindly, telling her that Guy was a lucky young devil and she must hurry up and get on her feet again, and her father had been very considerate about the whole affair.

When Mr. Smellie had heard the car leave, he crept back to the house and took refuge in his sanctum, where he sat wrapped in sad thought. "She'll be thinking of that young fellow, now," he said to himself. "Maybe she's writing to him this minute. She'll have forgotten her old Papaw already. It's natural enough, but it's hard, verra hard."

But Nesta Rowena had heard his slow step crossing the hall, and presently the door of Mr. Smellie's sanctum opened gently.

"Papa?" said Nesta Rowena. And she came limping across the room to where he sat, climbed on his knee as she had done as a little girl, and put her arms round his neck. "Dear Papa—"

4

"I have lived in *six* reigns," said Mrs. Lorimer impressively.

"Well, so have I—just," answered Miss Douglas. "What about it?"

"It makes me feel very old," said Mrs. Lorimer.

"Oh, I don't know. It's rather a young feeling, I think, to have lived in six reigns and still be in one's fifties. Our grandparents wouldn't have been able to make that boast, and still less our great-grandparents," said Miss Douglas, laughing.

The still November afternoon was all dove-grey and mother-of-pearl, except where, in the south-west, the last of the sun hung above a long hillside in splendour.

Miss Douglas had come over the fields from Thimblefield, and the two had gone for a delightful dawdling walk before settling down to talk until teatime.

Presently the door flew open and Colonel Lorimer appeared, wearing his oldest clothes and bringing with him a blast of cold air and a strong smell of bonfire.

"In here, are you?" he said genially. "Ha, Gray! Good afternoon. I thought you'd be out. It is a splendid afternoon. Splendid. You really ought to go out, Lucy."

"I have been out, Jack, and so has Gray," said his wife, looking rather sadly at the open door.

"Well, I won't interrupt your talk. I must get back to my bonfire," said the Colonel. He went out and shut the door, only to open it again and say: "You should come and see my bonfire, both of you. Have you got your garden rubbish burned yet, Gray? This is a perfect day for it. Perfect." And without waiting for a reply he withdrew, this time leaving the door open.

"That's another thing," said Miss Douglas as Mrs. Lorimer got up, went to the door and shut it with restrained violence. "Why does one close the door nowadays? Or feel warm? It isn't quite so bad as sitting on the couch in the lounge, certainly, but—"

"What on earth do you mean?"

"Well, personally, I *shut* the door and feel *hot*," said Miss Douglas.

"Do you? I wish I did," said Mrs. Lorimer, kneeling in front of the fire and banging viciously at a sullen lump of coal with a small black poker. "If Jack would sometimes remember to shut the door it might be easier to feel hot, or even warm!"

Gray laughed heartlessly. "You know you wouldn't change Jack for the most perfect husband that ever existed," she said.

"Well, no. Of course I wouldn't. I am used to him by this time. Though he has given me one or two surprises this summer, I must say," said Mrs. Lorimer. "The way he made Philly see reason, and Mr. Smellie too—and one or two other things that happened—"

"Very interesting for you."

"Oh, very. But a little disconcerting, after all these years!"

"Tell me how the family are," said Miss Douglas.

"Alice really seems to be quite strong again," began Mrs. Lorimer, pleased to retail her news to someone like Gray who was genuinely interested. "And Vivian can be trusted to look after her and see that she doesn't do too much. Mary writes very hopefully. She has now got a rather fierce ex-Nannie as cook, who is devoted to Thomas, and Mary is sure she will stay because she thinks that Thomas would die of neglect if she left. And Phillis is so excited at the prospect of a couple of years in Malta that she has no time to quarrel. So in the meantime everything seems to be going well. It won't *last*, of course, but after the summer I have had, I am only too thankful for present mercies!"

"Yes, poor Lucy! And yet the general opinion in Threipford is that it has been an exceptionally quiet and uneventful summer! What about Guy and Rona? Is their wedding day really fixed at last?" asked Gray.

"Really and truly fixed for the middle of December. They have been very good and patient. And I must say," said Mrs. Lorimer thoughtfully, "that having had to wait like this has probably been good for Guy, poor dear. They are delightfully happy, and I am really very fond of Rona now."

"I hear that when they are married Mr. Smellie says that he will sell Harperslea and buy a villa at Newton Mearns or somewhere like that, near Glasgow," said Gray. "Is that true?"

Mrs. Lorimer nodded. "Yes, and I am not surprised. He will be far happier there, in familiar surroundings. Those villas can be wonderfully comfortable, full of all the latest electric devices, and he will be able to have a first-class housekeeper and a good cook and give cosy little dinner-parties to his old business cronies— whatever cronies are. They sound more like Mr. Smellie than mere friends, somehow!"

"And he will be able to call his garden his very own," said Gray. "He will like that."

"Yes, poor little man. He never felt at home at Harperslea. I do hope he will be very happy, wherever he settles."

"And Harperslea will be for sale again," murmured Miss Douglas.

The two friends looked at one another in understanding silence.

Then Mrs. Lorimer said reflectively, "Yes it will be for sale again. I do love that house, Gray . . . When Guy is married there will be less room here than ever if they want to come and stay in a bunch. I wonder if I can manage to make Jack see reason about it?"

And they sat on until Nan came stumping into the room with the tea-trolley.

THE END

FURROWED MIDDLEBROW